STONED IN TEXAS

A NOVEL

JAMES EASE

First paperback edition

Cover design by Studio Bookmark
Book design by Brian Phillips Design

Print ISBN: 979-8-9910217-0-8
eBook ISBN: 979-8-9910217-1-5

Printed in the United States of America

Alta Real Publishing
jamesease.com | stonedintexas.com

1

THE ACTOR LAY IN BED NEXT TO A STRANGER in a cheap motel room that smelled of perfume and tequila along a lonely highway. He stared at the ceiling wondering how he got there, not how he arrived at this physical place, but how he found himself in the current situation. Below the bed was the evidence of a crime—a deadly crime—and he knew the killers would be swinging by at any minute to find out exactly what the actor witnessed. He felt the sunrise approaching and knew he should have been far away. He looked at the stranger's hips, curved like a bony mountain range under the sheets beside him. She'd already admitted she wasn't really who she said she was. He was desperate to leave but frozen; maybe it was because he promised to comfort the stranger or maybe he wanted to protect her, not from the killers who'd have no interest in her, but from the world outside. Car headlights slid across the wall through the blinds as he lay there paranoid and exhausted, replaying the events that brought him there. It all started back at the Coconut Club in downtown Austin.

· · ·

It was around noon on a Sunday. Our actor steered his tiny beat-up convertible through the streets of downtown. The air hung heavy. It felt like a monsoon would happen any minute. Even with a passing breeze, it was much too humid for late February. Our actor took a quick look at himself in the cracked rearview mirror and slicked his sandy blond hair back with the damp wind. It couldn't have been more than a few weeks since he'd driven downtown, but the whole place had changed. The freeway underpasses had been filling with tent cities for the past year, but now the parks and sidewalks were lined with people living in boxes covered in tarps. Shopping carts, camping chairs, burnt sleeping bags, chewed-up Styrofoam coolers, the general debris of street life overflowed. Towering above the rubble, brand new shimmering high rises of mirrored glass were being erected in every direction. Our actor didn't recognize any of it. This wasn't the place it used to be. It felt more brutal than ever. Maybe it was the hangover or the weather—neither were making anything better.

An Alan Watts speech played on his car stereo as our actor kept his eyes peeled for a parking spot:

"How does your head look to your eyes? Well, I'll tell you. It looks like what you see out in front of you. Because all that you see out in front of you is how you feel inside your head."

He liked the way Alan Watts could state the most universal truths in such an obvious way.

Our actor spied an open spot to his right between two cars. He pulled past the opening to parallel, but before he could shift into reverse, a neon yellow Lamborghini slipped in forward and backed up to straighten out. He watched the driver of the Lamborghini and his passenger, both a couple of clean-cut dudes who looked like they just came from a boat party jump out of the car. "Snaked by a couple of fuckin' tech bros," he muttered.

He watched the yuppies fumbling with the parking pay station in his rearview as he sat at the red light and wondered, *Where do they all come from?*

On the other side of the light, he noticed two available spots directly across the street from the Coconut Club. *Even better,* our actor thought as he pulled up to the curb. He decided to leave the top down even though it felt like a storm could happen at any moment. He figured this would keep him from staying too long and make him less of a target for theft, but more than anything there was a sense of freedom he felt by leaving his top down on the street: freedom from attachment, the same sense of freedom you get when you boldly walk upon a stage nude or even hypothetically nude. Plenty of nights, after the bars had closed, he'd find his car rifled through, though nothing was ever taken. Some nights he found other people's trash in his car, but it didn't bother him; he'd just toss it in the bin when he got home. All a small price to pay for the freedom he felt by leaving his top down on a public street.

He looked up at the street sign to make sure it was still free to park on Sunday—it was—and he walked across to the entrance of the Coconut Club, his shoulders cocked back with purpose. He tried to always be conscious of his posture, especially when crossing a street. There wasn't the usual amount of traffic since it was Sunday, but that didn't stop our actor from crossing the street like he was walking across a stage nude—or even hypothetically so.

A stairwell led up to the rooftop bar of the Coconut Club. A couple of drag queens were coming down as our actor made his way up. One was helping the other navigate the stairs in massive heels. They all flashed each other smiles. "Aye, I don't like being in cramped spaces with blondes," our actor heard the one needing the help say as they ambled past.

Our actor made it to the top and spotted his friend behind the bar. The patio was surrounded by the newly constructed sparkling, mirrored high rises stretching into the sky; some were condos, some housed tech start-ups with cheap logos.

"My man," the bartender said as he saw our actor strolling across the patio. "Jesse Strange in the flesh."

"Lipton tea bags," our actor said to his bartender friend as they slapped each other's palms.

"You just missed the drag show," the bartender, Ben Lipton, informed our actor, Jesse Strange.

"Aw, well, maybe next time."

A party of stragglers were scattered around the rooftop bar. A DJ blasted electronic dance music, pumping his fists as no one paid attention. The patrons who were still around looked like remnants from the night before—low energy, drunkish, haggard, whispering to each other in the corners of the patio. Last night would have resembled something like Austin's version of Studio 54, a flashy dance party on fire, but now it was time for the shift to change.

"You want a drink?" the bartender asked Jesse.

"Oh, certainly."

"Tequila?"

"With soda and a squeeze of lime, please."

"Of course," said the bartender as he fixed up a tequila and soda in a clear plastic cup.

He slid the drink to Jesse, who had a swig. The swig seemed to relieve something deep in the actor's soul.

"So, what'd you need anyway?"

"Probably just an eighth today," Jesse said.

"Just an eighth?"

Ben only tended bar on the side. His full-time job was dealing weed. He thought it was smart to have a legit gig for tax purposes. He sold weed out of the Coconut Club most nights anyway, so he figured he might as well take a bartending shift here and there to make some decent tips that he could write off.

They were interrupted by a straggler who had just come out of the bathroom. "Water, water, water, I need water," he shouted. His demands seemed like life or death.

"There's a water cooler down at the end of the bar," the bartender said in an assuring tone. "Help yourself."

"Is it free?"

"Oh, one hundred percent. Cups down there and everything."

"THANK YOU!" the spun-out patron screamed in relief, as if the bartender had just saved his life.

"Where do they all come from?" our actor asked.

"You mean that guy?'

"I mean the people filling up all these condos and the people living out there on the streets and in the parks. Seems like they all just appeared out of nowhere."

"Everywhere else, I guess," Ben Lipton said as he walked over to help a couple of dudes who seemed to be into the annoying dance music. They were bobbing along to it as they tried to decide what drink to order. Jesse's eyes glazed over as he saw his reflection in the mirror behind the bar. He drifted off into his drink. Everyone seemed desperate for something these days. Just getting a drink or free water was a huge win. Nothing came easy anymore.

After the bartender mixed a couple of tropical rum drinks for the dancing dudes, he came back to our actor.

"Anyway, what were we talking about?"

Jesse snapped out of his daydream. "Aw, just all the crazy shit."

"Yeah, shit's wild out there. Oh, speaking of, I bumped into Carla the other day on the street."

"Yeah?"

"I hardly recognized her. What happened?"

"Really not sure. I guess everything just caught up to her."

"Jesus, man, she was gone."

"I heard she was living in the park, but I haven't seen her in a while."

"You guys were a thing, huh?"

"I'm not sure what we were."

"I thought you two were gonna get married or something. You hear about Bobby?"

"Yeah."

"Living in the park, too," the bartender said, shaking his head.

"I saw his meltdown on the horn," Jesse said, motioning toward his phone that he had placed on the bar in front of him.

"Right there in the public eye. Same with PJ."

"Yeah, poor PJ."

"It's hard on people out there these days. Oh, here," the bartender said as he handed Jesse a small baggie consisting of an eighth of an ounce of beautiful marijuana flower.

Our actor cherished the companionship of his weed-dealing, bartender friend. Ben Lipton was a class-act barkeep. He always agreed with you and made you feel a little better by listening and getting you drunk and high.

"What's this stuff called?" our actor asked.

"Weed."

"Doesn't it have some goofy name like Return of the Jedi or something?"

"Oh, I'm sure it had a name, but by the time it gets to Texas, it's just called weed."

"Where's it imported from?"

"Colorado or maybe California. I get both."

"Seems like Texas will be the very last state to legalize it."

"Fine either way by me," said the bartender.

"You're not worried about losing business if it's legal here?"

"Nah, I'd still have my business. I mean, it's as good as legal in Austin, you just can't walk into a store."

"But if you drive five minutes outside of town . . ." the actor said with a grin.

"I do my best to avoid that. Hey, how's the movie going?"

"Didn't end up happening."

"What? It fell through?"

"They pulled the plug."

"Why?"

"Fucking tax incentives or something? I'm really not sure, just got the word from my agent it was over."

"Fuck, dude, I'm sorry. It sounded like that was gonna be big for you."

"Yeah, I suppose it would've been."

"The big break and all."

"Who knows?"

"What was the name of the movie?"

"*Mirage.*"

"Damn. Well, something else'll come through."

"Maybe."

"It will, dude. What else are you working on?"

"I'm doing a Sam Shepard play over at the Vortex Theatre."

"Now, how do I know that name, Sam Shepard?"

"Well, for one he's a national treasure as a playwright, but he's probably best known to the general public for his acting roles."

"So he wrote roles for himself?"

"Not really. He was more of a poet who wrote plays and then got into acting and screenwriting. There's really no one else like him."

"Oh, I think I was thinking of someone else then."

"And that's why I love you, you're not a film geek," said the actor to his bartender friend.

"That I'm not," the bartender said as he wiped down the bar. "Although, I do like a good story."

"Sometimes I can't stand the film world, so goddamn cerebral and boring."

"Yeah, that bad?"

"Ever been to a film festival?"

"Can't say that I have."

"They're boring as hell. They always have these wrap parties at the end and they're just awkward and dull as shit. I'd much rather hang around musicians and bartending weed dealers."

"That's true, you don't hang around many actors, do you?"

"Just on set or in my acting classes."

"Well, I look forward to seeing your play when it happens."

"I'll let ya know."

"I'm sure it'll all work out for you. All these film people moving here must be bringing jobs with them, right?"

"I don't know, man, doesn't look good as of now."

"No? You ever see yourself going back out to LA?"

"I don't know."

"You were out there for a few years, huh?"

"Yeah, but it's even more desperate."

"Seems like that's where the jobs are, at least for what you do."

"Probably, but good roles are hard to come by no matter where you are. Besides, you see the shit they're churning out these days?"

"They don't make 'em like they used to, huh?"

"Nope."

"How's your place?" asked the bartender.

"Got sold."

"Got sold?"

"The whole building got sold and they're doubling the rent."

"Are you gonna pay it?"

"Fuck, no. There's no way I could."

"What are ya gonna do?"

"No clue. Maybe get a job at a software company and buy a condo. That or move into the park with everyone else."

"Aw, man, you don't wanna do either of those. You just need that thing to click," Ben said, snapping his fingers.

Jesse stirred the little black straw around his cup of melting ice while he nodded his head in agreement to his image in the mirror behind the bar.

Ben Lipton slid down to serve some condo dwellers and take care of general bar maintenance. When he returned, he had a fresh tequila and soda for our actor. Our actor realized he always felt better after talking to Ben Lipton, a friend indeed.

"Can I be honest with you?" the bartender asked.

"Of course," Jesse replied.

"I feel like I've had this exact same conversation way too many times, and I have to say, I'm a little worried about ya, man …"

"Me?"

"I'm afraid you're starting to sound like one of those people."

"*One of those people?*"

"One of those people that's always talking about the way things *used to be*, and this town's overflowing with those people."

"Okay," Jesse said humbly.

"I mean, I've seen too many friends go down a dark road lately and I feel the responsibility to say something."

"Well, thanks for your concern," Jesse said before a brief silence fell between the two friends.

"Maybe you should get outta town, clear your head, go out to the desert."

"The desert?"

"Yeah, you ever been out to Delgado?" the bartender asked as he wiped the bar in front of him even though it was already spotless.

"No, but I've heard good things. Supposed to be magical or something."

"Yeah, things are different out there. It's like a void, massive and empty. You can really put things into perspective. You should check it out—it's only a day's drive away."

"Sounds great, but I don't see myself going on a vacation anytime soon."

"Sometimes you gotta prioritize, my friend."

"I need to stick around here and figure out what I'm gonna do."

"Maybe you could go work on a project or something?" Ben Lipton said, not giving in to his friend's apprehension. "At the very least, you could take some cool photos of yourself in the desert; I know you always need that," Ben said as he disappeared into a room behind the bar.

The thought was intriguing. Jesse had a flash of himself in

all black standing on a dusty road in the middle of the desert staring into the lens of a camera. He'd been dreaming of working on something to give his reel some depth ever since *Mirage* had fallen through. Something to showcase the full range of his abilities. Something he could write for himself to star in. The desert seemed like the place it could all happen, but the idea of leaving didn't feel possible.

Ben walked down to a skinny guy with dark stringy hair falling out of a black fisherman's cap. Jesse watched the deal go down between Ben and his client as they exchanged some grass for cash that Ben folded up and stuck in the pocket of his swim trunks as he walked back to Jesse. Ben was a party guy. He wore a bright floral shirt unbuttoned down to his navel that showed off his tanned chest.

"What if I told you that I'd be willing to cover a percentage of your trip out to Delgado? Would you go?"

"You'd pay for my trip?" Jesse asked.

"I could pay for some of it, but I'd need to ask a favor."

"Which is?"

"So, I'm investing in this big piece of land out near Delgado that me and my partner are turning into a lunar colony resort, stargazer paradise. This thing is going to be mind blowing!"

"A lunar colony?"

"Yeah, it's out in this chunk of desert that looks like the moon. We're putting in a series of dome houses that are connected to common areas with a pool and hot tubs. At night, the domes open to the sky and it feels like you're in space—like space on Earth. There's nothing else like it anywhere and it's going to attract people from all over the world. We'll have astronomers come out, give star tours and everything."

"Sounds cool, but how do I fit in?"

"As you know, I can't put my money in the bank, so I have to find other opportunities to invest in. We need all sorts of capital to get this thing off the ground. Wells need to be dug, permits need to get paid for, we have to hire a world-class architect, but the most pressing matter is retaining this local West Texas attorney to fight off an oil pipeline that is set to run right through the middle of our resort. The attorney can get the whole pipeline diverted for the right price, but I need to get my partner the cash ASAP for a down payment to lock in the attorney. I can't get out there for a couple weeks and I don't want to mail that much money."

"How much are we talking?"

"Eight grand."

"What about your partner? He can't drive it out?"

"No, because he's stuck out there working with the architect that's designing and building the dome structures. This guy is the best in the world, and he's there in Delgado now."

"I see, so you need a delivery driver," Jesse said.

"That's right, and there's not a lot of people I trust in our circle of friends with eight thousand dollars cash, but I trust you. Whaddaya say?"

"I'd need to think about it. Not sure that I can get away."

"I'd give you a ten percent delivery fee, eight hundred bucks. That'd pay for your gas to and from and put you up in a cool desert motel for a few nights. I have the money right here in my backpack in the office behind the bar."

"Wow, okay," Jesse said, feeling pressured to make a decision on the spot.

"It's cool if you need some time to think about it, but I have to get my partner the money in the next couple of days, so I'd need an answer soon, otherwise I'll have to ask my mom to do it."

"Give me twenty-four hours to kick it around and see if it's something I could make work."

"That's fine. Let me know in a day or two. Free vacation and you can check out the Star Colony—it's like nothing you've ever seen before."

"Okay, how much do I owe here?" Jesse asked.

Ben Lipton only charged him for the weed; the tequila was on the house. Jesse tipped for both and left the Coconut Club.

. . .

Waiting for the walk sign at a crosswalk, Jesse was startled by a lady who appeared out of nowhere. She looked out of her mind as she asked him for a dollar. He reached for his wallet but suddenly realized who had stopped him. He recognized her.

"Carla?" he asked.

"You gotta dollar, man," she repeated.

It was as if there was nothing on the other side of her once sparkling green eyes.

"Carla? It's me, Jesse."

She gazed at him with a blank stare. He wondered what happened. She always liked to party, she was a little wild, but no more than any of their other friends. This seemed to be more than just booze or drugs getting out of hand—she was a shell of herself. He thought about their first kiss at her apt on 13th Street, a few blocks away, over by the jail where he heard she'd been spending plenty of time lately.

"Is there something I can do to help?" he asked.

"You got ten dollars?"

He thought about it, but knew he gave everything he had in his wallet to his bartending friend upstairs.

"I can go to an ATM and get you some money."

Her eyes darted around like a trapped animal. For a split-second, they seemed to connect.

"Fuck you, pal," he heard her say as she walked off.

Jesse crossed the street and sat in his car, saddened by what he had just witnessed. He looked back and saw Carla panhandling a group of tourists on the sidewalk. He watched her in disbelief as she blended in with the other street people. He wondered what drove her here. She had talent and beauty and everything going for her, but it seemed to have all vanished. He kept his eyes on her as she walked in front of a billboard on the side of a building with bright golden postcard typography that read GATEWAY TO NOWHERE—DISCOVER MAGICAL DELGADO, TX. An infinite highway led into desert mountains bathed in the light of sunset. It looked like he could drive straight into it.

He got out of his car and walked back up to the rooftop bar of the Coconut Club. In a few minutes, he returned to the street carrying a blue vinyl bank bag. He jumped into the driver's seat and U-turned in search of Carla. He found her on the sidewalk a couple of blocks away and pulled up to the curb.

"Carla," he called to her, pulling a twenty-dollar bill out of the bank bag.

She approached the car with a suspicious gaze. He handed her the twenty. She inspected it for a moment, stretching it between both hands.

She looked back at Jesse and asked, "Can I get a ride?"

His first reaction was to open the passenger door, but he

stopped himself. He realized he could give her the twenty dollars and drive away or he could take her with him to the desert and get her out of here. He had a flash of the two of them on the open road, of Carla bouncing around the car with her own spastic energy and him wondering why he brought her. He knew she would alter the course of the trip in a chaotic manner and chaos was something he'd like to avoid. He wanted to help, but couldn't afford to get held up in town driving her around on drug errands. He needed time to himself out there in the emptiness. He reached into the bank bag, handed her another twenty, and drove away.

2

ESSE STRANGE WATCHED THE SKYLINE SHRINK in his rearview as he cut out of the city as fast as traffic would allow. In the passenger seat was a hard copy of Stella Adler's *The Art of Acting*. He listened to an audio excerpt of Stella herself reading from the book on his stereo.

"We have a dilemma. We don't want what we see to be flat and without interest. But we don't want to overdo it so people think we're "pushing." The answer is that we must be truthful. The more details we imagine, the more honest and believable and energetic our responses will be. Nine-tenths of your acting lies in the minute knowledge of what you see and what you do."

He felt this statement summed up the essence of the book and wanted to listen and read the line over and over because he felt that in it lay the key to the craft. He was excited to get out and study the actions of real people. In Austin, everybody was pushing to be an artist, a musician, a dancer, a developer, a manager, all opportunists in some capacity, all trying to "make it," all trying to hold it together in the public eye. He was filled with wonder by the prospect of real people doing real people things and couldn't wait to explore the honesty and humility of it, but before he could get out of town, a downpour erupted.

The tropical moisture had reached its breaking point and the rain fell hard. There wasn't much he could do but find shelter under a covered gas station awning, put the top up, and attempt to patch his back window, which was hung to the tan soft top with safety pins. He also figured this would be a good time to roll a joint while he waited for the storm to pass. In the time it took him to break up a pile of weed on the front cover of *The Art of Acting* and roll it up, the peak of the storm passed. He got back on the road and sparked the doobie. All he could see in front of him was clear blue western sky.

He felt he was doing the right thing, even if he was breaking the promise he'd made to himself. A few months ago he swore to only take acting jobs to make his way—no more waiting tables or serving drinks or anything that would keep him complacent with an easy paycheck. He'd managed to stay afloat this far, but there wasn't much on the horizon. He reasoned this delivery job he'd taken for Ben Lipton was different because it was just enough to cover the trip. He knew his cut of the money wouldn't go far, but it was comforting to know all that cash was tucked away in his suitcase in the trunk. Other than that, there were a couple of residual checks he'd been waiting on for a commercial he did that he didn't want to talk about and hoped no one saw.

The highway had him thinking about the classic Texas road movie *The Getaway* starring Steve McQueen and Ali McGraw. He worked himself into the mind of Steve McQueen's character Doc, calm and methodical in the eye of every gun-nut cop in the state hot on his trail, just trying to make an escape with his lady. He imagined Ali McGraw sitting beside him in a sexy brown overcoat, miniskirt, and boots. *God, she was something in that flick*, he thought. The film was directed by Sam Peckinpah.

"Peckpinpaaaahhhh!" he shouted out to the sky, God, Universe, void, whatever, in honor of the director's incredible contribution to the canon of American cinema. "Talk about a fucking madman," he said aloud. Peckinpah was up there with the greats for him. All the greats were outsiders, he thought. For actors, his favorites were the classics: Dean, Brando, Bogart, Hopper, Warren Oates, Harry Dean, McQueen, Paul Newman. Brando in *One-Eyed Jacks* was his ultimate style icon. He hoped there was still room in the world for actors of this caliber, but he was less sure every day.

He kept driving west, fantasizing about Ali McGraw's legs in *The Getaway* sitting beside him. All signs of the city had faded away and he was soon in a vast new landscape. The tree-lined hills slowly turned to scrub brush desert with glorious rocky purple mountains crowning the horizon to the south. *Mexico!*, he marveled. The air was thick with the smell of fracking and creosote.

He spotted a gas station sign in the distance, rising above the highway, with nothing else around. He was glad it was open when he pulled up, the tank was damn near empty and who knew what lay ahead? He sat at the pump and brought his awareness back to his actions, turned the car off, got out, and unscrewed the gas cap, conscious of his every maneuver. There was a garage next to the gas station and a couple of men were standing in the doorway, one inside in the shadow, the other outside in the sun. Broken-down cars littered a field behind them. Most were missing doors, tires, and hoods. Jesse noticed the two men and studied their movements.

Goddammit, there they are, he thought. *Real motherfuckin' people.*

They both looked the actor over and nodded to him. He nodded back with the hope that maybe they thought he was one of them, just an old desolate cowboy in a beat-up white Mazda Miata. He watched them out of the corner of his eye and tried to mimic the way they stood, both slightly hunched over. Both lean and dressed in loose denim. Their movements indicated they had nothing but time on their hands. What were they talking about, he wondered. Probably something about a horse or a coyote. Probably something about how the world had gone crazy. He continued watching them shuffling with their hands in their pockets, one in the sunlight, one in the shade.

"Son, you might wanna turn that pump off," one of the men called out.

"Huh? Oh, shit."

Gasoline was overflowing out of the tank onto the ground around him. Jesse regained his composure as he lifted the handle and placed it back on the dirty old gas pump.

"Sorry 'bout that," he called back to them.

They went back to their conversation.

"Think we're gonna see any rain?" he asked.

"We had a little storm yesterdee, but it don't rain too much around here."

"I was thinking of putting my top down."

"You'll probably be okay. Might wanna wear a hat though."

Good point, he thought. He looked out upon that vast desert getting baked by the unrelenting sun and decided it would be best to keep his top up for now, at least until sunset.

"You're gonna have to come inside to pay. Credit card slot don't work on those pumps no more," the fellow standing in the garage said to Jesse as he made his way inside the station.

Jesse found the man standing behind the counter in front of a large picture window with a view of the infinite desert.

"Beautiful view ya got there."

"Huh?" asked the man as he inspected the register, gazed out the window at the pump, and back at his cash register all in one slow maneuver.

"It's a nice view you have of the desert out there."

"The desert? Just a bunch a dirt," the man said as he double-checked his registers one last time. The actor paid close attention to the mechanic's every move and noticed how the man's leather skin sagged at the back of his neck as he craned his head to the pumps.

"Looks like twenty-five on the nose," he said as he squinted his old honker.

Jesse paid cash and the man counted out the change with his grease-coated talons.

Jesse Strange sat in his car and watched the man walk back to his friend still standing by the garage. They put their hands in their pockets and looked at each other, one in the sunlight, one in the shade. The actor left the station in awe of the cool simplicity of it all.

The road to Delgado bent south in the direction of the border. It dipped into canyons and rose to rocky plateaus with endless views. There were signs on the highway announcing the dried-up riverbeds it passed over; they had names like Diablo Wash and Horsehead Canyon. Massive yuccas lined the roadside with tall spindly stalks shooting up to flowers on the verge of blooming. Jesse found the joint he rolled earlier in his console and lit it again.

He continued twisting through the desert, listening to

nothing but the deafening roar of the middle of nowhere flying past. He saw the mountains of Mexico in front of him. Somewhere out there, the Rio Grande snaked along the bottom of the backbone that lay in the distance. He drove through a dried-up mining town with no signs of visible life. Shadows fell across the highway that ran between a few crumbling houses, an abandoned rodeo, and a couple of boarded-up gas stations. Our actor wished there was someone here whose character he could study, but there wasn't a soul around. He imagined the film that fell through taking place in towns like this. Nothing there but rattlesnakes, dust, and bullets. A violent movie set in what had always been a violent land. His starring role that got away, *Mirage.*

Mirage was a dystopian road thriller set in Texas and Mexico full of action, love, and savagery. It was an opportunity Jesse had always dreamed of, a physical role that would showcase his range. It would have been a huge boost to his career and brought him much attention. It had a hot new production company behind it and solid distribution but something didn't pan out. The financing fell through. Not an uncommon fate for an Indie production, but it was a blow to Jesse's confidence and he needed to get out of his head about it. These were the last days of his twenty-seventh year. He'd soon be turning twenty-eight and in his mind that may as well be the big one. There weren't a lot of opportunities on the scale of *Mirage* coming around and he wondered if there would ever be another one. A feeling of desperation was creeping in, and he knew desperation was a killer.

Out on the barren highway, something hit him out of nowhere—it was the urge. He dreamed of an old dusty saloon somewhere he could set himself right. He had tequila on the brain. The sun was blinding as it descended on the horizon, making it impossible to see anything but golden vapors a few feet in front of the car slithering along the road beyond him. He squinted his eyes and drove faster, knowing that it would get cold when the sun set. With night falling on the endless desert, he saw a rare sign of life flickering in the distance ahead of him. As it approached, he began to make out the flashing signal above the highway. It was three red neon ponies moving in succession. Below the ponies flashed the words OPEN—BEER.

3

HE PULLED INTO THE PARKING LOT and stopped just below the neon ponies blinking above him. It was an adobe building the color of rust, and now that he looked closer, it seemed to be on the verge of falling down. Maybe there would be something more inviting down the highway. *Don't be a chicken shit*, he told himself. *Open the door, and if something doesn't seem right, jump back in the car and get outta here. No problem.*

He thought about the money and weighed his options. Leave it in the trunk or take it inside with him? He got out, popped the trunk, and scanned the parking lot. There was one empty pickup truck parked beside the building. He didn't see anyone else around. He put on the tweed coat he had lying in the trunk and opened his suitcase. He took the cash out of the bank bag and slid it into the inner pocket of his coat. It was probably safer to have it on him than leave it alone in the parking lot of a highway bar.

He walked to the door with his shoulders cocked back. He opened it and paused to scan the place before stepping inside. The room was big and empty except for a couple of pool tables, a small stage in the corner, and a dimly lit bar at the back of the room. Jesse strolled back and sat down on a stool. He swung his head back and forth down the length of the bar, trying to imitate the mechanic he saw back at the gas station. There were a couple of tourists who looked like they'd been hiking around the mountains all day and a big black bartender with soft eyes who came down to where Jesse sat and asked, "What can I get ya, man?"

"Tequila soda."

The bartender grabbed a small glass from the mirrored wall behind him and filled it with ice from the well. Jesse knew instantly this man knew what he was doing. He slugged a heavy pour of tequila into the glass and picked up the soda gun. "Lime?" he asked.

"Yes, please," our actor answered.

The bartender slid the drink and Jesse Strange handed over a crisp twenty.

After handing Jesse his change, the bartender went back to the tourists at the other end of the bar.

"So, like I was saying," he continued to the tourists.

Jesse stared at the memorabilia covering the mirror in front of him and tried to look removed as he listened to every word the bartender said. It was hard not to, because the bar was silent otherwise.

"So, this cat walks in here in a duster jacket clutching his side. He looks like utter shit. Sits down right there and says, 'Let me get a bottle o' Bud.' I say, 'Sir, you look like you need a doctor.' He says, 'No, lemme getta bottle o' Bud.' He opens his duster jacket and shows me his bloodstained shirt. I say, 'Mister, you look like you need more than a beer. You been shot or something?' He told me he'd been gored by a bull training for the rodeo behind the bar and was waiting on the ambulance. I could hear the sirens coming closer and closer. He said, 'Gimme a beer before I'm stuck in that shithole, man.'

"You gave him a beer, right?" the male tourist asked.

"Hell yeah, I did. We've all been there, right?"

The tourists chuckled.

"He slammed his beer and I gave him another. Just then the ambulance pulled up and the paramedics rushed in. That old cowboy took his beer with him on the stretcher."

"Damn," said the tourists.

"They're a tough breed," said the bartender.

Jesse heard all of this and inched his way closer to the tourists and the bartender.

The bartender asked him, "You good, man? You need anything?"

"I'll have another whenever you get a chance," he answered.

"That's what I'm here for, my friend. Tell ya what, you strike me as the type of cat who might have all right taste in music. The jukebox over there is full of credits. We just need someone to pick some tunes. Why don't you hit us with your best shot and I'll whip you up another ranch water?"

"Oh, my pleasure," Jesse replied to the bartender.

He walked over to the jukebox on the wall and took a look. There seemed to be an equal mix of Country and Soul. Our actor was never a big fan of Country music, so he focused on the Soul. The first song that stuck out to him was "Needle In A Haystack" by The Velvettes. He followed that up with selection of classics by Junior Walker & The All Stars, Willie Mitchell, Martha and the Vandellas, The Ronettes, Smokey Robinson, Sam & Dave, and The Dramatics. A group of people entered the bar and walked over to order drinks. Jesse went back to the bar to retrieve his tequila. The bartender came by and said, "I had a feeling about you."

"Who's that cowboy in those photos behind you?" Jesse asked.

The bartender turned back to look and replied, "That's the owner."

"Looks familiar."

"He's been in a ton of films, bunch of Westerns and stuff. You've probably seen him in something."

The owner looked like a real cowboy, the type of cowboy who was as comfortable in front of the camera as he was on the range.

More people started streaming into the bar and grooving to the music playing from the jukebox. It was a mix of hip locals and tourists looking for something authentic in an inauthentic world. Jesse took his tequila to a pool table and started chalking a pool cue. He was never that great at pool, but tonight he wanted to get good.

As he took his time clearing the table, he was startled by a commotion outside that sounded like tires screeching uncontrollably across the pavement and slamming into a dumpster. Suddenly, the door burst open and in walked the person Jesse had come here hoping he would find. He had to do a double take, but it was her.

They met one night about a year ago in the bar of the Stanton Hotel in downtown Austin. An upscale place in which Jesse wouldn't normally find himself, but on this night he was there for a wrap party for a film he had just worked on called *Dust Devil Heat*. She was drinking by herself but didn't look lonely. He figured she must've been part of the production, although he didn't recall ever seeing her around the set. When he finally worked up the nerve to approach her, she said she didn't know what he was talking about.

"All of these people are part of a movie?" she asked, glancing around at the characters in the room without much interest. "That makes sense."

She was tall and blonde and looked like she just walked out of an Italian Neo Realist flick. He asked her what she was doing here. She said she was in town to see the bats, which he took for an obvious lie. She asked him the same question, and when he told her he was an actor, she didn't believe him. She was sophisticated but down to earth and full of a smart-ass confidence. She didn't seem to be searching for anything, just let it all come to her. She was rare in this world. They talked for hours drunk in a corner making up stories about themselves until the wrap party cleared out. Then she told him she was from Delgado and he assumed that was also a lie. She said he should come out and visit her. He asked where to find her if he did and she said the town wasn't too big. "If you ever made it out, there's a good chance we'd bump into each other." He believed her after she said this, because something in her eyes changed, as if she wasn't proud of it but it was just the way it was. When he went to the bar to order them another tequila, he turned around to see her getting into the back seat of a car on the street and disappearing into the night.

There were times he thought about driving out to Delgado to see if he could find her, but he always talked himself out of it. He never had the time or the money or a car that would make it. When Ben Lipton mentioned escaping to Delgado back at the Coconut Club, he didn't consciously think of her, but there was an excitement bubbling deep down that was about more than the desert landscape. About halfway out, she popped into his head and he wondered if he'd run into her, and *BAM*, there she was busting through the door with a brunette at her side who had the same fiery eyes and impenetrable air of confidence. Jesse leaned across the pool table with one eye on the cue ball and the other watching the girls as they walked past on their way to the bar.

Another song by Junior Walker & The All Stars came on called "Shoot Your Shot."

"Oh, my God, KT!" the blonde called out with her arms open.

The bartender came out and hugged both of the girls. "'Bout time you got back," the bartender said to them.

"You know we couldn't stay away from you for long," the blonde told the bartender.

"My Frankie and Nina are back," the bartender said. "Let's do a shot. What do you want?"

"Tequila," said the blonde.

"Mezcal," said the brunette.

The bartender lined up three shot glasses on the bar and poured two shots of blanco tequila and a shot of mezcal. The three of them grabbed their shots, raised them in a toast before tapping the bar, slammed them back, and brought their empty shot glasses back down on the bar.

A female tourist asked Jesse if he wanted to play a game of pool; she looked like an adult Girl Scout. She was with a couple other tourist friends who had taken over the pool table beside his. Jesse racked up the balls, keeping his eye on the blonde at the bar.

"You break," he said.

They shuffled around the pool table playing a slow game. He couldn't help but be distracted by the girls having a wild time at the bar. The tourists finished up their games and left our actor alone. He really tried to put a show on clearing the table, channeling his inner Paul Newman. He cracked a ball so hard it bounced off the table and rolled across the floor.

The blonde took notice and said, "Well, goddamned if you don't look like some sly devil," from across the room.

The brunette and the blonde approached him. He kept shooting at the remaining balls on the table. The two girls tried to get a read on him.

"So, you're just over here all by your lonesome?" the blonde asked. The brunette hung around like her shadow.

"I was just about to start the next game. You in?"

"I don't play," the blonde replied.

"What about you?" Jesse asked the brunette.

She shook her head.

He already had quarters in the slots. He pushed them in and proceeded to rack up another game.

"Where'd you blow in from?" asked the blonde.

He wasn't sure how to answer.

"Don't tell me, let me see if I can guess." She stood an arm's length away and began inspecting Jesse. "I can tell by your hands your not from West Texas, because they don't look like they've seen a day of hard work in their life."

Jesse disagreed but nodded anyway.

"People generally only come out here from a few places. Sure, you have random tourists from France or Japan, but for the most part they all come from the same handful of places."

She looked him up and down and said, "You don't look straight enough to be from Houston."

"No?" the actor asked as he broke without sinking anything.

"I mean people from Houston tend to follow the rules and you don't look like you always follow the rules."

Fair enough, he thought as he walked around the table looking for a shot.

"I could see Dallas actually," she paused, "but people from Dallas are a little dingy, like they've been hit by a train. You look like you've probably read a book or two, so I'm gonna rule out the Big D."

He couldn't disagree with her on that assessment.

"And you're definitely not from San Antonio or El Paso. Well, because you're not. Right, Nina?"

"Definitely not," said Nina.

"So, that leaves New York. I might detect a bit of New York. After all, you're wearing a black button-up shirt tucked into jeans and a tweed coat that looks like you bought it at a thrift store." The actor sunk the nine ball in a corner pocket. "But the thing is, the people who come here from New York are more the real estate investor, gallery owner types, more Manhattan and less Brooklyn and I'd say you're the opposite of that. That brings us to Los Angeles. Yeah, I could definitely see that. I can tell you care about your looks, but there's something telling me you drove into town in that beat-up white convertible in the parking lot and nobody from LA would drive around in something like that." The blonde was knocking Jesse off what little game he had. "Sure, plenty of people from LA drive white convertibles, but not in that condition. Besides, that convertible in the parking lot had Texas plates and no self-respecting Angeleno would drive around with Texas plates. So, the only other place left that people come here from is Austin. I'm gonna guess Austin. What about you, Nina?"

"That would be my guess," said Nina.

"You got me. You spent much time there?"

"Enough to know what it's all about."

"Do you remember the bar at the Stanton Hotel?"

The blonde seemed to freeze and squint her eyes as she further inspected the actor.

"Hmmm, doesn't ring a bell," she said.

The front door of the bar swung open and two guys and a girl entered the bar.

"Holy shit, it's a family reunion," the blonde cried out as she and the brunette met the new arrivals in an embrace in the middle of the room. The three newcomers looked like clean-cut city people in the type of clothes you'd pay a lot of money to work out in. They all made their way back to the bar to do more shots.

Jesse was left alone and continued to work on his pool game. He focused on the way he held the stick and trained his eyes on the pocket he wanted the ball to fall into. How were his legs planted? Was one leg more forward than the other? Was a knee bent? Did he move to his next shot knowing this one would fall or did he wait to find out? Did he put more effort into the reverse action or follow through? Had he been practicing all day or resting up in a hotel room? Did he have a fight with his girlfriend earlier? Had he had a couple of cocktails or was he stone-cold sober? Where did he learn to play? Denver or New Jersey? Who was he right now? He cleared the table and racked up another. Everything he had was riding on this game.

The blonde called out to the pool table, "What are you drinking, cowboy?"

"Same as you," the actor called back.

"KT, couple of añejos, neat."

She walked over with the two tequilas and sat one on the side of the pool table in front of him.

"We're all going to a little party in town when KT closes. You interested?"

"Yeah, but the thing is, I have no idea where I'm at right now. So, like, I don't even know where town is."

"That's okay, just follow us."

The bar filled with more locals and tourists. People kept asking Jesse where he was from. He didn't want to answer. He felt like he was in a distant land that was much cooler than where he came from.

Our actor got drunk and couldn't take his eyes off the blonde. He tried not to let her notice, even tried to make sure she saw him talking to a couple other girls, but at a certain point, he didn't care. They all continued to drink until KT closed the bar down. Everyone made their way out into the night and our actor followed.

He sat in his car in the parking lot breathing in the cold desert air and gazing into space. There were more stars than he recalled ever seeing in his life. He had the realization that he was in space, on Earth in space, and there was nothing separating him from what was out there. A large shiny black SUV pulled up beside him and the brunette in the passenger seat asked, "You following us?"

Jesse tried to say something, but nothing came out, so he just nodded and shifted into reverse. He followed the massive SUV out onto the highway and he saw the lights of a small town in the distance in front of him. The SUV pulled off onto the shoulder and Jesse did the same. He sat behind them on the side of the road and the blonde jumped out of the driver's side. She ran around and raised the back door of the SUV and started looking for something in the back. Jesse had his headlights shining on her. She was wearing a black fuzzy coat that her long thin legs stretched out of and fell into a pair of knee-high black leather boots. She found what she was looking for and ran back to our actor's car. "You want one?" she asked, holding a cigarette out to him.

"Why not?"

He put it in his mouth as she pulled a lighter out of her pocket and lit it for him. She ran and jumped back in her truck.

He followed the girls toward the twinkling lights of the town. The frigid air whipped across his face and through his hair. The galaxy stretched out around him. A strange frequency started pulsating out of his radio and he turned it up, trying to figure out what it was. A Delgado City Limits sign flashed by and the cars slowed to a creep through the small desert town. The place seemed to be crumbling and more rundown than our actor expected, but he liked it even more than the way it had been in his mind.

The SUV turned right onto a residential street. The girls parked and got out to walk across the lawn of an ancient house. He tried to catch up to them. When he made it to the party, he didn't see them anywhere. Someone standing in front of the front door handed Jesse a joint. He felt obligated to partake and ended up fucked up out of his mind, roaming around a party where he knew no one. Many of the same people from the bar were packed throughout the house. Jesse couldn't help but look for his friends, the blonde and the brunette. He caught a glimpse of them, then they disappeared. He found himself in a kitchen packed full of people. He did another shot of something and decided he needed some water. He sipped from a glass he filled in the sink. There was a girl standing next to him who said sweetly, "You're already drinking water?" He wondered what she meant by this as a small old lady appeared in the kitchen. She had white hair and grayish-brown skin with eyes that swirled like the Milky Way. She stood about four feet tall in a red smock dress and smiled gently at Jesse. Around her neck hung a leather strap connected to a Polaroid camera. She stared at Jesse. He and the girl next to him stared back at the little lady, entranced by her swirling eyes and spectral gaze. She brought the camera up and started to laugh as she pointed it at Jesse. The flash went off and he dropped the glass of water.

4

HE SWUNG HIS LEGS ONTO THE COLD HARD FLOOR and realized he was still fully dressed. God, he was hungover. How could he even be in this shape? The only thing that he could imagine would help was weed. He put his hands in the pockets of his jeans and pulled out a key for room 103 of the Hotel El Dorado. He was happy to find his wallet in his back pocket. He walked across the room, found the bathroom, and looked at himself in the mirror. He splashed cold water on his face and brushed his hair back with his fingers. "Where the hell are we, man?" The morning was a mystery, and he had to look for clues. Was his car outside, he wondered. Everything would be fine if his car was outside. He walked to the window and peered out onto a courtyard surrounded by other rooms with a pool in the middle. There was no parking lot in sight. His car had to be out there somewhere, but what about his keys or phone, he wondered. He looked around the room but couldn't find them. Maybe they were in his coat, but he didn't see that either. Then he remembered the more than eight thousand dollars in cash he crammed into the inner pocket of his coat. A panic washed over him.

He tried to calm himself down as he stepped out of the room into the blinding morning sun. His eyes squinted—he could barely tolerate the intensity, he needed his sunglasses. He assured himself that his car would be parked somewhere in front of the hotel and once he found it everything would be better.

He straightened out his body as he walked along the sidewalk that led through the courtyard. The pool was empty, there was sand in the bottom, and a few spiny weeds growing out of the cracks. The sidewalk led around a corner past the hotel office and out onto the street. He looked up and down the street for his white convertible. He walked around the corner and there was no sign of his ride. He walked down an alley in hopes that there was a parking lot behind the hotel, but it was just an empty dusty alley. He kept walking down the alley like a washed-up old gunslinger. *Why washed up?* he thought. *I'm the hot new hired gun in this town and I'm as fast as they come. I'm gonna find my pony and paint the whole place blood red.* At the end of the alley, he saw the town square to his right with a handful of storefronts and businesses scattered around it. To his left, he saw an open sign on the sidewalk in front of a café. There were cars parked on the street, but he didn't see his. The café had stoked an ember in his mind; coffee was sure to jog his memory.

He ordered up a cup, took it out to a small gravel-covered patio and sat down at a flimsy metal table in the shade of an ancient willow tree. Aw, the coffee was good and dark. *This'll help unlock some memories from the night before*, he thought, but all he had was a faint recollection of being at a party somewhere in the town. He realized he must have walked to the hotel from the party. He was certain that if he could find the party house, he'd find his car, the money, and everything else.

He was supposed to call Ben Lipton's business partner to

unload the cash as soon as he got to town, but he didn't have a phone or the cash. He sat contemplating what to do. A guy and girl dressed like they were in a Los Angeles rock band stepped out onto the patio. They both had long frizzy black hair and wore leather boots poking out of striped bell bottoms. They ambled around a bit hunched over and stoney. The guy spied Jesse and said, "Oh, hey, there you are. What happened to you last night?" he asked as he walked over.

"What happened to me?" Jesse asked with a nervous smile.

"Ha, yeah. We were talking on the porch and you were telling us about how the director of *Two Lane Blacktop* said that the only true movies are road movies and any movie that's not set on the road is just theater. I wanted to hear the rest but you were gone."

"Gone?"

"You walked away and I didn't see you again."

"Aw, well, that was pretty much the whole story," Jesse said, feeling terrible that he didn't remember any of this. "Any chance you know the address of the porch we were hanging out on last night?"

"I don't know the street number if that's what you're asking. It's Sam and Rita's house on South 3rd, I think."

"Yeah, South 3rd," the girl said.

"Is it an easy walk from here?"

"Yeah, it's only a few blocks. Just walk down to 3rd and take a right," the guy instructed.

Our actor stood up to leave and said, "Let's catch up later if you're around and I'll finish that story."

"We'll be around, but I thought you said you already finished the story."

"Oh, there's always more."

. . .

Out on the sidewalk, our actor walked south toward 3rd. There wasn't much activity happening around the town square. He assumed most people had sense enough to stay inside during the day around here. The sun was straight above and blazing. He wondered why his tweed coat wasn't in the hotel room. If he walked from the party, he would have needed his coat in the cold night air of the desert, he reasoned. He kept his eyes peeled in case he threw it off somewhere.

He passed the storefronts of Main Street, a pharmacy, a hat shop, a gallery. None of it looked familiar. On the corner, he came upon the town movie theater, The Delgado. On the marquee hung a few random letters that didn't spell anything. It looked locked up and empty. A poster was taped up in the window above the ticket counter for the movie, *The Border*. On the poster, Jack Nicholson was dressed as a border patrol agent in front of a fence and an American flag. Jesse didn't see any showtimes displayed but made a mental note to see this film if he got the chance. Even though he hadn't seen the movie, he could only assume that a Hollywood depiction of the border patrol in the early Eighties would most likely paint the agency in a less-than-positive light. That meant the Delgado Theater was giving a big fuck-you to the local border patrol by having this poster hanging in its window. Our actor had respect for the Delgado if that was the case.

He walked past an elementary school with a landscape mural painted on the wall that mirrored the surrounding desert. Parts of the stucco had fallen off the building, creating gaps in the painting. There was a large photo taken of the playground full of children in 1916 hanging between two wooden pillars, but the plastic frame around the photo had melted and made the whole thing look like a film burn you would see on actual celluloid. Brittle bleached wispy weeds grew out of all the sidewalk cracks. Windblown piles of sand were in every available space. The whole town seemed like it would slowly turn back into the desert if it wasn't actively maintained.

He came upon 3rd Street and took a right. Down about two blocks away, he spotted his car and almost sprinted toward it. He was filled with relief when he reached it and saw his copy of *The Art of Acting* safe in the passenger seat. His weed and sunglasses were still in the console and his phone was sitting in front of the gear shift. Lying on the back seat was his tweed coat. He checked the inner pocket and found the wad of cash; in the side pocket were his keys. He wondered what the hell he was thinking throwing his coat full of money in the back seat like that with the top down. He was concerned for himself and decided to put the top up to hide from the sun and the world.

He sat in the driver's seat and counted the money—it all seemed to be there. He knew he needed to give Ben Lipton's business partner a call and looked at his phone for the number Ben texted him. The text said: *Call Neil when you get to town 5129747301.*

The phone was almost dead, but he tried the number anyway. Neil answered right away. He had a deep and formal tone.

"Hey, this is Ben's friend Jesse. I'm here in Delgado and I have some money for you."

"Aw, bless you, my friend. Here's the deal, my architect and I had to come up to El Paso to check on a few things and we won't be back until tomorrow morning. Are you planning to be around there awhile?"

"I was planning to hang around a few days."

"Great, I'll text you first thing tomorrow morning with instructions on where to meet." Jesse sat there staring at the fat stack of cash in his lap and wondered what to do with himself. He got out, took the money to the trunk, and put it back into the bank bag in his suitcase. He thought he'd cruise around Delgado for a bit and see the sights. Maybe go back to that hat shop he saw on the town square. Hit up the Hotel El Dorado and find out what the deal was.

"Hey, there, Cool Hand," someone called out from behind. He turned to find the huge blacked-out SUV idling beside him. The passenger side window was down, and he saw the blonde calling out to him from behind the wheel.

"Heading down to the hot springs today. You wanna take a ride?"

"Why not?" Jesse said with zero deliberation.

The rear passenger side door swung open, a couple of guys got out and shuffled around to get into the third row of seats. Jesse unzipped the bank bag and attempted to cram the cash into the front pocket of his jeans but he had to break it into two wads and fill both pockets. He walked over and jumped into a second-row seat directly behind the brunette riding shotgun. There were the two guys sitting in the back row, a girl sitting next to Jesse, and the blonde and brunette in the front. All of these people were at the bar last night.

The brunette turned around to Jesse and asked, "You been to the hot springs yet?"

"I haven't been anywhere yet except for that bar and my hotel."

"Do you remember our names?"

Jesse thought about it before saying, "Sorry, I don't."

"I'm Nina," said the brunette.

"And I'm Frankie," said the blonde.

"Daniella," the girl beside him said. She was wearing shorts and had long dark legs that took up half the back seat. Every now and then they would bump up against our actor's legs and he would inch his way closer to the door.

"Dante."

"Brian."

Jesse nodded to all of them as they introduced themselves.

"And who does that make you, cowboy?" asked the blonde as she navigated her tank of a truck out of Delgado and into the desert.

"That'd make me Jesse Strange."

"Jesse Strange. I can see that."

"Yeah, I can see that," the brunette agreed.

The paved road leading out of town turned to a rocky dirt pass meandering up into the mountains south of Delgado. Tall golden grass and the spears of new Yucca blooms shot up along the hillsides. The mountains were shades of brown, red, and blue and crowned the horizon in every direction. The peaks varied in shape and altitude. They didn't seem to follow any of the traditional mountain patterns or formations that our actor was familiar with. He'd been to most parts of Texas and all over the US West, but he had never been here and never seen mountains like this. There was an overwhelming chaos of earthly design. He felt disoriented and out of place and suddenly his hangover hit him like a shock wave. His plan was to not say much and attempt to remain mysterious, just keep his eye on Frankie, the blonde, and try to figure her out, but he was feeling shaky and knew that he could use something to help his hangover soon.

"Say, there wouldn't happen to be a place we could stop for a refreshment of some sort on our way to the springs would there?"

"If the Pueblito store's open, we can stop there, but they only open up when they feel like it," said Nina.

"There's a cooler back there full of drinks. Pass me up a Topo," Frankie instructed.

Dante opened the cooler and Daniella grabbed a glass bottle of sparkling Mexican water and passed it up to the driver. Jesse gazed over at the open cooler and spied many cans of Modelo Especials sharing the ice with the Topos.

"Let me get one of those Modelos. It's too early for sparkling water for me."

He got a chuckle from the others with that one, even though it wasn't much of a joke.

"Ooh, me, too," said Daniella beside him.

"I'll have one," said Nina.

The two guys in the back passed out the beers and everyone cracked them open.

Frankie drove slower as the road became more banged up and rocky the higher they went.

"So, you guys all from around here?" our actor asked, trying to distract himself from Daniella's legs. He already felt better with the Modelo in his hand.

"Frankie's the only who's from out here," said Brian in the back.

"I'm from San Antonio and Nina's from down in the Valle. These two are from Dallas," said Daniella.

"I'm not technically from here," Frankie corrected. "I spent plenty of time growing up around here, but I've lived all over."

"What about you?" Daniella asked our actor.

"Jesse Strange is from Austin," Nina informed her.

"Born and raised? I didn't think anybody was actually from Austin."

"There are a few." Jesse never cared for such small talk and regretted asking the question to begin with. He didn't mind getting to know people and shooting the breeze, but he was always uncomfortable with such a direct line of questioning.

"I could never live in Austin. I mean, I like to go there and party and I've boned a lot of hot guys there, but it's just so overrated these days," Brian chimed in.

"Oh, my God, the traffic's fucking horrible," Daniella added.

Jesse looked onto the infinite otherworldly landscape stretching out in all directions. The elevation was high enough that there were trees now. Twisted piñon pine and junipers grew thicker and a flowing stream ran down the side of a mountain and across the road that must have been coming from a nearby snow melt. This was about the point where they crested a peak and had a view of what seemed like all of Mexico laid out in front of them. It was breathtaking.

"I have some weed if anyone has a paper," Jesse felt inspired to say.

"Of course the guy from Austin brought weed," said Frankie.

"Is that not a thing people do around here?" our actor asked.

"No, seventy-five percent of people are cool out here, it's just the other twenty-five percent are cops or border patrol and they're trying to bust everybody," Nina said.

"It's fine since we're going down to the border, but when we go back you should probably get rid of it. The cops and border patrol pull everybody over on this road going back to Delgado and they will fuck with you for the tiniest amount of weed," said Frankie. "Like, take all of us to jail if they even smell it."

"I didn't know cops cared about weed anymore."

"These cops do, and being this close to the border, they have extended powers and a federal jurisdiction to pretty much do whatever they want."

"They've also spent their entire lives playing cowboys and Indians and now that all of the liberal states have legalized it they feel like it's an assault on all that they hold dear and right in this country. It's fine if you keep it in Delgado, just don't want to drive around with it outside of town. Especially close to the border."

"Last I checked, California also shares a border with Mexico, but I don't wanna go get anybody locked up or anything. Guess I'll have to get rid of the evidence before we head back."

"Probably smart. They'd be happy to ruin your life to feel like they're serving some greater patriotic purpose."

"I'm pretty sure it's also how the local PD makes all its money: speeding and weed."

The road descended down toward the Rio Grande and came to a T. Frankie turned right and there was the Pueblito store without a soul in sight.

"Looks like they're closed," Nina said.

They twisted back through some gravel roads and drove down into a canyon shaded by ancient cottonwoods and finally came to the entrance of the tiny hot springs resort. Frankie parked her tank of a truck in front of the main adobe structure. Everybody got out. The air was as dry as it could be and warmer than back in town. A lady came out of the building saying, "Oh, hey, y'all! I was hopin' somebody'd pay me a visit today."

"Hey, Charlie! Thought we'd come down and have a soak."

Charlie hugged Frankie and Nina. She looked like a true, tough-as-nails Texas cowgirl, obviously not a recent transplant from the city, but someone who'd been out here for a lifetime. She had the leather skin and dry sun-bleached hair to prove it.

"The place is all yours. No one's been out here for days that I'm aware of. Supposed to pick up soon though. Y'all need anything?"

"You wouldn't happen to have a pack of rolling papers lying around for this cosmic cowboy?" Frankie motioned toward Jesse.

"Oh, sure, I can find something for ya. Come on in and let's take a look around the storehouse."

Jesse followed Charlie inside the building through a front office and back to a room that resembled a kitchen pantry.

"People leave all manner of accouterments behind here."

On one wall was a metal shelving unit full of random supplies that you'd want at a place like this; half-full bottles of booze, packs of cigarettes from every known brand, old ball caps, sun hats, sandals, water shoes, jewelry, books, knives, towels, and a few water pistols.

"We keep all this around in case anyone comes back for it, but mostly just give it away to whoever's in need, people like yourself." Charlie found the rolling paper section of her stash shelf.

"Got a few different types of Zig Zags, some JOBs, these are for rolling some type of cone up, these are pretty." She pulled a pack of glittery paper cones with iridescent tips.

"I'll take one of those."

"I've got a few glass pipes, too, if you want one. People bring a lot out here that they don't wanna take back with them. You'd be surprised at what we find. I've got a walk-in cooler full of beer and unopened bottles of wine, full boxes of wine, you name it. Here take one of these bottles of tequila, sugar." She handed Jesse an opened bottle of tequila.

"Wow, okay. Can I pay you for this?"

"No, no, that wouldn't be legal. Just go out there and have a good time. Let me know if y'all need anything else."

"May I ask what's the weirdest thing you've found someone left behind?"

"Well, there's been plenty of dildos of different shapes and colors and sex toys that I couldn't manage to figure out how they were even used. The weirdest thing might be this though."

She opened up a cabinet and pulled out a large rubber bunny mask. "We found this on a bed next to a red and black satin robe. Still can't put that one together. We get some pretty freaky characters out here."

"I can imagine."

Our actor walked to the screen door leading out of the office.

"You been running with that crew long?" Charlie asked before Jesse walked out.

"What do you mean?"

"The friends you're with. You known 'em long?"

"Just since last night."

"That's kinda the impression I got. You'd be wise to proceed with caution is all I'll say."

"Caution?"

"That's all I can say without saying too much," Charlie said with an uneasy smile.

"Señor Strange, you coming?" Frankie called to Jesse from the parking lot.

Jesse left the building and met Frankie and Nina at the trail that led from the parking lot into the hot springs. He thought Charlie must have sized him up and underestimated him, thought he was out of his league or something.

"We thought we should probably save you from Charlie. She's a little too isolated out here and doesn't see many people. She'll corner you if you let her," Nina told Jesse.

"She's such a nut," Frankie said.

The girls led Jesse down a shady trail that led to a small stream. He was mesmerized by Frankie now that he saw her beyond the driver's seat. She would turn back and look at him with her piercing sea green eyes and smile. She was flirting and he just followed along, out of touch with his better mental faculties. He couldn't help but wonder if she indeed had no recollection of their night together at the Stanton Hotel bar or if she was fucking with him.

Along the stream were rock pools for soaking in the warm mineral water.

Daniella and the two guys were already sitting in one of the pools drinking beers.

"Oh, shit, looks like Charlie hooked you up," Dante called out.

Jesse remembered he was holding a bottle of tequila in his hand and held it up to show it off before turning it back and filling his mouth with the warm agave. He offered it to Dante when he reached the others. The two girls took off the small pullover dresses they were wearing. Jesse tried not to focus on what they were wearing underneath as he stripped down to his underwear and got in the soaking pool with the others. The water was cooler than he expected and smelled of sulfur.

Frankie sat down right next to him, her hips touching his. He felt lightheaded and took another pull from the tequila before offering it to Frankie. She took a swig and passed it to her right. There was just enough room for the six of them in the pool. It was cozy.

"So, Jesse, what do you do back in Austin?" asked Brian. "You a musician or something?"

Jesse instantly felt the dread he knew it was important to overcome when answering questions about himself.

"I'm an actor."

Everyone in the pool seemed intrigued.

"An actor!" Daniella said.

"Like in movies?"

"Movies, theater, commercials if I can get 'em."

"Ooh, anything we would have seen?" Nina asked.

"Probably not."

"I was in a movie once," Dante said.

"Shut up. What was your character?" asked Brian.

"My character was Dante. I just played myself. They needed a black gay guy from Dallas and I was a natural."

"A lot of the greatest actors just played themselves," said Jesse.

"So, you just do indies in Austin? Do you make a living?" asked Nina.

"That's mostly what they shoot there and I guess I carve out a little something."

"So you have aspirations to go out and make it in Hollywood?" Daniella asked.

"No, but I'll go anywhere for the right part."

"You act full-time? Like you're not a waiter or a bartender on the side?"

"For better or worse, I decided to cut off all my other side gigs and focus on what I love full time"

"Wow, that's cute."

"Wow, that's brave in Austin."

"Okay, that's enough grilling Jesse for now. You guys talk about something else," Frankie told the others.

The others had no problem talking about themselves to each other.

Jesse knew these people were different from his typical group of friends back in Austin. They weren't members of scuzzy underground bands, drunk painters, set decorators, skate videographers, moonlighting screenwriters, or weed-dealing bartenders, but they seemed all right by him.

"Now that you know what I do. What about you? How do you earn a paycheck?" our actor asked Frankie.

Everybody in the pool seemed to almost spit out their Modelo.

"Frankie's an influencer," Brian said.

"I'm not a fucking influencer."

"Look her up, she has like a million followers."

"You mean like someone who travels around the world and asks for free meals at expensive restaurants no one else can get a table at?"

"Yes, exactly that."

"I'm not an influencer. You could say I'm in sales."

"Whaddaya sell?" Jesse asked.

Everyone grew quiet.

"Tell him, Frankie."

"Can we please talk about something other than what we all do for a living?" Frankie asked. "I get it, you're trying to make small talk, but it's just not that interesting of a story."

"Okay, now I'm intrigued," said Jesse.

"Can we please change the subject?" Frankie asked with equal parts fluster and humor.

Nina stood up and announced she was going to a hotter tub upstream. Frankie stood and put her wet bikini butt in our actor's face on her way out of the tub. Everyone got out and milled around the pools along the trail. Jesse got up, wrapped a towel around himself, found his weed, and stuffed the cone he got from Charlie on a nearby picnic table. He lit it up and went back to the pool he'd been siting in and took a few hits before putting it out. He lay back and closed his eyes and relaxed into the water. His hangover had fully left him. He took a deep breath, filling his lungs with the clean desert air. He listened to the leaves of the cottonwood trees fluttering in the breeze above him. He realized that he was finally chilled out. It felt like this moment was the ultimate reason for his journey and it was all worth it. He let himself get lost deeper and deeper into a blissful state. He heard the rustling of his friends around him and people getting into the pool.

"Mind if we join ya, pardner?"

Jesse opened his eyes to see a middle-aged cowboy and a lady climbing in. The cowboy was wearing an oversize T-shirt, swim trunks, and a Stetson hat. He was lean with tan skin and he had a hook nose like an eagle's beak. The lady was in a one-piece swimsuit with a frilly skirt thing around the waist. She had sun-bleached blonde hair devoid of any moisture. They both sat down on the rock ledge in the tub before our actor could answer, "Not at all."

The couple took a moment to tell each other how good the water felt. Then the man asked, "Whatcha got there?" He nodded in the direction of our actor's right hand. Jesse looked over and saw the joint he was holding.

"You need a light for that?"

"Mine's on the picnic table over there," Jesse answered.

The lady grabbed a lighter sitting on top of a pack of Marlboro Lights next to her and handed it to Jesse. He lit the joint, took a puff, and passed it to the cowboy.

The cowboy took a big hit, held it in his lungs, and blew it out slowly.

"Ahhh, the good stuff. Not the Mexican brick weed you get around here. This must've come from California."

"Yeah, most likely."

"It's hard to complain about all the tourists when they bring mota of this quality."

The lady pulled a big bottle of white wine from her bag and started pouring a couple of cups.

"Damn, Cleeve, it's not really nice to call someone a tourist, at least not to their face," the lady said with a slowness. "You wanna cup?"

"Sure."

"I didn't mean anything bad by it, but dammit, now that you mention it, it does sound insulting, so I'm sorry about that."

The lady handed our actor a clear plastic cup of white wine and they all had a sip.

"It's cool, I'm a tourist. I curse the tourists all the time back where I live. They all drive like shit because none of 'em know where they're going."

"Ha, yep! That's true."

"Yep," said the lady.

"I guess all the cities are just as full of tourists as this place.

Hell, it's actually probably a lot worse. My daughter grew up here and moved off to New York and then to Austin, but she's thinking about coming back here because it's gotten so damn crazy out there."

"So, you guys are natives, huh?"

They both chuckled.

"Natives, that's a way to put it. She's a transplant but I guess I'm about as native as you can get—part Mexican, part Apache, and part European mutt redneck. Now, if you look down south through this clearing" —he turned to the south and pointed to a clearing in the trees with a view across a desert valley in the distance that Jesse hadn't been aware of until now—"you can see a mountain out there. That mountain is in Chihuahua, Mexico. My family has owned most of that valley between here and that mountain on both sides of the border for more than three generations. There's hardly anything between here and there except for a handful of goat ranches. There are about three hundred Mexican black bears that live on that mountain and plenty of big cat mountain lions that would love to get their paws on those goats. Sorry, it went out." The man passed our actor the unlit joint.

"I'm good."

"I'm good," said the lady.

"I guess I'm pretty well roasted myself."

Everyone chuckled and sipped their wine. The lady poured them all some more.

"When I was a kid, no one really paid any mind to a border. There was the river, but on both sides were just family and friends. People came and went as they pleased. People lived and worked and went to school on both sides and nobody recognized the two separate countries. It was just all one place as far as anyone around here was concerned. All of that changed in my lifetime.

"Near the base of that mountain lived a lady who was what we call a *curandera*. There were times when I would go and visit her. It would take me three days to walk through that desert, and when I arrived, she'd have cookies waiting for me that she'd just baked, which were cooling and just the perfect temperature. She not only knew I was coming but at exactly the moment I would show up. She didn't have a phone or telegram or anything—there was no way to contact her. She just knew when people would be showing up. There's a lot of people with abilities like that around here. I guess you'd call it psychic, but I think it comes from being so unexposed to the day-to-day elements of civilization. It puts you in touch with something that we've lost. I think we all have higher psychic capabilities than we're aware of but we lack the mental and physical space to be in alignment with them."

Jesse stared out across the desert and onto the mountain in the distance. It looked like it could have been a hallucination, it was so faint.

"More and more the world seems to be finding this place. I don't mind though, don't mind at all. Probably only help my little town turn into something that could attract a few tourists," the cowboy continued.

"Which town's that?" asked our actor.

"The old Soledad ghost town about a thirty-minute drive from here."

"We're soaking with the mayor of Soledad," said the lady.

"Mayor, hell, I own the damn thing."

"Wait, you own a ghost town?" Jesse asked.

"That's right, an old mining town that they turned into a movie set back in the Fifties and Sixties. It kinda fell apart after that because no one maintained it. I bought the whole thing a few years back as part of another larger property and didn't think much of the old ghost town, but lately I've been working to bring it back to life, maybe get some movies shooting there again."

"So, the ghost town's also an old movie set? Do you know what was shot there?"

"Oh, a bunch of Westerns. I couldn't tell ya all the names, but they're all written down in a ledger. There's a scrapbook with all sorts of memorabilia. You and your friends should stop by and check it out. It's on the way back to Delgado if you take the river road back to the east. I assume that's where y'all are coming from."

"Holy shit! Yeah, I'd definitely love to see this place."

"I have the saloon fully operational now. You guys come by and have a drink."

The cowboy and the lady looked up to see Frankie and her crew coming back down the trail to the pool. They got out and started drying themselves off.

"Jesse Strange, you ready to start heading back soon?" Nina asked as she approached.

Jesse got out of the pool and wrapped a towel around his waist.

"My friends here have invited us to stop by their ghost town on the way back to Delgado."

"Oh, yeah?" asked Frankie.

"It's not my ghost town," said the lady as she moved her things to the wooden picnic table.

"Yeah, the old Soledad ghost town over on Route 17. You guys are all welcome to swing by," said Cleeve, the cowboy.

"They shot Westerns there in the Sixties," our actor informed his friends.

"I don't like to take that road because the cops are really bad," Frankie said.

"Cops? On 17? Those guys are a bunch of chumps. Ain't nothing to be afraid of. They won't mess with you."

"Every time I take that road back I get pulled over, and this Austin hippie," motioning to Jesse, "brought some Mary Jane with him."

"Actually, I'm clean now. We just got rid of it."

"I'd like to see it. They shot movies there?" asked Nina.

Frankie gave her a look.

"Yeah, they shot a ton of Westerns back in the day. I couldn't tell you all the names, but I know James Garner, James Coburn, some of those guys were there. I'm trying to restore it to its former glory."

"Ooh, I wanna see it, too," said Brian.

"Fine. Since everybody wants to go, we'll go, but don't blame me if we get hassled by the border patrol and sit on the side of the road for an hour while they do a background check on everyone."

"Oh, those guys are all about as smart as a fuckin' sack of rocks. Don't worry about 'em," Cleeve said.

Jesse put his jeans on, careful not to spill or expose the cash in his pocket. The gang walked back up the trail and piled into the truck. Charlie came back out of the main building and walked to Frankie's window.

"You guys taking off?" she asked.

"Yes, ma'am," Frankie answered.

"Were y'all talking to that cowboy and that lady?"

"Our friend back there was buddying up to 'em."

"Well, that was the mayor of Soledad, but I've never seen that lady in all my life and it definitely was not his wife, so I was trying to get the scoop."

"Uh oh, secret rendezvous," said Dante.

Everyone in the truck laughed at this piece of juicy gossip.

"We'll let you know if we find anything out," Frankie assured her.

. . .

Frankie drove along a bumpy road that ran beside the US side of the Rio Grande. After a few miles, the road split: One road went south into Mexico and the other was Route 17 heading North back toward Delgado. Route 17 was a paved two-lane highway that climbed back into the mountains.

"I'm telling you guys I've been here, it's just some old buildings that are falling down. I don't think you'll be impressed," Frankie told everyone as she took a right onto a tiny dirt road just past the sign for Soledad. There were a few disappearing adobe homes and the remnants of an old mining operation up on a hill above the town. They drove past a small cemetery with a few white wooden crosses marking a handful of ancient graves. Giant black boulders surrounded the town. Prickly pear cactus and a couple of twisted cottonwoods were the closest signs of life. Then they saw the remnants of the film set. The Soledad road ran right into the center of it. The stone façade of a church with an arched chapel stood at the entrance of the movie set. There was a town jail, a Banco building, a couple of random crumbling structures, and at the end of the street was the saloon. Frankie stopped the car and everyone got out to take a look around.

"This is it?" Brian asked.

"I told you," said Frankie, "not much to look at."

For Jesse, it felt like a dream. He'd never been on a Western film set and it was as if he had come home to something. He ran around to the structures and peered inside the buildings. Everything was covered in a thick layer of dust and sediment. Looking back down the main street they drove in on opened to a vast window into Mexico. A banged-up baby blue Seventies pickup truck came up the road driven by Cleeve the cowboy without his lady friend. His tires slid across the gravel road as he pulled to a stop in front of the saloon.

"Come on in and have a tequila," he said to his visitors. Jesse followed him into the saloon.

The photos on the walls were mostly historic photos of the town of Soledad and its residents.

"There were fifteen hundred people living here in its heyday," Cleeve said as he opened up a bottle from behind the bar and poured a few glasses. "They mined silver up on the hill to the east until about 1940, when the mining company shut it all down because it stopped making money."

"When'd they start shooting movies?" Jesse asked, walking to the bar to retrieve his tequila.

"First one was probably in the late Fifties, early Sixties. The people I bought the town from left a ledger with a list of everything that was made here. The problem is I can't find the damn thing after I hired a lady to come out and clean the place up. It's around here somewhere." Cleeve looked around for the ledger behind the bar.

Frankie and the gang came inside the saloon and took a look around. "We should probably head back," she told Jesse.

"Hey, you just got here. I got whiskey, some mezcal. Let me pour you something."

"I'll have a mezcal," Nina said.

"Coming right up," Cleeve said as he got to work. He seemed lonely out here in his ghost town and excited to have some new young friends around.

"Okay, guys, one drink then we have to hit the road," Frankie obliged everyone.

"What can I get you?" Cleeve asked Frankie.

"I'm good," she said.

Jesse went outside to take a look around. He stood in the doorway of the saloon, leaned on a wooden pillar, and gazed up and down the main street. In his mind, he could see the arc lights and the camera crew and the other actors. He stepped off the saloon porch and walked with caution through the main street as if a bloody shoot-out would erupt at any moment. He heard a sound and turned quickly to his right to see two doves fly out of the Banco building. He caught his reflection in the broken window of the building and the thought hit him that maybe he could shoot something here. He stared into his eyes in the broken window and everything seemed to be aligned, like he was exactly where he was supposed to be in space and time.

"Are you in your happy place now?" Frankie called out from the porch of the saloon.

Jesse walked back to her and took her hand as she walked down the steps. When she reached the street, he twirled her around. He put one hand on her lower back and held the other out to dance with her. She seemed impressed by his move but not enough to allow herself to get lost in it. She stopped him after a couple of steps as her friends came out of the saloon.

"You're all welcome back anytime," Cleeve said as he followed everyone out. "I've got big plans for the future of this place. Wouldn't be right to let it all fade away."

Jesse went back to Cleeve.

"Hey, man, thanks for having us. Not sure how long I'll be around, but I'd love to come back and discuss filming something here."

"Come back anytime. You know where to find me," Cleeve said. "Any chance you could leave me with some of that green?"

"That's all I brought with me from back home, but I'll try to track some down in Delgado and bring it back to you."

"Hell yes, please do. Bring me some weed and you can do whatever you want out here, especially some of that good California shit."

"You got it, my friend."

On that, they gave each other a firm shake.

. . .

The sun set on the road back to Delgado. Jesse stared out the window onto the rocky desert mountains and thought of a concept. A short film, maybe just a scene that he could write and star in, like a screen test, something for his reel. He figured he could find some weed in Delgado and bring it back to Cleeve as an excuse to hang around the abandoned film set and see what he could come up with. He wanted to make something unique, like nothing he'd ever done, and it felt like Soledad was the perfect backdrop.

The others in the truck talked about their big workday

tomorrow. They were all gearing up for some trip out of town. When Frankie dropped him off at his car, Jesse had to walk around the front of her truck.

"There she is, cowboy," Frankie said with her window down.

"There she is. Do you happen to know the best way back to the El Dorado Hotel?"

"Take a right at the next street and drive until you see it," she said, pointing in the direction his car was facing. "Hey, if you're really interested, you should come by the warehouse some time and I'll show you what we do."

"Yeah, where's the warehouse?"

"Gimme your number and I'll text you the address."

He did, and Frankie put it in her phone.

. . .

Jesse parked at the El Dorado and walked into the office. He was greeted by a nervous fellow wearing big Buddy Holly-style horn-rimmed glasses with shorn black hair standing behind the front desk. It was a small room with cement walls and a couple of the same rust-colored Naugahyde chairs in the corner. There was an old blocky computer monitor and a keyboard on the front desk. Our actor couldn't tell if this was some retro artifact or an actual functioning computer. The front desk clerk stared at Jesse without saying anything.

"Hi, I stayed here last night and I still have this room key," Jesse said, pulling the key out of his pocket, "and I'd like to pay for another night if I can."

"You've already checked in?" the clerk asked.

"I believe I checked in last night. I'd just like to pay for another night?"

"Which night would that be?"

"Tonight."

The clerk looked confused.

"When did you check in?"

"Last night?"

The clerk began clicking on the tan keyboard that looked about thirty years old.

"And your name?"

"Strange, Jesse."

He kept typing.

"Is there another name the room would be under?"

"No, just mine."

"What room was it?"

"103," Jesse said, putting his room key on the desk.

The clerk inspected the screen in front of him and looked back at Jesse and the key briefly before staring back at the monitor.

"Your room has been taken care of for as long as you'd like to stay by Miss Hammer."

Who was Miss Hammer? Jesse wondered, but stopped himself from asking the question out loud. *Better to just play along*, he thought.

"So, everything's taken care of for tonight?"

"Everything's taken care of."

He had questions but didn't want to blow his free room for the night. His best inconspicuous response was to ask, "Do you happen to know Miss Hammer?"

"Yes, sir, she's the owner of the hotel," said the clerk.

Jesse went back out to his car to gather his things. He wondered what was happening. Who was this Miss Hammer, the owner of the hotel, and why was she paying for his room? He still had no recollection of getting the room last night and now there was more to the story. *None of it made sense, maybe the front desk clerk was confused*, he thought. His options were to go in search of another place or take his things with him back to room 103, which he did. He could always figure something else out tomorrow.

Inside, he pulled the wad of cash out of his pocket, put it back into the bank bag, and stuffed it in the bottom of his suitcase. Carrying around all of this cash was making him uneasy, and he looked forward to unloading it in the morning. He felt like he'd be able to enjoy himself more without all this money on his mind. He kicked off his boots and flipped on the TV. Turner Classic Movies had a Brigitte Bardot movie on called *SHALAKO*. He watched most of it before drifting to sleep and dreaming of her dressed in a Western outfit on the ghost town film set. He followed Briggitte down the main street as she looked back at him. He felt eyes on him, like he was being watched from the windows of the ghost town buildings. Brigitte turned around to face him with a pistol in her hand, but she had morphed into Frankie in the same outfit, the same red lips and flowing blonde hair in the wind. She looked at him with death in her cold eyes. She brought a finger to her lips and made a "shhhh" sound as she shifted her eyes to her upper left. Jesse followed her gaze and noticed a gunman in a second-story window pull up a shotgun and aim at him. That was the end of the dream.

5

JESSE HEARD THE SOUND OF A KEY being jiggled into the lock, but the bolt wouldn't turn. The door knob turned erratically back and forth, but it didn't open. Then there was a knock. *The jig's up*, he thought. *May as well let 'em in.* Maybe they'd be generous enough to let him get cleaned up before he got the boot. He got up and peeked out of the front window and saw an old man standing at the door who looked like a farmer holding a Styrofoam cup of coffee. Jesse opened the door.

"Well, what are you doing in my room?" the man asked.

Jesse Strange stared at him, not sure what to say.

"Dale, leave that man alone and get away from his room," an older lady in a Mexican dress called out as she walked down the courtyard sidewalk, also holding a Styrofoam cup.

"I wanna know what he's doing in my room."

"That's not your room, we're in 106 now," she said irritated.

The man continued to stare our actor down as the lady reached them.

"Sorry, we *were* in this room, but we finally got one with a kitchenette last week. We went to get some coffee from the office, and he just got confused as usual. Sorry he bothered you, sir. Come on, Dale."

"No bother. How's the coffee?"

"About what you'd imagine."

The lady pulled Dale down a few doors, where they put their coffees on a blue metal table outside of their room.

Jesse was relieved and decided to take a shower in case someone did come along to give him the boot. He opened a small window in the shower that looked out on the dusty alley. A cool, dry morning breeze blew in that complemented the hot shower. He took deep breaths of the fresh desert air as he rinsed off.

He got cleaned up, wrapped a towel around his waist, crawled back into bed, and grabbed his phone off the nightstand. There were a couple of lengthy texts from Neil that said: *Good morning, amigo! It's your sky captain, Neil. I want to meet you but I don't want you to bring the package. Please leave it somewhere secure and meet me in an hour. Leave South on Hiway 17. When you get to the Delgado High School set your odometer. Drive 23 miles until you see a white sign that says Star Colony with an arrow pointing right. If anyone tries to stop or question you tell them you are a lost tourist, nothing else. Continue down the road for 10 miles until you see another Star Colony sign. Stop in front of the black iron gate and I will meet you.*

As he got himself dressed, he looked at the text from Neil again. He wondered why he didn't want him to bring the "package." It seemed odd, but he assumed Neil had his reasons. He left the money in the suitcase under the bed and walked out the door.

He drove out of town on Route 17 and set his odometer like Neil asked when he reached the high school on the south side of Delgado. The highway ascended into golden hills that grew rockier as it climbed in elevation. It was a vast beauty that was almost blinding. He drove for about twenty miles before turning right onto a dusty white rock road that ran flat along a mesa. After a slow drive, he came upon the Star Colony sign and pulled up to the black iron gate. The land was flat and chalky. He saw the resemblance to the moon, but there was no sign of construction, just open desert. Red veins ran through white rock boulders surrounding the mesa. He heard an engine coming up the road and turned back to see a small blue pickup pulling to a stop near the driveway.

The driver got out of the truck. He looked like a tall thin hippy, wearing loose white cotton pants and a white tunic. The passenger wore black jeans and a blue button-up, binoculars hung around his neck, and he carried a leather attaché case. He seemed a bit older.

"Our friend!" the driver exclaimed as he approached Jesse with his hand out. "Love the car," he said. "I'm Neil." He used both of his hands to shake Jesse's. "This is Gil Phillipe, the world-renowned architect."

Gil Phillipe walked past Jesse and Neil and through an opening beside the gate. Neil waved his hand to Jesse toward the opening. Jesse walked onto the other side of the property.

"Have you ever seen anything like it?" Neil asked as he walked beside Jesse out into the open lunar landscape.

"No."

"Ten dome structures will be arranged in a polygon connected through a series of tunnels that link back to a communal oasis in the middle with a pool, restaurant, and bar," Neil explained excitedly.

The architect came back with a pad of paper and showed Jesse the sketches of the domes he'd made. "You see, it forms a star," said the architect with a French accent.

"There will be nothing else like it on the planet. The only problem is we've found out a massive pipeline project is set to go straight through the middle of the colony. That's why it's important we pay the attorney who's actively fighting to stop the pipeline or at the very least push it further to the east."

Gil Phillipe walked between them and brought the binoculars to his eyes, "There they are," he said.

"And you see even now we are being watched," said Neil, motioning to where Gil Phillipe had his binoculars pointed.

A big white SUV was parked in front of a wrought iron gate about one hundred yards to the east.

Gil Phillipe continued staring at the SUV through his binoculars.

"Being watched?" Jesse asked.

"Have a look," said the architect as he handed Jesse the binoculars from his neck.

Jesse saw two guys that looked like bouncers sitting in the front of the SUV. The passenger was staring back with his own set of binoculars.

"Who are they?" Jesse asked.

"We're not sure. Could be agents working for the pipeline, could be spies."

"Could be the FBI," said Gil Phillipe as he took the binoculars back from Jesse.

"Whoever they are, they seem to be monitoring our communication. That's why I didn't want you to bring the package right away. I wanted to meet you in person to avoid a phone record. Turn away from them," Neil instructed.

All three of them turned around, facing away from the SUV in the distance.

"What I want you to do is go back to where you're staying, enjoy yourself this evening, just keep the money safe. Tomorrow morning around this time, take the package to the Delgado Theater on the town square. Keep an eye out in case anyone's following you. Slide the money through the slot in the ticket booth and make sure it falls off the counter and onto the floor—give it a good shove. That's it, we'll take it from there."

"Got it," said Jesse.

"You're the man! We'll make sure you get a voucher for a free stay when the resort's up and running. It's gonna blow your mind. For now, just head back to town and we'll keep an eye on the spies," Neil said, nodding in the direction of the SUV.

Jesse turned his car around and drove past the spies in the white SUV. He made sure not to look at them though he felt their eyes. Whatever was going on at the Star Colony wasn't anything he wanted to be involved in, and he was glad he'd be through with his side of the deal soon. He'd rather spend his time with this beautiful desert backdrop making his screen test happen, which was becoming clearer after his dream about Frankie last night.

. . .

Back in Delgado, he pulled into a parking spot on the street in front of the hotel. As he walked through the courtyard, he noticed the older lady in the Mexican dress sitting at the metal table outside of her room a few doors down from his. She had a small red glass in front of her and held an unlit cigarette.

"Hey, darling, you got a light?" she asked as he reached his door.

Jesse felt the pockets of his jeans and said, "I have one inside."

He pulled the room key out of his pocket and stuck it in the door knob.

"You have a cup or something in there? I accidentally poured too much of this and I could use some help."

She held up the glass in front of her.

"Oh, sure, yeah I'll find something."

Jesse grabbed a lighter off his nightstand and blew out a clear plastic cup off the bathroom sink. He noticed that his bed had been made and his room tidied up. He thought it was a good sign that housekeeping had been by and he still had his room. Before he walked back outside, he pulled the suitcase from underneath the bed and had a quick look to make sure the cash was still there. It was.

Outside, he found the older lady standing next to the metal table in front of his room. He lit her cigarette.

"Thank you, sweetheart. Here, let me see your cup."

She poured about half of the clear liquor she had in her glass into Jesse's cup.

"Mind if I join you?" she said, sitting down at his table.

Jesse sat down with her. "Not at all."

He raised his plastic cup to his mouth and was hit with the ferocious aroma in his nostrils before he tasted the tequila.

"Cheers," she said, holding up her glass.

"Cheers."

"There's ice over at the office if you want it."

"This'll do, but that's good to know for later."

"I'm really sorry about this morning."

"Don't be. I needed the wake-up call."

"I'm at my wit's end with that man." She blew out an air of exasperation and cigarette smoke. "I don't see you wearing a ring, so I'm gonna assume you're not married."

"Not married."

"You ever been?"

"Nope."

"Well, if you ever do, make sure it's to someone you're willing to take care of when they're old and out of their mind, because that's what happens to every single one of us. My old man doesn't know where the hell he is or what's going on from moment to moment. I'm just thankful he can still wipe his own butt. He just sits out there in his truck all day listening to sports."

Our actor was pretty sure he parked next to her husband's truck in front of the hotel.

"What brings you to Delgado?" she asked.

"Just getting out of the city, I guess."

"What city would that be?'

"Austin."

"Boy, has that place changed. I guess everywhere has though. You remember hearing about tropical storm Desiree? It hit the coast a few months ago, did a bunch of damage to all the towns down there."

"I think I remember that one."

"Well, it pretty much wiped out the entire town we live in, including the home we've had for over forty years. The house we raised our family in. The whole thing gone in an instant."

"Sorry to hear that. What town?"

"Port Olivia, just up the beach from Corpus Christi. Most people haven't heard of it."

"Can't say I have."

"I think it broke something in my husband. After that happened, he just kinda lost touch. We came out here to Delgado because our kids are here. They run an art gallery called the Desierto Lodge."

"I'll have to check that out."

"It's a cool place. They show artists from all over the world. Our son and his wife run it. They don't have a lot of room in their house, so we just stay here in this hotel waiting on the insurance settlement to come through."

"You gonna rebuild down there in Port Olivia?"

"To tell you the truth, I don't know what we're gonna do. I wouldn't mind staying around here, but the houses are about the cost of what you'd pay in Austin these days. Things have gotten so expensive, especially with all the Californians and New Yorkers moving in. I don't know what we're gonna do. I may have to put my husband in a home, I don't know."

They both finished their tequila.

"Let me see your cup and I'll pour you some more."

Our actor passed her his plastic cup, she took it to her room, and was back in a flash with a couple of half-full tequilas.

"Thanks for listening to me complain. I just need a cognitive adult to talk to every now and then."

"Well, thank you for the tequila, and I'm sorry about your house."

"The storms are getting stronger and stronger," she said, gazing off across the hotel courtyard. "You smoke?" she asked.

"Cigarettes?"

"Yeah, you happen to have an extra? That was my last one."

"I don't smoke."

"Well, that's good. I only started smoking again after the hurricane, but I *need* to stop."

"Do you happen to know a good restaurant to take a girl on a date around here?"

"Nothing comes to mind, but I've heard there's some fancy

places around. We always go to the same Mexican place a few blocks away. I couldn't tell you the name. It's just a couple of old ladies in the kitchen whipping up the best enchiladas I've ever had in my life. We found that place and didn't see the need to try anything else."

"Jodorowsky said the closest thing you can find to heaven on earth is a Mexican restaurant."

"I don't know who that is, but I'd have to agree." The lady polished off the last sip of her tequila. "That one went down way too easy," she said. "I'd better go check on Dale. Make sure he didn't drive off into the sunset or something."

"Good luck."

"I'll need it. I'm Barbara, by the way. How long you sticking around this place?"

"Jesse. A couple days at least."

"I'm sure I'll be seeing you, Jesse."

"Hey, do you know the lady who owns this hotel?"

"Nope. The place could use some work though. See ya."

. . .

Jesse went inside and lay down in his bed. He looked at his phone and texted Frankie: *Anything happening around here tonight?*

After a couple of minutes, she texted back: *Don't know. Out of town until Thursday.*

Jesse recalled talk of Frankie and her crew leaving town for a few days in the truck on the way back from the hot springs yesterday.

He replied: *Oh yeah, maybe Thursday then?*
Let's meet up when I'm back. I'll text you.
Cool.

What do we do now? he asked himself. He thought about Cleeve, the cowboy out on the ghost town movie set. He remembered telling him he'd bring him some weed, and he wanted to follow through on that. There had to be some floating around Delgado, and if he was going to hang out around here waiting to see Frankie again on Thursday, he'd need something to keep him entertained. He decided it would be a good idea to go out and buddy up to some locals when drinking time came around. Until then, it was probably a good idea to rest up and keep an eye on his room at the El Dorado.

. . .

Around sunset, he spent some time on his phone looking for a bar to hit up. He wondered where the weirdos hung out on a Tuesday night in Delgado. He found something called Bodhi Wind just a short walk away and decided he'd give it a shot.

Bodhi Wind was a 1950s concrete block house with a pool in the backyard. The interior of the house was decorated in a space-age Palm Springs style with white shag carpet throughout. An ancient TV played black-and-white moon landing and rocket launch footage in the living room. There was a bar set up in the kitchen, but no one was around. Jesse wandered around the empty house before he spotted the pool bar in the backyard. He walked out of the sliding glass door and across a small grassy lawn to the pool as the sky turned pink on the horizon. He realized that just below the back of his neck, there was a tension missing in his muscles, a feeling that was always so present in the city you never really noticed it, but now it was completely gone. There was a calming connection to the natural world you felt in a faraway place such as Delgado. An early evening breeze drifted across the backyard from the east. The place was empty except for one bartender setting up his station. Around the pool were a number of table and chair setups.

"Hey, glad you stopped by," the bartender called out to Jesse as he approached.

The bartender looked like another guy in a Los Angeles rock band and Jesse wondered what was up with that.

"What are you having?" the bartender asked as he slid him a one-sheet cocktail menu.

"Oh, just make me something with tequila, please." He never liked reading those cocktail menus—too much information for something as simple as a drink.

As the bartender got busy whipping something up, he said, "Dude, so I watched the original *Texas Chainsaw* last night and I totally saw what you were saying about it having a double meaning."

"Double meaning?" Jesse asked.

"Yeah, you were talking about how it was really about the hippies in Austin being surrounded by hostile rednecks five minutes outside of the city."

"Yeah, that and technology slowly rendering the agrarian lifestyle obsolete but when was I talking about that?"

"The other night at Sam and Rita's, you were talking about how it was the first true indie film to be made in Texas."

Jesse had no recollection of this but he went along with it.

"Yeah, the people who made it were UT students who made a film before that, a completely unwatchable hippie movie with no plot, at least not one that anybody could figure out. Then they decided to make a genre flick that ended up being an allegory on the sociopolitical landscape of Texas. Up to that point, any film made in Texas was a Hollywood studio picture that shot on location. The majority of the movies set in Texas weren't filmed here."

The bartender slid our actor a purple drink in a small glass with a slice of blood orange floating on top. "Well, it's still a pretty crazy movie. I feel like it stands up better today than most of the other horror movies made in the Seventies and Eighties."

Jesse took a sip of his drink. "I agree, and the allegory's still relevant. What's this one called?"

"Breath of Medusa."

"Makes sense," Jesse said. "Hey, what's up with that old theater on the square? They still show movies?"

"The Delgado? Yeah, they show movies whenever they feel like it. That girl Nina programs it."

"Nina?"

"Yeah, I saw you hanging out with her the other night."

"That Nina? I didn't know she was a film person. I saw *The Border* was playing but I didn't see any show times.

"That played last month. I'm the one who got her to show that film."

"No shit?"

"Yeah, my dad was in it. He played a border patrol agent."

"Your dad was an actor?"

"No, that was the only movie he was ever in. They shot it in El Paso and needed extras. It's funny, because he was a hippie who hated the border patrol and he only got to be in the movie because he got Jack Nicholson weed on set. You want another?"

"Yeah, but can I do a tequila soda?"

"You got it."

"That's an amazing story, man. Speaking of, do you know where an out-of-towner could find some around here?"

"Weed?"

"Yeah."

"I can get you some of that," said the bartender as he slid our actor his tequila soda.

"Treasure of the Sierra Madre," Jesse said.

The bartender went to mix a couple of drinks for some recent arrivals to his bar. The tables around the pool filled up with city people on vacation. Our actor sipped his tequila soda and thought about going out to the ghost town film set tomorrow. His idea was to shoot a one-act Western-style screen test, something like a one-act play for one actor. He didn't have a solid premise at the moment, but he knew he wanted it to be sincere with a touch of surrealism. He hoped by spending time out on the film set, something would stir in him.

"I text my guy. How much do you want?" the bartender asked.

"Oh, an eighth'll probably do. I'm sure you told me the other night, but could you tell me your name again?"

"Ram."

"Jesse."

Ram looked down at his phone and said, "He'll be over soon. You want another?"

"Please, sir. Do you know any camera people in town? I'm looking for someone to help me film something."

"Most everyone who's serious moves off to work somewhere else."

"I don't even care if they're serious, just someone with a camera."

"You should talk to Nina, she probably knows someone."

Jesse continued drinking tequila into the night at the poolside bar until the weed guy finally arrived, a tall West Texas cowboy who walked up with his arms wide open. He stood there staring at Jesse, waiting for him to stand up. When our actor stood, the cowboy instantly wrapped him in his arms and gave him a big hug. He smelled of leather and weed with a faint hint of manure.

"Hey, we must've met at the party," Jesse said when the cowboy let him go.

"What party?" the cowboy asked.

"A couple of nights ago."

"Wasn't me, man. Anyway, how much did you want?"

"An eighth."

"Tourist special. Hug me again."

Okay, Jesse thought, and hugged the cowboy. He felt the hand of the cowboy slide into his back left pocket.

"This way anybody watching thinks we're old friends. Put the cash on the bar in front of your drink."

"That's a new one," said Jesse.

"Ram, gimme a shot a rye."

"How much do I owe you?" Jesse asked.

The cowboy looked Jesse up and down and said, "How's fifty dollars sound? That's my friend deal since we go back a couple nights and I appreciate you keeping a toned backside."

Jesse pulled two twenties and a ten out of his wallet and put them on the bar in front of him. The cowboy threw back his shot and picked up one of the twenty dollar bills, waved it at Ram, and said, "Uno más."

Ram poured him another shot and the cowboy downed it before picking up the rest of the cash.

"Okay, I'm outta here. If anybody asks, you didn't see me," the cowboy said as he quickly clomped back along the edge of the pool and through the house in his muddy Ropers.

A drunk girl jumped into the deep end of the pool in a long

black dress and floated around like a dead body before spitting out water at the other people at the tables.

A chill was settling in, and Jesse realized he'd be wise to head back to the El Dorado and see what was on Tuner Classic Movies tonight. He thanked his new friend Ram for the help and settled up for his drinks.

"Come see my band this Saturday if you're still in town," the bartender said.

"If I'm still here I'll be there. What's your band?"

"The Talking Walls. We play Austin all the time, usually Hotel Vegas and the Electric Church."

"Ah, I've probably seen you there."

Jesse weaved through the house, between the tourists and locals, and out into the frigid night. He took deep breaths full of the pristine air and wondered at the Milky Way stretching out above him as he strolled through the empty park on the town square.

Inside room 103, everything seemed to be on the up and up. He felt a sense of accomplishment as he sat on the bed and rolled a joint on the small in-room *TV Guide* magazine. The buds were a bit dry and lacked any color beyond a few shades of green, but they broke up easy—he'd seen worse. He grabbed the remote and flipped on the TV as he sprinkled the grass into a rolling paper. The default on the TV was the cable provider's news station that played in a small box at the top right-hand corner of the screen. There was an interview with some West Texas sheriff talking about marijuana legalization in other states. "Do whatever you will in California and Colorado, New Mexico, Arizona, or wherever else, just don't bring it back into Texas, because you will be arrested and prosecuted to the full extent of the law. We have illegal smuggling coming over the border here, and any amount of marijuana is still very much illegal in the state of Texas."

Jesse lit up the joint and scrolled down the channel guide to Turner Classic Movies. The Michelangelo Antonioni film *Red Desert* was on. He'd always liked Antonioni even though most US critics seemed to consider his films all style, no substance. He was a big fan of *L'Avventura*, *Blow Up*, and even *Zabriskie Point*, and he of course thought Monica Vitti was a dream goddess, but though he enjoyed the cinematography, he found the plot hard to follow and it wasn't long before he drifted to sleep.

6

"**EVERYTHING IS BASED ON ACTIONS.** *An actor develops a character from the things he does. That's why the actor must understand actions. Every action you do has its nature, its truth. In order to be truthful onstage, you must know the nature of what you're doing, and it must be truthfully done.*"

Stella Adler's voice emanated from the speakers of our actor's car as he made his way south out of Delgado up into the rocky high country in the direction of the Soledad ghost town. Stella was talking about how to make actions truthful. In order to make an action truthful, you must understand on a conscious level the details of the action. She used the example of opening a jar. What were the muscles that are used in opening a jar? Was it more in the wrist or the forearm? How much pressure was applied and how much did the jar weigh in the hand that wasn't turning the lid? You didn't just pick up the jar and poof, it opened—there was effort, and we had to be aware of this effort.

Jesse reflected on his actions on his way out of town this morning. He stopped at the Delgado Theater, and did as Star Colony Neil instructed. He kept his eyes peeled to make sure no one was watching him as he took the blue bank bag full of cash to the ticket window. He thought about the weight of eight thousand dollars in cash in a bank bag. It took a certain amount of force to give the bank bag enough of a shove to make it slide off the counter and onto the floor. Then it was done and he felt a sense of relief knowing that his official business in Delgado was wrapped. He got back in his car to drive south in the direction of Soledad. Every action must have its nature, its truth.

At the crest of Midnight Pass, he shifted into a lower gear. He was aware of the exact amount of pressure it required in his left foot to depress the clutch and the muscles that were used in his lower right leg to gently let off the gas pedal. His right hand shifted the stick from fifth gear down to third. His left hand kept steady at the top of the wheel. He paid extra attention to the balance of easing off the clutch and pressing on the gas again. When the action was complete, the RPMs evened out and he ascended smoothly to the top of the mountain. An endless view of the South sprawled out in front of him.

He weaved down the other side of the pass for close to fifteen miles until he saw the sign for Soledad and turned left off Route 17. He drove until he saw the crumbling adobe structures and parked next to a couple of old dusty pickup trucks in front of the saloon. One of them he recognized to be Cleeve's 1970s baby blue Ford F-150.

As Jesse approached the saloon doors, he could hear a few men shooting the shit in a raucous sort of way.

"You don't know what the fuck you're talking about," Jesse heard as he opened the wooden saloon doors. The chatter paused, "Looks like my tourist friend from California's back."

Our actor saw no need to correct Cleve. The cowboy was joined at the bar by a couple of pals who looked like they hadn't seen a day outside of this calloused chunk of the Chihuahuan desert their entire lives.

"I've come to fulfill my side of the bargain," Jesse said walking to the bar.

"The grand bargain," one of the pals proclaimed.

Jesse Strange pulled two medium-sized joints from his front shirt pocket and placed them on the bar in front of Cleeve.

"Well! Pull up a seat and let me pour you a glass," Cleeve said as he stood and walked around to the other side of the bar. "Our friend, Nestor brings this stuff up." Cleeve nodded down the bar to Nestor. Nestor nodded in Jesse's direction. Cleeve took a glass from the counter behind him and filled it with ice from the basin. "Our tourist friend here has brought some fine Mota from far away," he said as he pulled a big brown clay jug from down the bar, poured a half glass of milky liquid over the ice, and passed it to Jesse.

"I actually found it in Delgado."

"Aw, in that case, it could've come from anywhere."

Jesse took a drink of the frothy white liquid and fought his stomach from instantly spitting it out. Something seemed wrong, but he let it settle, and a soothing wave hit him.

"What was that?"

"Pulque. Comes from agave like tequila, it's just made a different way. People have been drinking this around here as long as anything."

The next sip went down easier, although he did detect the aroma of lighter fluid and fought off making a tormented face.

"That's the drink of the gods," said the cowboy sitting a couple of barstools away.

Cleeve picked up one of the doobies and lit it.

"Now, you're gonna have to forgive me for calling you my

tourist friend, and I know you told me your name, but remind me what it was again."

"Jesse."

"That's right," Cleeve said as he took a pull off the joint and exhaled it. "And I'm Cleeve, in case you suffer from a similar lack of name-remembering ability. That's Cisco and Nestor, as I said before." He pointed the joint at both of them as he said their names.

Jesse nodded to them all again and Cleeve passed him the joint.

Jesse was excited to be in the midst of these real deal cowboys. He paid close attention to their actions, how they sat, what they said, how they drank their pulque.

"Now, if I'm not mistaken, you showed up here the other day with the hammer girl," Cleeve said.

Jesse wondered what Cleeve meant while he took a puff. The question echoed around his brain as he passed the doobie to Cisco, the cowboy sitting to his left, and exhaled, "Who's the hammer girl?"

"Hammer girl?" Cisco said as he took the joint.

"Pretty sure that was Bob Hammer's daughter."

"As in Robert L?" asked Cisco.

"That's right."

Jesse registered the Hammer name and its attachment to the El Dorado Hotel. As in, his room was supposedly being taken care of by a "Miss Hammer."

"You get involved with her and you may end up owning half the town of Delgado," said Cleeve.

"You might end up owning Soledad itself if her old man had his way," said Cisco, passing the joint to Nestor. Nestor took a puff and handed it back to Cleeve.

"It'd take a cold day in hell for Bob Hammer to get his greasy palms on this place," said Cleeve, taking a toke.

"You're talking about Frankie?" Jesse asked.

"Is that her name? She seems like a sweet girl. I just don't hold her father in high regards."

Cleeve passed the joint to Jesse.

He took a puff and passed it to Cisco.

"I'd have to say I'm good and baked," Cisco said.

"What's so bad about her old man?" Jesse asked, trying to come across as an old dusty rustler like the others.

"Just a lot of rumors flying around these days, who knows if any of 'em are true. By the way, I finally found that ledger with all the films that were shot here," Cleeve said as he pulled out a notebook from next to the cash register and handed it to Jesse. Jesse inspected the entries, all of which were handwritten in pencil by what looked to be the same hand:

A Pale Horse Wanders - 1965

Greetings from the Other Side - Winter 65

Death Warmed Over - May 66

The Desert Has A Place For You - ?

The Devil's Drifters - Feb 67

Stray - Spring 67

Apparition - August 68

Hell In Texas – 1973

"Wow, these all sound amazing, but I haven't heard of a single one," Jesse said.

"I don't recall seeing any of these myself, except maybe *Death Warmed Over*, that one sounds familiar," said Cleeve.

Cisco looked over the ledger and said, "Yeah, I think I remember *Death Warmed Over*, don't know about the others though."

Jesse snapped a photo with his phone. "I'll look these up later."

"Yeah, look 'em up and let me know if there's anything good in there. I'd like to see this place in its silver screen heyday. Looks like it was a busy place in the late Sixties. I found this photo with the ledger," Cleeve said, turning to pick up a wood-framed eight-by-ten photo off the counter. He took a look at the photo and passed it to Jesse. "Hard to make out what's happening."

It was an out-of-focus behind-the-scenes film still. A blurry black-clad gunslinger was frozen in the air with his pistol pointed to the sky in his right hand. The gunslinger's body was contorted as if he had just taken a bullet fired by someone out of frame. There was a large film camera on sticks and a couple of crew members in the foreground to the right edge of the frame. The ghost town buildings in the background were the same set of buildings currently facing west today; they were in focus but overexposed. A black-and-white Palomino was tied up in front of the Banco building across the street. It appeared as if the on-set photographer infinity focused with a wide open aperture from the porch of the saloon. Jesse flipped the framed photo over and saw it was signed *Bear Jenson March 1967 on the set of Stray*.

"Not the greatest photo ever taken, but I thought it was pretty cool," said Cleeve.

Jesse took another look and passed it to Cisco. Cisco took a glance and handed it down to Nestor.

"Qué tipo de películas te gusta ver?" Cleeve asked Nestor

"Los películas de narcotraficantes," Nestor answered.

Cleeve laughed, "Nestor says he likes the movies about drug smugglers."

Nestor handed Cleeve back the photo, and Cleeve walked around the saloon trying to find a home on the wall for it. "Would be nice to get some productions happening here again."

"It's interesting that so many classic Westerns were set in Texas but didn't shoot a single frame here," Jesse said.

"Like what?" asked Cleeve.

"You ever see the *Wild Bunch*?" asked Jesse.

"I definitely remember that one," said Cleeve holding up the photo on the wall behind the bar.

"Yep," Cisco chimed in.

"It was set right here in a town on the Texas-Mexican border, but the whole thing was shot a few hours away in Durango, Mexico. The opening title in the John Ford film *The Searchers* says TEXAS 1868, but it was shot in Monument Valley, Arizona. Same with *Rio Bravo*."

"Now, that's a good one," said Cisco.

"They filmed it in Tucson and the back lots of Burbank. The list goes on with movies *and* TV."

"That's because the whole shebang's a fucking myth. The mythos of Texas is more romantic than the reality of the place. One of the reasons it's so hard to make anything happen here in Soledad is because there's better tax incentives in all the surrounding states. I've been researching the tax incentives and the geniuses who wrote the damn thing put in a provision that says they can deny incentives to any project that portrays Texas or Texans in a negative fashion. I mean, how juvenile is that? The biggest problem facing this state are the stupid fucking politicians that run it."

"Why don't you tell us how you really feel, Cleeve?" chuckled Cisco.

"I can't stand the fucking morons who run this state. Just a bunch of Ivy League brats pretending to be cowboys, ain't a one of 'em seen an honest day's work in their life. They don't have any ideas on how to lead, they're just in the pocket of the big corporations, and they play to their constituents' openly racist and regressive fears. Fuck 'em. I hope they all get voted out soon. Fuck 'em for being a bunch of Neanderthals. That's how I really feel, now who wants another drink?"

All three of the saloon patrons pushed their empty glasses to Cleeve. Jesse liked Cleeve even more now. The mayor of Soledad filled up the glasses with ice and poured another round of pulque. Everyone had a drink. Cleeve lit up the half-smoked joint again, took a couple of puffs, and passed it to Jesse.

"What part of California you from?" Cisco asked.

"Me? I'm from Austin."

"I thought you told me you were visiting from California," said Cleeve.

"Nope."

"Well, Austin may as well be in California these days," Cisco mused.

"People keep saying that, but it's still in Texas as far as I know," Jesse said as he passed Cisco the joint.

"I'll have to pass. Me and Nestor need get back down to the resort."

"I was wondering why you knew so much about movies that weren't filmed in Texas if you were from California," Cleeve said.

"That's just my focus."

"You in the movie biz?" Cisco asked.

"Yeah."

"Well, how do we get some movies rolling out here in Soledad?" asked Cleeve.

"I'd like to talk to you about that," Jesse said.

"Let's talk."

"Well, we gotta get going. Me and Nestor can't sit around here getting any more fucked up," Cisco said, rising from the bar.

"They both work on a ranch at a resort down on the border that caters to a bunch of energy execs from Houston," Cleeve informed Jesse.

"Among other forms of slime," said Cisco.

All four gentlemen stood and made their way to the swinging saloon doors.

"Gracias por la pulque," Cleeve said as he clamped down on Nestor's shoulders.

"De nada, traeré más la próxima vez," Nestor said.

"Eso espero!"

Cisco and Nestor climbed into an old white pickup and headed south down the road out of Soledad. Our actor noticed a sticker on each side of the bumper as the truck drove off: NO WALL. NO PIPELINE.

. . .

Jesse scanned the buildings of the ghost town and envisioned the full-scale productions happening in the late Sixties and wondered what it must have been like to be part of them.

"So, what'd you have in mind?" Cleeve asked.

Jesse thought about it for a moment.

"Hold that thought," Cleeve said as he went back into the saloon and returned with a couple of bottles of Bud. He handed a bottle to Jesse. "Let's take a walk."

They stepped off the porch of the saloon and eased down the main street of the ghost town.

"When I first saw your place, it inspired me to want to make something myself here."

"Yeah?"

"Yeah, it spoke to me."

Next to the saloon was the two-story façade of the Inn, propped up by a series of planks on a cement foundation. Cleeve and Jesse stopped to take a look at the Inn.

"To tell ya the truth, I'm surprised this thing has stayed up as long as it has. Seems like a strong wind would've knocked it down by now. I guess they did something right. They built the front here for the film set in the Sixties, but the foundation looks like it goes back to the mining days. You said the place spoke to you—what'd it say?"

"I was hit by a flash of seeing myself working out a piece here on the set. Like déjà vu, but in the future."

"Like a premonition?"

"Maybe that's what it was."

Cleeve squinted his eyes and nodded, "I think the same thing happened to me."

They crossed the dirt road on the other side of the Inn and walked toward a small adobe brick church.

"Now, this church goes back to the old days of Soledad. This is the original town church, built around the turn of the century, 1910, I think."

They stopped and took a look inside. It was one empty room with the sun streaming in from holes in the roof.

"As you can see, it'll take some work to restore this place."

They walked across the main street to the jail building. Jesse saw the cemetery in the distance down the road out of town.

"Now, what are you thinking? You wanna film a big feature with a crew or what?"

"Just me and a cameraman. I'd like to write a short piece and film it here, a screen test. I have a couple of people who help me get acting work and I wanna make something that shows a bit of depth to what I do. Something I can add to my reel and give to my people to shop around. You probably wouldn't even know we were here."

They walked back up the main street toward the saloon.

"You have my blessing, but if there's any way you could use your movie thing to help me promote this place, tell all your film biz friends, agents, or whatever about it, that'd be great, because I'm trying to make some shit happen around here."

"Absolutely. I'll tell everyone I know."

They came upon the post office, next to that was the general store, and then the Banco building directly across the street from the saloon.

"When are you thinking?"

"Sometime in the next few days. I was thinking I'd come back in a day to two around sunset to scout the light. I could bring you some more weed."

"That works for me. I'm out here all the time these days. Speaking of," Cleeve pulled the rest of the joint out of his shirt pocket, sat down on the porch of the general store, and lit it. Jesse joined him and took a look around the ghost town, making note of the way the light was falling.

"Now, the story goes that right here on these steps," Cleeve passed the joint to Jesse. Our actor took a bigger hit than he intended, which resulted in a hacking fit that he had no control of. He took the last swigs of his beer, but it didn't help. Cleeve sat patiently as the coughing subsided.

"There was a shoot-out that happened, not a film set shoot-out, but a real-life shoot-out between about twenty mine workers and the sheriff's men who were paid off by the owners of the silver mine. There was a collapse in the mine that killed a few people and set off a strike over unsafe working conditions. Some miners got together to protest and rally here in town and over the course of a few days, things escalated to a gun battle, and a number of women and children were caught in the crossfire. The majority of the cemetery down there is filled with the miners and their families that were lost in that shoot-out."

Jesse found it hard to wrap his head around the story. It filled him with a fear, a fear of the brutality of the desert. Anxiety washed over him. He was more stoned than he preferred and thought he should probably go lie down in a cool dark room and chill out for a while.

"There's a lot that's changed since those days," Cleeve spoke softly, "and then, there's a whole lot that's stayed the same fucking way."

They heard a truck in the distance on the road coming into town getting closer. A brown and tan Bronco came barreling toward the ghost town.

"That's Mary," Cleeve said, standing up.

When the Bronco came to a stop in front of the saloon and the dust settled, Jesse recognized the lady he'd met with Cleeve at the hot springs.

"I should probably hit the road," Jesse said.

They both walked over toward the Bronco in front of the saloon.

"You don't have to rush off."

"I'll be back in a day or two."

"I'll be here. Wait a sec," Cleeve said as he swung through the saloon doors.

"Oh, hey there," Mary said to Jesse as she got out of her truck.

"Hey."

"Hey, there, beautiful," Cleeve said, coming back out of the saloon with three bottles of Bud. "Here, one for the road," he said to Jesse, handing him a beer.

Jesse nodded in gratitude. Cleeve gave the other to Mary.

"Be seeing ya, amigo!"

. . .

Jesse Strange sat in his car and took a sip of his beer. The idea of driving through the desert back to Delgado was not appealing. He felt much too high to make any logical sense of the journey or the surreal landscape that he would be required to navigate. He looked through his phone and decided to play a talk by Alan Watts in hopes the philosopher's playful words would soothe his mind. He started the talk and eased his car down the road out of Soledad and onto Route 17. Alan Watts's voice speculated out of the speakers on the genesis of the universe and how stars had been created out of planets with highly advanced civilizations that had destroyed themselves through nuclear war that in turn created more planets orbiting these new stars. It was already too much for Jesse's sensitive state, and he stopped the talk. He decided the sound of the road was all he needed.

The wind whipped through his hair and around every contour of his head. It was pleasant at first, but as he made his way to the top of the pass, the road and wind became deafening. He considered the word "deafening." It felt like his eardrums were going to explode. He reached the peak of Midnight Pass and took in the view of the cratered basin to the north. He rolled into a turnout on the highway and stopped. He wasn't sure why he pulled off the road; it was an unconscious action on behalf of his body. He took the opportunity to get out of the car, slam the beer, and pace around. He could see the faint image of Delgado shimmering on the golden plain another thirty minutes in front of him.

He needed soothing music to get him there. He got back in the car and put on Caetano Veloso's Transa. Brazilian music from that era always made things better. He pulled onto the highway and continued toward his destination. He felt cool and regained a sense of confidence behind the wheel as he made his way down the winding mountain road. He steered around a couple of hairpin curves, and as the road turned back onto a straightaway, he noticed a cop car sitting on the side of the road, a blacked-out Mustang with what looked like a massive cattle guard on the front grill. He breezed past the cop, but was soon startled by the sight of the police cruiser circling around and charging up behind him blaring its siren and lights. He looked around to assess what he had in the car. He was glad he tossed the beer back at the turnout, but he remembered he had the rest of his weed in the console. He calmly found the bag in the middle console and stuck it down his pants as he slowed the car to a stop on the shoulder of Route 17.

Jesse felt his heart pounding in his throat. A tingling hot, needling sensation consumed his body. Confusion overwhelmed his mind as he made a mental attempt to slap himself in the face and realign his center. Every thought was irrational. "Breathe," he commanded as he saw both the driver and passenger side doors of the patrol car swing open in his rearview.

A couple of out-of-shape, gut-busted, real-deal Texas cowboy cops stepped out of the cruiser. One hung back on the passenger side and the other marched right up along the driver's side of the car. Jesse looked over at *The Art of Acting* sitting face up in the passenger seat. He flipped it over, knowing it would not be favorable for him if the cops saw the title of the book and the image of Stella Adler in a theatrical stance on the cover.

"Keep your hands on the wheel where I can see 'em," he heard the cop coming up the driver's side say. Jesse kept his palms in place and tried not to grip the wheel in a nervous manner.

The cop now stood directly over him. He wore Ray-Bans with the bottom wire rim, Clubmasters, and held his shoulders back like a real badass.

"What do we have here?" he asked in a way that felt like he accidentally spoke his thoughts out loud.

Our actor looked at him blankly with a dull gaze and nodded. He knew if the cop asked him to take his sunglasses off he'd be in trouble. Luckily, it was bright, so he hoped he could naturally squint enough to mask the redness in his eyes.

"Where ya headed today?"

"Back to my hotel in Delgado," he said in an understated Texas manner.

"Where you coming from?"

"Oh, I was just out sightseeing. I haven't been out this way before."

"Sightseeing? Can I see your license and proof of insurance?"

"I'll need to reach into the glove box for the insurance."

"That's fine. My deputy's got ya covered."

Jesse felt the deputy behind him on the passenger side tense up and place his right hand on the pistol in his holster. Jesse opened the glove box and found the insurance card. Both cops glanced into the compartment to see what else was in there. He left it open so they could get a good look and pulled his wallet out of his back pocket. He retrieved his license and handed over the documentation to the officer. The officer wore a sheriff's badge over his left shirt pocket. Above his right was a golden name tag that read D.W. SPEED. He inspected our actor's license.

"You're a long way from Austin, Mr. Strange."

"Well, I needed to get a long way from Austin. Came out here to this beautiful countryside for a much-needed vacation."

The cop behind him chuckled. "Beautiful countryside?"

"Now, you're driving from the south, heading north. The only thing south of here is Mexico and the border. So, what were you doing down there?" asked the sheriff.

"I didn't even make it that far, just drove over the pass and turned around."

"Just drove over the pass and turned around, huh?"

"Pretty much."

"Pretty much?" The sheriff held up his license and insurance to the deputy and motioned for him to take them. The deputy came around and took the documents back to the cruiser. "See, the problem with that story is we've been sitting in that same spot for over an hour and we haven't seen anybody come up from the north, especially a little white convertible driven by you."

"I stopped in that ghost town back there to check it out. I'd always wanted to see an old mining town like that. I must've been there a couple of hours just looking around."

"So, you went to Soledad?"

"Was that the name of it?"

"You were there a couple hours and you don't know the name of the place you were at?"

"I don't think I ever caught the name."

At this point, Jesse realized he was fabricating his story to some degree and he knew he'd be coming back to Soledad to work on his screen test. He thought maybe he should come clean and tell the cop he was location scouting the ghost town for a possible film production that would bring some funding to the area.

"Do you have any marijuana in the vehicle?"

"No, sir," the actor blurted without thought.

"If you're lying to me, it's a federal crime being this close to the border, so I'll ask again. Do you have any marijuana or anything else illegal in your vehicle?"

"No, sir."

The deputy came back with the license and insurance. "One arrest, no warrants," he said to the sheriff. Jesse was relieved that was all that showed up.

"What were you arrested for?"

"Disorderly conduct," said the deputy.

"I asked *him*, Grady. What was the arrest about?"

"I got in a fight downtown a few years ago, just in the wrong place at the wrong time."

"Got in a fight, huh? You a tough guy?"

"No, sir."

"You mind if we search your vehicle?"

There was a Texas cop that came to Jesse's mind. The cop was a legend for how many drug busts he'd made on the highways of West Texas. He set records for the amount of money he made for his department in drugs and confiscated merchandise. He was one of the top narcotics officers in the country. At some point in this cop's career, he realized everything he was doing was wrong and that he was ruining more lives than helping and he decided to become a marijuana advocate. He produced a series of instructional videos on how to avoid getting busted. The videos were full of practical information on what not to do on a Texas highway if you were in possession of weed. Jesse remembered that one of the key takeaways he learned from the cop-turned-marijuana champion was to always let a cop search your vehicle if he asked, that was as long as whatever you had was well concealed and hidden. If you refused a vehicle search, it was a sure sign to the cop that you had something to hide and they would not stop until they found it.

"Not at all, sir," Jesse answered.

"Take your keys out of the ignition, put 'em on the dashboard, and step outta the vehicle, Mr. Strange."

Jesse got out of the car. His legs were gelatinous and barely held him up.

"Walk back there to the front of my patrol car and stand next to my deputy."

Jesse walked back to the deputy. On his way, he noticed the two alert, pricked-up ears of a German Shepherd in the back seat of the police car. He felt his knees might buckle. The sheriff walked over to the back driver's side door and let the dog out. He led the canine by a short leash to Jesse's car. The dog sniffed around excitedly.

"He's already hit on something," the sheriff called out.

"What does that mean?" our actor asked the deputy.

"That means the dog smells something in your car, and just so you know, we have a federal jurisdiction being this close to the border. If you lie to us and we find something in there, it's an instant felony. Now I ask you, is there anything at all in your vehicle that you don't want us to find?"

"Nope."

Jesse was overwhelmed with fear and adrenaline. He suddenly realized anything could be in his car. He had no idea what might have gone down in there on any given night he left his top down on a downtown street. He was certain they would find something and felt like he might pass out.

The dog jumped into his car and sniffed all over. It started pawing in a fervor at the back seats.

"One of these keys open the trunk?" the sheriff asked.

"Yes, sir," Jesse said deflated.

The cop took the keys and led the dog back to the trunk. He fumbled with the keys until he found the one that worked and popped the trunk. The dog instantly jumped in.

"He's on to something. Mr. Strange, now would be the time to let us know what's in here before the dog finds it," said the sheriff.

"Have you ever smoked weed?" asked the deputy. "It's okay if you have. I know you're from Austin. You can tell me."

"No, sir."

"You've never smoked weed?"

"Nope."

"Remember what I said about lying."

"Do you mind if I ask the reason you guys pulled me over

to begin with?"

"We don't need a reason. Anybody coming from the border is subject to inspection."

"But I wasn't coming from the border. I just stopped off in Soledad."

"Soledad? What were you doing there?" the deputy asked.

"I was location scouting."

Before he could explain his story to the deputy, the sheriff said, "Mr. Strange, you're free to go," as he led the K-9 back to the patrol car.

The cops got back in their cruiser and Jesse was left confused on the side of the road. His keys were lying on the front seat as he got in. The cop car did a U-turn in front of him and the sheriff gave him a mad dog look as he sped off in the other direction. Jesse sat rattled in his car. The cops had tested his acting abilities and he failed. He gave a piss poor performance, but at least he was free. He drove the rest of the way back to Delgado in silence.

. . .

The sun began to set as he reached the town. He was still stoned and a little nervous, which caused him to drive extra slow, as if in slow motion, through the stop signs of Delgado. He crept his way back to the El Dorado and took a long shower. He filled his lungs with the clean desert air blowing down the alley through the window in his shower and was relieved that he had his own place to return to.

That night he drowned himself in margaritas and a heavenly plate of enchiladas at the place his neighbor at the El Dorado, Barbara, recommended. It was probably the best Mexican food this side of the border. He sat in a booth at the back corner of the restaurant and had a vision of the behind-the-scenes photo he saw earlier at Cleeve's. He thought the photo could serve as good inspiration for his screen test, maybe a place to start, but instead of a screen test, he should write a play. A play to be filmed at the ghost town. Maybe the play could be from the perspective of the gunslinger in the photo who had just taken a bullet, like one long death sequence. It opens with him on the ground, then he gets up slowly and stumbles through the town on his way to the church or cemetery. He gives a monologue, and the audience isn't sure if he's alive or dead. Or maybe it's everything leading up to the moment the gunslinger is shot.

The piece should show his physicality. All of the films he'd been in thus far were dialogue driven, easy to film around Austin, low-budget indies. The role he wanted was like the lead role in *Mirage*, a physical character based more on action and less on words. All in the eyes, all in the posture. This was the direction he could see his career going. The inspiration was coming, and he vowed to spend the rest of the evening and day tomorrow working on the play.

7

ACT 1 OF 1

SETTING: *A black-clad gunslinger lies down on the main street of Soledad, TX, a silver mining town in the badlands of far West Texas. He has just been hit by a bullet fired by an unknown assassin. The fearful townspeople observe the fallen gunslinger from the windows and porches of the businesses of Soledad. There are eyes everywhere. The gunslinger begins to slowly move his body and reawaken to the world. He mumbles something:*

GUNSLINGER
(mumbling)

THAT WAS AS FAR as our actor got last night on the play. He was still waiting on his character to wake up and say something. Who was this gunslinger stranger? Where did he come from? Why was he shot in the middle of main street Soledad and who shot him? He was hoping something would hit him in a dream, but there was no dream that he could recall, just a long unconscious nothingness of a night's sleep. What was he trying to say with this piece, he asked himself. How could he state something pure about himself through this gunslinger allegory? The questions swirled as he got out of bed and made his way to the coffee in the office.

The lobby was empty as he filled up a white Styrofoam cup with the burnt sludge. Jesse found himself staring into an abstract black-and-white photo that hung above the coffee pot. He tried to make sense of what he was looking at. It seemed to be an aerial view of a massive circular rock formation that looked like an inverted volcano. The sharp rock cliffs ran in repeating patterns that gave the impression of looking into a flower. Jesse kept looking deeper into the photo as the brooding hotel clerk came out of a door behind the desk.

"Still here," Jesse said to the clerk.

The clerk nodded.

"The room still squared away?" Jesse asked.

"Yes, sir, Mr. Strange."

"All taken care of by Miss Hammer herself?"

"Yes, sir."

"We're old friends from way back, me and Miss Hammer."

"I'm sure you are," said the clerk.

"Say, is there a library around?" Jesse asked. He wanted to read some other plays, maybe something Western to help the words spring forth.

"The library's on Pine Street, a few blocks to the north. Would you like a map?"

"I can find it. Want me to check anything out for you?"

"Not today, Mr. Strange."

Jesse had a sip of his coffee and took another look at the photo before heading back to his room in the morning sun.

"What's he doing going into our room?" he heard his neighbor say as the older couple approached from behind.

"That's not our damn room, Dale," said the wife, Barbara, as she pulled her husband down to room 106. "Morning," she said in passing.

"Morning."

Dale looked back confused as his wife dragged him along.

. . .

It was another perfect day in Delgado, the sun was out, the breeze blew gently. The town moved by slow and quiet. No one was ever in a hurry here. The library was a white stucco building with small blue tiles surrounding the front door and windows. Jesse took the time to fill out the paperwork to obtain a Delgado library card and found the theater section. He browsed through the classic theatrical works of Shakespeare, Arthur Miller, Samuel Becket, Neil Simon, Anton Chekhov, and the like, but he couldn't find exactly what he was looking for. There weren't many plays written like Westerns from what he could tell. Since he went through the trouble of getting a library card, he thought he should check something out. He found an ancient Greek tragedy by Euripides called *Orestes*. It was the oldest play he could find, from around 400 BC. It was originally performed in the Athenian Theatre of Dionysus, the birthplace of theater. *Why not go back to where it all began?* he thought. He checked it out and walked over to the town square to sit on a bench in the shade and read the play.

He read the beginning, and right off the bat, it was intense and disturbing. A story about a kid who killed his mother in retaliation for her killing his father and now the kid was haunted by spirits who were tormenting him for the murder of his mom.

He was interrupted by a text from Frankie that said, *Do you want to meet at the warehouse today?*

Where you work? Jesse replied.

Yeah.

He wasn't interested in the warehouse, but he wanted to see Frankie, so he agreed.

She gave him the address and told him to come by in an hour.

The warehouse was on the western edge of town, across a gravel lot from a pair of massive grain silos that sat on the side of the railroad tracks. On the outside, it was just a big corrugated metal building. Jesse parked his car next to a couple of old white pickup trucks and walked over to an open bay door on the side of the warehouse.

What the hell does she sell, livestock feed or something? he wondered.

The front room was empty and unassuming. Beyond that, he saw a much larger room with floor-to-ceiling industrial shelving containing cellophane-wrapped pallets full of cardboard boxes and other indecipherable items. He recognized Brian walking out of the back room in his expensive workout clothes. "Oh, hey!" Brian said as he approached our actor. "Fancy seeing you here. You come to see Francine?"

"If Francine is Frankie, then yes I've come to see Francine."

Brian laughed and walked past Jesse and through a door to the right.

A moment later, Frankie stepped out of the same door. She wasn't in workout clothes. She was wearing blue jeans and a black turtle neck that fit her frame perfect. She walked out of the door holding an unlit cigarette like a French model from the Nineties.

"You made it," she said with eyes of excitement.

Frankie lit the cigarette as she reached the bay door. Jesse followed her outside the warehouse. Her hair blew in the wind as she looked back at him, exhaling the smoke, like she was thinking of something to say. They both tried to get a read on each other.

She stared into his eyes and held out her cig offering him a puff.

He shook his head.

"What ya been up to?" she asked.

She's making small talk, he thought, *a good sign*.

"Aw, just seeing the sights."

"The sights? Which ones?"

"I drove back out to the ghost town yesterday."

"You went back there? Why?"

"I wanna film something."

"Yeah?" she asked, uninterested or lost in her own thoughts. She flicked her half-smoked cigarette into the parking lot. "Come on, I'll show you around."

She led Jesse back into the warehouse.

They walked through the empty front room to a black door on the right. She took a key from her back pocket and opened the door. On the other side was a large bright office with modern furniture and lighting. There were several desks, art on the walls, a couple of big brown leather couches, circular fluorescent lights hung from the ceiling. It looked like a showroom.

"Señor Strange," Nina called out from behind one of the desks. She was standing next to Daniella, who was sitting down in an office chair.

"This is where it all happens," Frankie said.

Jesse was intrigued now. Obviously, there was money in whatever they were doing. Then again, there was no shortage of start-ups in Austin with massive amounts of seed capital that fizzled out in a year. Just about everyone he knew had worked for one at some point, himself included.

"What is it you sell anyway?"

"We sell the dream."

He wondered what that meant exactly. Houses in the suburbs or something?

"The dream, huh? What, the American one?"

"I'm not sure what that is," she replied.

"Me neither."

Frankie led them to a back door in the office that opened up to the warehouse room he saw Brian walking out of when he got there. He gazed around at the merchandise on the shelves.

"What is all this stuff?"

"It's all the collateral merchandise we acquire."

"You buy and resell this stuff?"

"Something like that. I think you'd be good at it."

"Good at what?"

"At what we do. It's like acting. I mean, there's a script you follow and everything."

"I don't know about that. Sure, there's a level of acting to everything, but acting to move people is a completely different thing." He wanted to make that clear without saying too much.

"You'd probably make a lot more money doing this."

Now that was just insulting, he thought. It seemed like she was trying to sell him something.

"Do you wanna have dinner tonight?" he asked.

"What, like a date?"

"Call it whatever you want. Is that a thing people do around here?"

"Go on dates?"

"Yeah."

"Sure, people go on dates, I guess."

"Well?"

"I need to get back," she said, nodding her head toward the office door. "I'll walk you out."

They walked back through the warehouse in silence. He wondered why she asked him to meet her here. He wanted to come out and ask, but he kept his cool. They made it out the front doors into the blinding sunshine.

"Meet me at Horizon Gardens at eight," she said.

"Okay, but I have no clue what that is."

"Look it up."

"I will. See ya there at eight."

"See ya there," she said with a smile and turned away to walk back inside.

On his way back to the hotel, Jesse wondered why Frankie invited him to the warehouse. Was she trying to impress him with her operation? Though the bigger question on his mind was who was Miss Hammer and if it was Frankie, why was she comping his room? He'd have to get to the bottom of it all tonight at dinner.

. . .

Later that evening, Jesse got ready. He'd spent the rest of his day reading Orestes and searching for inspiration for his screen test. The idea was becoming more solidified in his mind. He stood in a towel in front of the bathroom mirror and brushed his hair back with his hands. He had left Austin haphazardly without putting too much thought into what to bring, so his clothing options were limited. It was his fourth day in Delgado and he needed to do laundry, but it was too late. He'd have to throw on his old faithful black button-up shirt tucked into jeans with black cowboy boots and a tweed jacket, the same thing he was wearing his first night in Delgado—it would have to do. He wished he had some tequila to calm his nerves, but he hadn't had the foresight to get anything for his room.

He drove out of Delgado in the last light of dusk. The town was rimmed by distant mountains on all sides. To the south, the mountains stretching into Mexico were much taller than the ones to the north that eventually feathered out into the plateaus and flatlands of Texas. Delgado sat in a vast golden bowl that had now turned magenta. The evening chill was setting in fast on this high desert highway.

By the time he parked at the Horizon Gardens, the sky was full of stars. He walked through a stucco archway along a path lined with massive olive trees following the signs for the restaurant. The entrance to the restaurant was through two large wooden doors, and directly inside was the host stand. He peered around the dimly lit restaurant, but there was no sign of Frankie. He got a table for two tucked away in a corner near the fireplace. As he sat down, his phone went off. It was a message from Frankie that said *Leaving now.* Jesse ordered a margarita, which he sucked down and ordered another before Frankie appeared twenty minutes later striding across the room like she owned the place. She wore a white cotton desert dress that gently hugged the contours of her curves. When he saw her, a chill ran up his spine.

"Did they sit you here?" she asked as she reached the table.

"Yeah, I guess." He thought he picked the best table in the house.

"I usually sit on the back patio," she said, motioning to a hall leading out to the patio. "The view's better and it's more private."

Frankie walked back to the host stand and brought the hostess who guided them to a table on the patio in the back. The patio had an open view of the surrounding desert and night sky. You could hear the yaps of coyotes echoing around in the distance. They sat at a table by the outdoor fireplace and both agreed it was better than inside.

"So, what are you filming at the ghost town?" she asked.

"Just a screen test for my reel, something my agents can use to get me more work. The moment I saw the place, I knew I wanted to shoot something there."

"You have agents? That sounds serious. How do you get agents?"

"They found me actually. They approached me after seeing a film I was in that played at a film festival in London."

The waiter came around and Frankie ordered a steak and a French Pinot Noir from deep down the wine list. Our actor ordered another margarita and the ceviche.

"So, what was the movie that played in London? Must've been a good performance if it got you an agent."

"It was a movie called *Welcome Home, Gilley*. I played Gilley."

"And who's Gilley?"

"Gilley's a guy who just returned home to Austin after fighting for a brief time in an endless imaginary war. The whole film takes place at a surprise coming home party his friends have thrown for him, but he finds it hard to relate to any of them after seeing what he saw in the war. Everyone he talks to says they haven't seen him in years, but he was only away for six months. He came back hoping he could move in with his girlfriend, but she tells him it's not gonna happen. His best friend confesses that he's been dating his girlfriend and Gilley does everything he can to win her back. His best friend is shipping off to the same war the next week and he pleads with Gilley not to try to get back with her. Gilley is conflicted because he wants to talk his best friend out of going to war but he also sees it as a chance to get his girlfriend back. The girlfriend ends up getting with some other guy at the party and things spiral into chaos. Then, *It* happens."

"*It* happens? What?"

"You'll have to see the movie and find out."

"Okay, where can I see it?"

"That's the tricky part. It hasn't been picked up for distribution *just* yet."

"So has anyone seen it?"

"Yeah, it played festivals all over the world, even won a few awards. The agents saw it and liked it, and they've been trying to get me parts ever since."

The waiter brought the drinks to the table, and they each had a sip.

"Well, I hope to see it one day, sounds like a pretty serious drama."

"Yeah, a lot of people said it was like Buñuel meets Cassavetes, but I never thought that. It was more Altman than anything."

"So, have they got you anything? The agents?"

"Not really, to be honest." Jesse took another swig of his margarita. "I was up for something big, but it fell through."

"Something big?"

"A feature for a company that's hot right now. I had two auditions and it seemed promising, but at the last minute, they pulled the plug. It had a decent budget, too, so that was hard to swallow."

"Yeah, I bet."

"What about you? You said you were from here but grew up all over?"

Frankie took another sip of wine.

"Yeah, my dad worked in oil, so we moved around a lot. I spent time in Abu Dhabi and Qatar as a kid. Then we lived in London and New York in my teens. He was from Houston and always wanted to come back to Texas, so at some point we bought a ranch out here. We'd go back and forth a lot. I went to college outside of Paris for a couple of years, then moved back to London for work and started splitting my time between there and New York before coming back here about three years ago."

The waiter showed up with the food, and they both took a moment to inspect their entrees and take a bite.

Normally, Jesse found talk of academic matters boring, but he asked anyway, "What did you study?"

"Finance, but I'd been modeling since I was a teenager, so that really took over in Paris and that's what brought me back to London and New York. I worked for one of the top agencies and just got swept away in that world."

"So, that's why your friends called you an influencer."

"Well, it's not hard to get followers when you're in the public eye like that."

It was clear to Jesse that he was dealing with more than a pretty, well-traveled girl from West Texas. Frankie was something else.

"At a certain point though, I decided to give the whole thing up and come back here."

"Why'd you give it up?"

"There were a lot of reasons, but honestly, I got burned out on the lifestyle. I couldn't help but wonder where the longevity was in anything I was doing, and I wanted a change, so I decided to get away from it all and focus on the family business. I cut ties with just about everyone I knew in the modeling industry and got offline. Then I came here. Not sure if it was the best decision, but I decided to stick to it."

Frankie cut into the steak that she had ordered rare.

"What about you?" she asked. "Did you study acting somewhere?"

"I did a couple of workshops in New York and LA."

"And you don't want to go to Hollywood?"

"Not really. Why should I?"

"Because that's where an actor goes."

"I mean, I've spent plenty of time there. I'd just rather focus on where I'm at."

"Where's that?"

"I'm here. I'd be in Hollywood if I felt I needed to be, but I don't see the point."

"You don't wanna be famous?"

"I don't care about that?"

"So, you're an actor who doesn't want to be famous?"

"I guess so."

"Bullshit."

"You think that's all I want?"

"I call it like I see it."

He admired her for that and couldn't help but feel like he could use someone like her in his life to keep him honest. He finished his third margarita and caught the attention of the waiter.

"Do you want another?" he asked Frankie.

"Sure."

Jesse motioned for another round.

"Do you make a living as an actor?" she asked.

"Yeah, it's paying the bills. I get some decent residuals from a couple of commercials I was in."

"How much do you make a year?"

Frankie was beginning to stare into Jesse's eyes so intensely that it felt like she was trying to burn a hole in the back of his head.

"I couldn't tell you off the top."

"Do you have an accountant?"

"At the moment, no."

"If you don't have someone doing your taxes for you, then you're not making much money."

"You know some people would argue there's more to life."

"And those people are liars. Do you wanna make money?"

"I'm not opposed to it."

"Then come work for me."

The waiter came back with their drinks.

"I'm still not even sure what it is you do."

"Everyone on the team thinks you'd make a good addition."

"Okay."

"And I agree with them. I think you'd be good at it. Come work for me and you'll make real money."

"I'll think about it, but I'm not sure it'll be for me," he said in hopes the conversation would change to another topic.

Jesse could tell Frankie's second glass was going down way faster and she was stuck on him working for her. He wondered if she was just getting drunk. The waiter came back and she ordered both of them a mezcal neat.

"So, you don't aspire to go to Hollywood or anywhere else making a living as an actor would be an option, but you do think that going out to a ghost town in the middle of nowhere to work on an audition reel or whatever will get your acting career on track? I don't see what's so special about that ghost town anyway."

"It's the kind of abandoned film set I've always dreamed of. Just sitting out there collecting dust."

"Seems like it's collecting a bunch of old drunk crusty cowboys. I don't see the allure."

"Jeez, do you always make people feel like shit for doing what they love?"

The mezcal came and Frankie smiled.

"I'm sorry," she said, staring into his eyes sincerely. "I really do have a role in mind for you though. I hope you'll think about it."

"Hey, speaking of a ghost town in the middle of nowhere, you were right about the cops on that road."

"Wait, what happened?"

"I got pulled over on the way back from Soledad and I thought they were going to plant something on me and haul my ass away. They had the K-9 out and everything."

"Shut up! I told you that road's bad news. Did you have anything on you?"

"Just some weed."

"But they didn't find it?"

"No."

"Lucky for you the cops are dumb around here, right?"

"They seemed pretty dumb."

Frankie stared into Jesse's eyes and nodded. "Texans."

Jesse returned a nervous nod.

"They're easy to manipulate, huh?" Frankie said as she finished her mezcal.

Their conversation was interrupted when the waiter appeared with the check. Jesse reached for his wallet, but before he could pull it out, Frankie grabbed the leather-bound check holder and put her credit card inside.

"Let me get this," Jesse said.

"It's fine, I got it. You're visiting."

"No, let me pay," Jesse said, taking the check holder back.

Frankie put her hand on it. "I'll take care of it, don't worry about it."

"Seriously, I'm paying," he said, unwilling to budge. He took her credit card out and started counting out twenties from his wallet. He couldn't help but notice his wad of delivery fee cash getting lighter. When the waiter came back, Jesse handed him the bill.

"Fine, but I'm buying the drinks wherever we're going next," Frankie said, taking her credit card off the table.

"Okay, where are we going?"

"Somewhere in your car really fast with the top down."

. . .

As they made their way through the courtyard and into the parking lot, Jesse asked, "What about your truck?"

"It'll be here tomorrow," Frankie said.

They jumped into Jesse's convertible and took off down the highway in the direction of the lights of Delgado.

"Your car's really cute!" Frankie yelled over the roar of the wind. "I bet you pick up all kinds of girls with it!"

Jesse nodded with a confident shrug that said, "I do all right."

"Let me guess, you paid like eight hundred dollars for it?"

"Yeah, something like that," Jesse said as he shuffled through his phone and stopped on The Stooges' *Fun House*. He paid fifteen hundred dollars for the car three years ago. He had never driven it beyond the city of Austin and was impressed the thing had made it this far. He turned up the volume as Iggy's voice came grunting and hooting out of the speakers like a wild animal let loose from its cage.

Frankie was getting loose in the passenger seat, shaking her head back and forth to the music. The road was a straight shot back to Delgado and Jesse drove at top speed. When they reached the edge of town, Jesse slowed the car and asked, "Where are we going?"

Frankie fixed her windblown hair in the mirror of the passenger side visor and said, "Turn left here."

They made their way through the deserted streets until they came upon the town square. Frankie directed him to park behind an old three-story brick building just off the square. Jesse followed her down a set of cement stairs that led to a basement door in the back of the building. Before she opened the door, she said, "No one knows about this place, so keep it a secret."

On the other side of the door was a small dark cocktail bar. There were paintings of horses framed on the indigo walls and little lamps on the tables that illuminated the room in a soft red glow. The place was empty except for a few couples sitting in the corners speaking quietly to one another. Frankie led Jesse to the bar where they were met by a bartender with slicked-back black hair and dark piercing eyes. "Two Ready Fire Aims, please," Frankie ordered.

"What's that?" Jesse asked as the bartender went to work

on their drinks.

"A cocktail they do here. It's a little spicy, but if you don't like it I'll buy you something else."

"I'm sure it'll blow me away."

"That's the spirit."

The bartender mixed the cocktails and slid them over. The two of them walked to a table in a corner. They sat down and both had a sip.

"Ready, Fire, Aim," Frankie said as she made her hand into a gun and pointed it at Jesse's face.

"So, I'm staying at this hotel called the El Dorado," said Jesse. He'd been looking for an opportunity to bring this up all night, but he kept stopping himself. Now he was just going with it.

Frankie was attentive. "After my first night there, I went to the office to pay for a couple more nights because I liked the room so much, but the guy at the front desk told me my room had been taken care of for as long as I'd like by someone named Miss Hammer."

"Yeah?"

"Yeah, then the guy at the front desk told me Miss Hammer was the owner of the hotel. So, I'm trying to figure out what kind of hotel Miss Hammer's running if she just lets strangers from outta town stay for free."

"Miss Hammer sounds like a nice girl," Frankie said.

"Do you have any idea why she'd be paying for my room?"

"Maybe because you were a drunken mess the first night you got to town, but you had a way of charming everyone you came in contact with at the party you stumbled into," Frankie said as she put her hand on our actor's knee. "Maybe because you were trying to drive and didn't have a clue as to where you were going and maybe Miss Hammer had a room in her family's hotel she could put you up in for a few nights and maybe she's always been the type of girl who isn't afraid to take in a stray animal if they look like they could use some help."

"Stray animal?"

"You looked a bit stray. Are you telling me you don't remember any of this?"

Jesse had no recollection, but to avoid looking like a total fuckup, he said, "That night got a little hazy."

"Uh, Nina and I carried you to your room."

"Well, I thank you for the room, but I like to pay my way," he said.

"It's no big deal, there's always an empty room at the El Dorado."

"That's fine, but I'd prefer to pay."

"You wanna pay? Go get us a couple more drinks," Frankie said.

"What would you like?"

"Whatever you're getting."

"I'm getting a beer."

"That's fine."

Jesse went to the bar and came back with a couple of Negra Modelos.

"I think we make a good team," Frankie said, putting her hand higher up on Jesse's thigh.

He contemplated his best approach to get her back to the hotel room she was comping for him. It seemed like a sure thing, but he didn't want to blow it. What was his line, he wondered? She took her hand off his leg and they drank their beers in a moment of silence as they calculated their next move.

"Should we go back to the El Dorado?"

"Come to work for me tomorrow."

They spoke over each other.

"I should go," Frankie said as she pulled her phone out of her purse.

"Go where?"

"Home, to bed."

She typed a message to someone and hit send.

"I'll give you a ride."

"No, I have one."

"Your car's at the restaurant. I'll take you back there."

"Don't worry about it, I have a driver. Walk up to the street with me."

They left the bar and climbed the stairs to the street level and stopped on the sidewalk.

"I had a good time," Frankie said with a slightly drunken distant slur.

"So did I."

There was an uneasiness between the two of them now. Jesse wondered what else he should say. A clean black Lincoln pulled up to the sidewalk in front of them.

"I'd like to repay you for my room somehow," he said.

Frankie gave him a quick hug and said, "I need to take things slow, okay? You understand?"

"Sure, of course."

"Come to the office whenever you wake up tomorrow."

Jesse agreed, but he wasn't sure why.

"So, I'll see you in the morning?"

"Yeah, I'll be there."

Frankie got into the back seat of the Lincoln and the car

drove away.

Jesse stood dazed on the sidewalk before walking back to his room.

In his bed, he thought about his evening with her. He had zero memory of Frankie and Nina getting him to his room on his first night here. They must have driven him in Frankie's truck. *What happened when they got me here?* he wondered. Did they hang out or did they plop him on the bed and leave? Did he do anything to embarrass himself outside of being blackout drunk? Frankie was still speaking to him, so he couldn't have embarrassed himself too bad. She even went on a date with him and wanted him to work for her. And what was the deal with her putting so much pressure on him to come work for her? Did she feel sorry for him? Was there a worker shortage out here or something? He wasn't interested in a job, but he wondered if there was any harm in exploring the position. Maybe it would be easy money—he could use a bit of that. It was at least an opportunity to hang out with Frankie, and he could talk to Nina about getting some camera help for his shoot. He didn't like the idea of someone paying for his room though. He felt there was an unspoken obligation there that left him uneasy. He decided to insist on paying for his room or find another hotel for the remainder of his time in Delgado. He continued lying in the darkness. As for tomorrow morning, he was conflicted.

8

HE STARED AT HIS FACE IN THE BATHROOM MIRROR, still wondering what to do. His sleep was uneasy. He'd been in his head most of the night about going back to Austin with dwindling cash and no real financial prospects awaiting him. Maybe Frankie was right, he thought, and he'd be good at whatever it was her company did. He'd already taken the delivery job to get out here, so what was the harm with making a little extra to go home with? He started putting his clothes on and getting ready for a day at the office. "Remember, you're going in on your own terms," he told himself in the mirror. "Don't take any of it too serious. If nothing else, it'll be a chance to spend the day getting close to Frankie." He did his best to look professional despite the hangover.

At 10:26 a.m., he fired up his car on the street in front of the hotel. It was Friday and he felt the overwhelming presence of weekend tourists pouring into town. He drove with the morning sun on his back to the warehouse by the train tracks. In the parking lot, he parked next to a rusty white pickup with another bumper sticker that said *No Wall*. As he walked toward the warehouse, he had a strong feeling to turn around. He didn't want to be a salesman. Maybe spending the day working on his screen test would be a better use of his time, he thought. He could get stoned and drunk on tequila with Barbara and hide out in his room writing.

He found himself standing inside the warehouse in front of the door that Frankie led him through on the tour she gave him yesterday. He turned the knob and stepped in.

"Well, look who it is," Nina said as she stood up from her desk. "We didn't think you were gonna show."

Frankie was sitting at her desk across the room on the phone. She looked up and saw Jesse, raised her finger, and mouthed, "One minute."

"You want anything?" Nina asked. "Coffee, water?"

"Coffee'd be good," he answered.

Nina led him back to a small break room, where there was one of those coffee machines you put the little plastic pods into. It wasn't his favorite, but he played along.

"You're still here," she said.

"Still here."

"You been out wandering the range?"

"I have, and I was told you might be someone who could help me find some camera equipment, possibly even a camera person."

"Maybe. Is it for something you're shooting?"

"Yeah, out at the ghost town."

Frankie showed up at the break room door and asked, "Do you wanna get started?" She was all business. "Come with us," she said to Nina, "I'm gonna have you go over the drill with him. I have to leave for lunch and I can't be late."

Nina nodded, clear in her role.

Jesse and Nina followed Frankie to a desk behind a waist-high cubicle. The rest of Frankie's crew were busy on their phones at desks scattered around the office.

"Sit here and you'll go down this list and dial the numbers on the spreadsheet," Frankie instructed. On the desk was a computer setup and a monitor with a spreadsheet open. The spreadsheet contained a list of names and phone numbers. Next to the monitor was a phone. Frankie picked up a laminated eight-by-ten sheet of paper that was lying on top of the keyboard and gave it to Jesse. "This is your script. You call these numbers and read the script. Super easy. Nina will show you what to do from here. I gotta run but I'll be back at some point."

Frankie left Jesse and Nina at the desk. Jesse sat down in the rolling leather office chair and took a look at the script.

"So, what are you filming out at the ghost town?" Nina asked, leaning against the cubicle.

"A scene for a play I'm writing. One act for one character. I'm trying to shoot it in the next few days. I met a guy at a bar who told me I should talk to you, said you might know someone who could help me film the thing."

"Well, all the good DPs in town that I'm aware of moved away, but I have a camera you can use. It's an Arri."

"Wow, Arri, must be nice."

"Yeah, it's nice. We bought it to film interviews with a few locals for a documentary I wanna make about the Delgado Theater. It's one of the oldest movie theaters in Texas."

"I heard you were in charge of that place."

"Frankie's dad owns it now, but he lets us do whatever we want there. Hey, maybe we could show one of your movies?"

Jesse leaned forward excited and said, "Now you're speaking my language."

He liked Nina. She was like Frankie's shadow, because

Frankie literally towered over her by what seemed like a whole foot, and Nina was always at her side, her right-hand lady. It seemed like she had to take a lot of mental notes on Frankie's professional and social life to keep things in order. Deep down she seemed like a sweet, innocent girl from the Rio Grande Valley and Jesse felt like he might have more in common with her than he had with Frankie.

"Anyway," Nina said, directing Jesse's attention back to work, "your job's easy. All you're doing is making sure that the person you're calling has received a letter from the Friends of the Basin Eco Survey Group. Then you're making them aware that the Tex-Mar pipeline will be running through or near their property. If they want more information, you just push this button and connect them to line two," Nina pointed to the button for line two on the phone.

"So, I'm letting people know there's a pipeline coming to their property?"

"You're just spreading awareness. Frankie's dad has an environmental law group that is standing up for ranchers and homeowners to help them fight against the pipeline. There's more information in the script. Everyone on this list"—she motioned back to the spreadsheet—"should have received a letter from us with all of this information. You're just following up and asking if they want to know more. If so, switch them over to line two. If you pass someone on to line two, mark the line in the spreadsheet green; if you just talk to someone or no one answers mark the line yellow. If you get a voicemail, recite the script and leave the callback number." She pointed to that number on a sticker on the phone.

"I thought I was selling something."

"Nope, not today. Oh, and feel free to make up a name to introduce yourself with. We don't use our real names."

"What name do you use?"

"Roslyn Tabor. Rose for short."

"Great name, very classic."

"It was Marilyn Monroe's character in *The Misfits*."

"I should have recognized it. Marilyn's last dance."

"We play it at the theater every summer. Anyway, gotta get back to work. Let me know if you have any questions."

Nina walked away and Jesse took a look at the script.

Hello Mr/Mrs ___________,

My name is ___________ and I'm calling you today to confirm you received a letter from the Friends of the Basin Ecological Survey Group letting you know that the proposed Tex-Mar pipeline will be running through or near your property. Your property may need to be purchased by the US government for the construction of the pipeline. It has come to our attention that the US government is under-appraising many properties in the pipeline's path and offering owners less than a fair market rate. If the property owner does not accept the government's offer, their property may be seized through eminent domain. The Friends of the Basin Ecological Survey Group is here to help. Would you like to find out more about how you can protect your property from government seizure?

If YES: Please stay on the line and a representative will be right with you.

If NO: Thank you, and have a wonderful day.

He was struck by the odd coincidence that he came here to deliver a legal retainer for protection from a pipeline. Was this the same law firm that Neil and Ben Lipton paid to stop the pipeline from running through the Star Colony, he wondered? This wasn't what Jesse was expecting, and he was insulted that Frankie would even compare this telemarketing spiel to acting, but he was intrigued to find out more. He took a look at the first name on the spreadsheet and dialed the number. Someone answered right away.

"Hello, am I speaking with Mr. or Mrs. Deanie Rust?"

"Who is this?"

"My name is Joey Barbarella." Jesse forgot to come up with a name and this was the first one that popped into his mind—he had no idea why.

"Your name is what?"

"Joe."

"Joe?"

"Yes, I'm trying to reach Deanie Rust."

"Not interested."

The person on the other end of the line hung up and his first call came to an end. Was he helping property owners fight the pipeline, like his friends at the Star Colony, he wondered? That wouldn't be so bad. He dialed the next number.

"Hello?"

"Hello, could I please speak with Dennis L. Toothman?"

"He's speaking."

"My name is Sergio Fulci and I'm calling you today to confirm you received a letter from the Friends of the Basin Ecological Survey Group letting you know that the proposed Tex-Mar pipeline will be running through or near your property."

"Look, kid, whatever it is you're selling, I don't want any," Dennis L. Toothman said as he hung up.

"Hello, may I please speak with Garner Sly?"

"This is him."

"Mr. Sly, my name is Chip Marblewood and I'm calling you today to confirm you received a letter from the Friends of the Basin . . ."

"How did you get this number?"

"I'm calling to let you know that the proposed Tex-Mar pipeline . . ."

"Listen, you punk, you take me off your goddam list right now."

Jesse turned Garner Sly's line in the spreadsheet yellow.

This was the way the majority of the calls went down.

"Hello! I'm trying to reach Sylvia Sanchez . . ." CLICK.

"Hello, may I speak with Vivian Tar please?"

"Who is this?"

"My name is Jack Cahuenga and I'm calling you on behalf of the Friends of the Basin Ecological Survey Group . . ."

"I already gave you people money." CLICK.

"Hello, my name is Jerry Rosenblit and I'm calling to speak with Roger Escareno."

"El es Muerto!" CLICK.

On and on and on, every line was marked yellow, until . . .

"Hello?" a soft sweet voice answered.

"Hello, I'm calling to speak with Millie Evelyn Jones."

"This is she."

"My name's Dean Starwood and I'm calling you today to confirm you received a letter from the Friends of the Basin Ecological Survey Group letting you know that the proposed Tex-Mar pipeline will be running through or near your property."

"Yes, I received the letter."

"Great!" Jesse said and continued with the script, "Your property may need to be purchased by the US government for the construction of the pipeline. The US government is under-appraising many properties in the pipeline's path and offering owners less than a fair market rate. If the property owner does not accept the government's offer, their property may be seized through eminent domain."

"They're going to take my home, aren't they? I've lived here in this same house for over fifty years. We've raised livestock, chickens, horses, and a child on this property, and I always knew they'd come to take it away one day."

"Well, ma'am, the Friends of the Basin Ecological Survey Group is here to help. Would you like to find out more about how you can protect your property from government seizure?"

Jesse felt stupid saying this now. What the hell was he even talking about, he wondered?

"Yes. Yes, I would like to find out more."

"Okay, can you please hold on the line?"

"Yes, I can hold."

Jesse switched the old lady over to line two. He felt some sense of reward and accomplishment even though he had no clue as to why. He marked the line green in the spreadsheet and dialed the next number.

"Hello, my name is Monty Cliff . . ." CLICK.

"Hello, my name is Deanie Rust, can I please speak to . . ." CLICK.

The next hour went by with little human interaction. Frankie came back through the front office door around 2:30 p.m. and pulled up a chair close to Jesse. He was excited to see her.

"How's it going?" she asked.

"Well, most people hang up before I can actually say the thing."

"That's okay, we're just spreading awareness. Let's call it a day. It's Friday and everyone wants to get out of here early."

"Okay by me," Jesse said, rolling his chair closer to Frankie.

"Hey, I had fun last night."

"Yeah? Me, too. What are you doing later?"

"I can't tonight. I have to attend something with my family. Another night soon though. Are you up for working tomorrow? I have a special assignment for you."

"Special assignment? More telemarketing?"

"No, this is fieldwork, where I think your talents will shine. Can you meet me here tomorrow morning?"

"Just let me know what time."

"Is ten too early for ya?"

"Ten a.m. call time, I'll be here."

"Nina said you did a really good job. She said you veered off the script a bit but did a good job overall."

"She could hear me?"

"Yeah, she was listening to your calls."

They both got up from their chairs at the desk as Nina came by.

"I'll bring you the camera tomorrow morning," she said.

For the camera, a few hours of telemarketing was worth it.

. . .

Jesse sat in his car in the Friday afternoon parking lot sun. He wasn't sure how he felt about this job business with Frankie and how it was tied to the law group fighting the pipeline. It seemed like the goal was to wrangle clients for her dad's law firm. He didn't see any harm in it if it was helping local land owners, but he was curious to find out more tomorrow. For now, he had an open late afternoon evening he wanted to make use of. He pulled out of the parking lot in the direction of the El Dorado. When he got to his room, he rolled a doobie and put on the clothes he would wear for his screen test: black jeans, black boots, and a black button-up long-sleeve shirt. He wanted to emulate his screen icon, Brando, in *One-Eyed Jacks*.

He jumped back in his car and headed south out of Delgado. There was a mild sense of paranoia about his drive to the ghost town, but he knew the cops would most likely pull him over on the way back headed north. He only brought the one joint, which he could easily throw into his mouth and swallow if for some reason the cops stopped him on the way to Soledad. He drove up into the high country and watched Delgado and the full and flat basin floor fade away in his rearview mirror as he reached the top of the pass. On the other side, all of Mexico stretched out beyond him. He cut around the curves and turned onto the dusty road to Soledad. There had been no sign of the police or border patrol the entire way. Jesse breezed into the ghost town and parked in front of the saloon next to Cleeve's baby blue pickup and a couple of other equally beat-up and rusty trucks.

"Hey! Our actor friend's here," Cleeve exclaimed as Jesse entered the saloon. The gang was all there, Cleeve, Mary, Cisco, and a little boy about five or six. Cleeve stood behind the bar and told Jesse to grab a stool. Jesse sat down at the bar next to Mary, pulled the joint he rolled out of his shirt pocket, and held it up to Cleeve.

"Mi amigo! What are you having?"

"Anything's okay by me, man."

Cleeve grabbed a bottle of Bud from the cooler in front of him and poured a shot of whiskey. He slid the beer and shot to Jesse and said, "Cowboy special."

Jesse took a swig of the beer and thanked him.

"Jesse here's gonna help me turn this place into a movie shooting Mecca. He's bringing that big money from Austin and Hollywood," Cleeve told his friends in the saloon. "What's new?" he asked Jesse.

"I think I found a camera, so I wanted to work on my screen test if it's all right by you."

"By all means. We'll do our best to stay out of your way." The little boy had come over to Jesse and stood at his legs, staring up at him with a blank expression. "That's Cisco's boy Hadley."

"Hadley, leave that man alone, he ain't got nothing for you," Cisco called down to his son.

"Daddy, I gotta pee," Hadley said.

"Well, go outside then." Cisco got up and walked down to his boy. "C'mon, I gotta go, too," he said as the two of them walked out of the saloon doors.

"You mind if I light this?" Jesse asked Cleeve holding the joint up.

"Please do." Cleeve picked up a clear orange lighter and handed it to Jesse.

Jesse lit the joint and took a long drag before passing it to Cleeve.

"So, I got pulled over on my way back to Delgado the last time I was out here."

"Yeah? What happened?" Cleeve asked, blowing out a lungful of smoke and passing the joint to Mary.

"There was a cop sitting on the other side of the pass. They followed me for a while and pulled me over about halfway back to Delgado."

"Was it the police or border patrol?"

"Po Po."

Mary passed the joint back to Jesse.

"Speed?" Cleeve asked.

"Speed? No, I was way under the speed limit."

"Sheriff Speed."

"Oh, yeah, actually, it was Speed."

"Fucking Darrel Wayne, that little pussy."

"They grilled me for half an hour on the side of the road. Had the drug dog search my car and everything."

"They didn't find anything?"

Jesse passed it back to Cleeve.

"I put everything I had down my pants, but the dog went crazy on my car, left claw marks all over the door, the little shit."

"Thing about those dogs is they'll hit on anything. They just use them to have probable cause to search your car."

"I had a cop follow me all way up Route 17 today to the door of the saloon out there," Mary said.

"They've been making their presence a lot more known lately. Not sure what's going on. They've driven through here at least three times today. I used to never see 'em, now they're out there all the goddamn time."

"They said they had some sort of federal jurisdiction being so close to the border."

"Who did?" asked Cleeve.

"The sheriff *and* the deputy said that as they were searching me. They said if I lied to them it was a federal offense."

"That's a load of bullshit. They don't have no federal juris-diction. They just say that to scare people. They don't even have the jurisdiction to come into Soledad. Here's the deal with D.W. Darrel Wayne Speed, he was an ace fullback for the Delgado football team back in high school. He was so good he got a scholarship to some school in New Mexico, which was a big deal because that was back when Delgado was a six-man team and there weren't a lot of scholarships given out to schools that small. Anyway, he didn't last a year or two before he beat up some girl, flunked out, got kicked off the team, and came back here to torment all the townspeople he grew up with."

"Sounds like a real piece of work," Mary said.

"He's a piece of shit if you ask me," Cleeve said.

As much as Jesse enjoyed chatting with Cleeve and Mary, he came out here to put some work in, and the sun was getting low.

"I'm gonna get to work," Jesse said as he stood up and took the shot of whiskey.

"Don't let us hold ya back," said Cleeve.

. . .

He stepped off the porch of the saloon and stood directly in the middle of main street Soledad, facing south. He stretched out his arms and felt the ends of his fingertips. He summoned the power of the mountains all around him. He took in the setting laid out before him. He knew if he went through the motions and put himself in the situation, the words would follow. He visualized the bullet speeding toward him. Who fired it didn't matter; it may as well have been fired from outer space. He felt the bullet hit him right in the gut. He crouched over and hit the ground. He lay there feeling the hot lead sear his insides.

He felt the blood saturating his shirt around the bullet hole and pooling on the ground below him. He emptied his mind of all thought. He lay motionless, splayed out upon the gravel road of main street. The white rock and dirt pressed into his face. He meditated like that for a moment and let himself drift away before bringing his attention back to the physical place he was in.

"Don't think of words, just go through the motions," he told himself.

He slowly moved the fingers on his right hand; it was the first part of his physical being to come back to life. He opened an eye and took in the world around him. He felt his toes in his boots and moved one foot around in a slow circle. Planting his hands on the rocky ground, the sharp stones penetrated his palms. He used his hands to lift his torso while pulling his knees closer to his torso. He looked around knowing there was most likely still a piece of steel trained on him, but he wasn't giving in to the danger. He sat up and felt for the bullet wound on his abdomen and examined his blood-soaked hand. "Looks like you got me, Soledad."

He managed to stand up on his feet, but his legs felt too weak to hold him up for long. He took one stumbling step and then another until he eventually found himself resting against a stripped cedar post that supported the awning of the saloon. He gazed all around the buildings of the town. He looked into the windows of the Banco building and the general store but didn't see a soul. He looked beyond the post office at the cemetery in the distance. He had the feeling that his assassin must be waiting in a second-story window of the inn just above him to the south. He stepped back into the street and continued in the direction of the graveyard. He felt the cold dead eyes of his killer staring down on him to his upper right. He applied pressure to his side to help slow the bleeding. He grew lightheaded but kept inching forward. He spied the church down the street, on the right, just past the inn. He knew he could make it to the church but probably not much further than that. He braced himself, knowing that at any second he could be hit by another. He dragged himself closer to the church with each step.

Then, BLAAMM! Jesse jumped at the sound of what seemed to be a real gunshot echoing around the mountains. He snapped out of his trance and looked around quickly in all directions. The gunshot was so close his ears were ringing. He heard something on the other side of the post office to his left. He looked around the corner of the building and saw Cisco and his boy standing there looking at the ground.

"Don't think too hard about that, buddy. It don't mean nothing," Jesse heard Cisco say to his son.

He realized that Cisco was holding a pistol in his hand and the two of them were standing over what looked like a dead dog.

"What the hell was that?" Cleeve said, coming out of the saloon.

"Goddamned coyote!" Cisco called back.

Cleeve and Mary came over to see the poor animal. Everyone took in the scene.

"Why'd you go and shoot it? You have a hard-on for death or something, Cisco?" Cleeve asked.

"Thing was coming right for the boy."

"That poor animal wasn't coming for your boy."

"Sure as shit was, Cleeve, it was coming right for us."

"Well, you could have just as easily thrown a rock or something. I think you just like to shoot things. Now you need to do something with the carcass."

"I know where to take it," Cisco said.

"I'm sure you do."

"Come on, son let's go get the truck."

Everyone walked back over to the saloon.

The sun had dipped below the western rim of the mountains, erasing all of the harsh shadows that fell across the ghost town. This was the best time to film, a half-hour prior to now and a half-hour after, the full magic hour.

Cisco and his son hopped into his truck and drove over to the dead coyote behind the post office.

"He used to shoot coyotes for the government," Cleeve said as Cisco drove off.

"For the government?"

"He worked for this program called Wildlife Services that killed coyotes and mountain lions to stop 'em from preying on livestock for the ranchers. The government paid for the killing. I think he still has that job in his mind."

They all watched the wiry Cisco struggle to lift the dead coyote into the bed of his truck as his son looked on.

"Guess I'm gonna hit the road," Jesse said. "I'll be back in a day or two to start filming."

"We'll be seeing ya, then."

"Bye, hon," said Mary.

"Bye."

"Oh, if you see Darrell Wayne Speed, tell him Cleeve said he can go fuck himself."

"I hope I don't have the opportunity."

. . .

He made it back to Delgado unscathed as the stars began to appear in the early evening sky. He passed a neon-lit liquor store on the edge of town, did a U-turn in the middle of the street, and pulled into the parking lot. Inside, he found the tequila aisle and bumped into the friends he met but didn't remember at the party the first night, the guy and girl who helped him find his car that morning after.

"Hey, you're still here?" the girl said with a sweet, stoney lilt.

"Still here."

"You're practically a local now," said the guy.

"If you're still here tomorrow night, we're playing at a place called Bodhi Wind," said the girl.

"Oh, yeah, I hung out with your bandmate who bartends there a few nights ago."

"You should come by. We'll play at nine or ten."

"I'll be there for sure."

The couple walked away and Jesse found a bottle of tequila. He was looking forward to a night alone drinking and working on his play.

. . .

Back at the El Dorado Hotel, Jesse went to his room, grabbed the ice bucket, and filled it up at the ice machine next to the office. In his room, he scooped up a clear plastic cup with ice and poured enough tequila to fill the cup three-quarters of the way. He sat back in his Naugahyde chair and sipped the agave. He wondered what he was trying to say with his play. On the surface, his story was about a gunslinger who was shot by an assassin hiding in a window above the street, and the gunslinger stumbled to the church to hopefully redeem his soul after a lifetime of killing. Below the surface, he felt there was something to say about the creative will, though he wasn't sure how to articulate this. He pondered the sentiments long enough to drain his cup of nothing but ice.

He filled up another while his thoughts drifted to the strange sense of accomplishment he felt from his day at the office. He couldn't figure out the angle or shake the feeling that something was off. Frankie seemed like much more of a capitalist than an environmentalist. Where was the money to be made in protecting property owners from a pipeline? Maybe her dad's firm was building a case to sue the pipeline company. There must be gobs of cash in suing petrochemical companies. Without thinking, his hand picked up the remote on the nightstand and flipped on the TV.

Rio Grande was on TCM, another movie set in Texas but filmed elsewhere, beautifully directed by John Ford, starring John Wayne. This one took place just after the Civil War on the banks of the Rio Grande, but instead of the actual river on the border of Texas and Mexico, it was shot on the Colorado in Utah. Why didn't John Ford shoot in Texas? Jesse wished he could ask the great director. Maybe it was because ninety percent of the state was a humid bug-infested flatland that had the visual appeal of Kansas? Maybe because the only part of Texas that truly passed for the West was in the far southwestern tip of the state at the northern end of the Chihuahuan desert, the area in which our actor was currently sipping tequila in a plastic hotel cup and enjoying a black-and-white Western from 1950. Was there anywhere else in the world, he wondered, that had this many films set in it that weren't actually filmed there?

9

JESSE PARKED NEXT TO FRANKIE'S SUV in the gravel lot outside of the warehouse. Inside the bright office, our actor found Frankie standing at a desk organizing paperwork.

"Morning," said Jesse.

"Hey! Thanks for coming in on a Saturday. You feel like taking a drive?"

"Sure. Where we going?"

"You're flying solo on this one, but I'm certain this is where your immense talents will really pay off."

"Okay, where am *I* going?"

"You're gonna drive out to Vista Acres, about half an hour from here. Save any receipts you spend on gas and I'll reimburse you. We need to get some papers signed, and I feel you're just the man for the job."

"Whatever you need."

Frankie had the paperwork in her hand, about ten printed pages held together by a silver paperclip. She handed them to Jesse.

"I'm texting you the address now," Frankie said, typing into her phone. She half sat on the edge of the desk. Jesse felt magnetized to her as he turned and leaned on the desk moving closer. Frankie's text came through and he took a look at the address.

"You got it?" she asked.

"Yeah, just drive out and get someone to sign these," Jesse said, holding the paperwork.

"Yep, all we need is a signature. Text me when you're headed back. What are you doing later?"

"Thinking of checking out a band at Bodhi Wind."

"Cool, let me know. Maybe I'll stop by."

"You should. I'll text you on my way back."

"You're gonna be good at this," Frankie said as she stood up and walked across the room to another desk. "I can just tell. I'll see ya later, okay?"

"Okay. So, I'll see ya back here when I get these signed?" Jesse asked as he stood up from the desk.

"Like I said, just text when it's done," she replied, distracted by some other task.

. . .

In the parking lot, Jesse put the paperwork in his passenger seat and looked up the address on his phone. The destination was thirty-three miles away and would take forty minutes to get there. He fired up the car and headed in that direction. He drove due east for a while before turning south toward Vista Acres. He passed the bar he stopped at on his first night just outside of town. Maybe he'd pop in on his way back, he thought. The road stayed flat and straight as he drove east. When he turned right onto Ranch Road 623 heading toward the border, the two-lane went up over a mountain pass before dipping back down into a big desert valley. RR 623 went up and down over and over like a roller coaster until it eventually bottomed out just before he passed a faded wooden billboard that read WELCOME TO

VISTA ACRES. On the east side of the road, he started to see large estates surrounded by old-growth poplars, Italian cypresses, cottonwoods, and junipers. The estates stretched from the valley floor up into the base of a mountain to the east. He turned left onto a bumpy gravel road and slowed down to minimize the damage to his shocks. Five miles could seem like forever on a road like this, and it did. A giant pickup truck blew past him in the opposite direction that left a cloud of dust in its wake for a mile. On the other side of the dust, he came to the driveway of the address. He turned right and could see a house in the distance on a hill. Both sides of the driveway were lined with tall cottonwoods and barbed wire.

Jesse drove slow along the sandy gravel avenue as he made his way up the hill to a modest white farmhouse. He reached the house and turned off the car. There was a gold Lincoln town car in the carport next to the house that looked like it hadn't been driven in ages. He was having trouble breathing through his nose and looked around for something to clear his nasal passages into. He found an old napkin in the glove box and blew out a healthy amount of blood-crusted desert dust. He threw the napkin on the passenger floorboard and took a look at the paperwork sitting beside him. It was the first time he had given it much attention and noticed the name at the top of the contract: Millie Evelyn Jones. The name was instantly familiar, but it took him a minute to register that this was the lady he spoke to yesterday, the only person he was able to get through his full phone script with. He sat puzzled for a moment, wondering what this all meant until an old lady appeared from around the other side of the house walking with a white Great Pyrenees. The lady and the dog had the same color hair and moved in a similar rhythm. The lady was thin and the dog looked to have issues with its back legs. Jesse grabbed the paperwork and stepped out of the car.

"Mrs. Jones?" he asked.

"That's me. Now, who are you?"

Jesse paused, unsure if he should use his real name or an alias. He remembered the name he used with her yesterday because it sounded ridiculous but at the same time like a quintessential 1950s actor's name, and he was impressed with himself for making it up on the spot. He decided to go with it.

"Hi, Mrs. Jones. My name's Dean Starwood and I have the paperwork for you to sign."

"What paperwork?"

The dog fell back and rested on its tail, panting, staring at our actor.

"I'm really not sure, ma'am, I was just told to bring it to you to sign."

"Well, you'll have to come inside and read it to me. I can't see to read too well and I don't want to stand any longer in the sun," she said as she started up the steps to her front door. "C'mon, Myles," she said to the dog. The dog struggled for a moment but eventually managed to get back up on all fours and follow the lady into the house. Jesse followed the two of them.

"That's Myles," Mrs. Jones told Jesse as he entered the house. "He's damn near as old as I am."

The front room of the house was split between a living and dining area. There was a minimal amount of furnishings in both areas. A couch, an old box TV, a lamp on the living side, and an oval wooden table on the dining.

"Have a seat and let's take a look at what you have there,

hon," she said, motioning to the table. "Would you like a cup of coffee or tea?" she asked, continuing into the kitchen.

"I'll have a cup of coffee, thank you."

Jesse laid the paperwork on the table and took a seat. There was a ceramic bowl of sugar and a jar of honey on the table. The honey was covered in tiny black ants that ran along a path from the door, along the baseboards, and up the wall to the table.

Millie came back with two small white cups of coffee and placed one in front of Jesse, "How do you take yours?" she asked.

"I'll take it just like this, thanks."

Millie took a spoonful of sugar and swirled it around her cup. The coffee tasted like it came from a bygone era of American history.

There was a five-by-seven framed photo on the wall centered above the table. In the photo, a boy rode a horse in the desert with the white farmhouse and mountains in the background. Behind the farmhouse, a few other horses ran around a pen. The photo and frame looked like they were from the Seventies.

"That's my son, Robert, when he was about twelve," Millie said with eyes of love on the verge of tears. "He used to be a big help around here. He loved riding those horses. He moved off to the city years ago to start a life of his own." Millie fell silent, then snapped out of her reminiscence and asked, "Now, what is it that you have there?"

Jesse inspected the paperwork. There was a line with her name at the top that listed her as the owner and an address below that.

He read aloud from the document, "*THE PROPERTY together with all rights, privileges, and appurtenances, pertaining thereto, included but not limited to, water rights, claims, permits, strips and gores, easements . . .*" He read more to himself but had no idea how to translate the legalese. "Honestly, I'm not really sure what all of this is about, Mrs. Jones. From what I gather, this is a contract that will protect your property from being seized by the government for the construction of a pipeline, but I didn't write this, and I'm not an attorney."

"My husband always said that one day they'd come in and try to take it all away. He was a *very* smart man. He said they'd probably find oil one day in this valley. We moved out here in 1962 to breed and raise horses, and that's what we did until I couldn't manage to take care of them on my own anymore. Do you like to ride horses?"

"I've never been on one."

"You never rode a horse?"

"No, ma'am."

"Well, the stables and corral are still there out back. We had twenty-five horses here at one time, but it's a lot of work taking care of that many. It's a lot of work to take care of *one*, to tell ya the truth."

"I'm sure it is."

"If this agreement will allow me to hang onto my home, so it's here for our son when I'm gone, I'll sign it. I've just always hoped that I could leave this place to him. It's not much, but it's all I have."

"I think it's a beautiful place you have here."

"Well, it won't be beautiful if they build a big ugly pipeline through it, so gimme something to write with and tell me where to sign."

Jesse felt his pockets, knowing that he didn't bring a pen.

"I'm sorry, ma'am, but I don't seem to have a pen."

"You didn't bring a pen?"

"I must've lost it," Jesse said, wondering the point of any of this.

"Let me see if I can find one," Mrs. Jones said, standing up from the table. She went into the kitchen to look through a drawer.

Myles sat curled up on the floor staring at the stranger at his dining room table. Jesse looked back through the contract and felt that something wasn't right about all of this. He was in no place to explain this contract to Millie and she had no idea what she was signing. He didn't like the position he found himself in.

Millie came back with a pen.

"Found one," she said, sitting back down at the table.

"Are you sure you wouldn't like to have an attorney take a look at this for you? Just so you know what you're signing?" Jesse asked.

"Well, I thought you told me what I'm signing."

"I feel like you might want to get another set of eyes on it. Is there anyone you trust to do that? Maybe your son?"

"My son lives in San Antonio and he's busy with his own business."

"Could you give him a call and see what he thinks?"

"I'm sure he's at work right now. I don't want to bother him."

"In that case, my advice is to hold off on signing this until you have someone that you trust to take a look at it for you."

"I guess I can give Robert a call this evening."

"I would do that," Jesse said, standing up from the table. "I'll leave the contract here with you for now and I'll come back in a couple of days after you've talked to someone. Thank you for the coffee."

"You're welcome, sweetie," Mille said as Jesse saw himself out.

. . .

Jesse got back in his car, turned around in the driveway, and headed back down the cottonwood-lined lane. He felt he was doing the right thing. It was a big contract and he didn't want to be responsible if there was something in there that wasn't favorable to Millie.

Down the hill, he saw a big white full-size SUV sitting on the side of the road just to the right of the driveway. He continued down the driveway, and as he turned left onto the dirt road, he made out the face of the driver. When Jesse drove off, he noticed the SUV turning into Millie's driveway and heading up to her house. It made him a little uneasy. The truck was familiar, he thought. Then it hit him—it was the same truck and driver he saw through the binoculars at the Star Colony. The same goons Neil and the architect said were watching them. Something didn't seem right.

He continued down the bumpy dirt road in the direction of the highway contemplating what he should do. He pulled to the side of the road and decided to call the cops. Just before he dialed 911, he noticed a police cruiser stopped where the dirt road met the highway about a mile in front of him. He made his way to the cop car and pulled up beside it. He rolled his window down, as did the officer, and Jesse recognized the deputy from his traffic stop a few days ago. The deputy was in the car alone and stared blankly at Jesse.

"I think there may be a lady in trouble about three houses back down this street on your right. Can you go check on her? I saw a couple of sketchy-looking guys driving up to her house."

"Yeah? Which house?"

"105's the street number. It's a big white farmhouse on a hill, the Jones residence. There should be a white Chevy Tahoe in the driveway; that was the car the two guys were driving."

"And what brings you out here?" the cop asked in a suspicious tone.

"I was visiting the lady's house on unrelated business."

"You were visiting her house?"

"I was hired to deliver some paperwork to the homeowner and I noticed the guys driving up the road to her house on my way out. It just felt like something was off. Would you mind going over and checking it out?"

The cop stared at Jesse for a moment before putting his car in reverse, spinning around, and driving up the bumpy dirt road in the direction of Millie's. Jesse watched the cop disappear into the dust and reasoned there wasn't much else he could do as he pulled back onto Ranch Road 623.

He worked to put the current situation into perspective on his way back to Delgado. He was sure he had just seen the same meatheads he saw at the Star Colony driving up to Millie's house after he took her the contract. They must have been thugs from the pipeline company, he concluded, out to shake down the property owners who were standing in the way of their construction project. He wondered if they went after everyone who signed a contract for Frankie's dad's Eco Law Group. He wondered if Frankie and her dad were aware of any of this. He may not have a signed contract for Frankie, but he did have some intel on the pipeline dicks trying to railroad the Eco Group's protection plan. He was conflicted because he felt he needed to fill Frankie in on what he knew and get Millie's number to check in on her, but at the same time he wanted to take a moment to collect his thoughts. He drove back over the mountain pass into the Delgado Basin. Something didn't feel right, and he found himself driving back to the Hotel El Dorado to lay low in the darkness of his room and think things over.

He couldn't get the old lady in the desert off his mind, and he wanted to check on her somehow. He looked up the number for the Delgado PD and called them.

"I'd like to check on an incident I reported earlier," he said when the operator picked up.

"What was the incident?" the female operator asked in a raspy West Texas twang.

"There was a lady I thought might be in trouble at 105 Vista Acres Lane."

"What kind of trouble?"

"Well, there were these two men who looked like they were going to rob her or something."

"What time did you report the incident?"

"I was planning to call 911, but then I saw a Delgado police officer on the road by the lady's house and I stopped and told him about it. I think he went to check on her. I just wanted to see if there was any news about the case or the lady."

Jesse could hear the operator typing on a keyboard as he spoke.

"I don't have an incident reported for that address. What time did you say you talked to the officer?"

"Around eleven this morning."

"There's nothing showing up for that address from today. What's your concern?"

"I just wanted to make sure the lady that lives there is okay."

"Well, she's probably okay if nothing's been reported. Did you have anything else?"

"I guess not."

"Thanks for calling the Delgado Police. Have a good day."

The operator hung up.

Jesse stared at his phone and decided to wait for Frankie to reach out to him instead of calling to fill her in.

. . .

That evening, Jesse got himself nice and high and took a walk through the breezy desert night over to Bodhi Wind to see his pals in The Talking Walls perform. The town had swelled to three times its population with the weekend tourist influx. The restaurants and shops were packed with city folk wearing expensive hats and getups. They all came out here seeking the same escape our actor sought, though he felt that a week here had somehow separated him from them.

At Bodhi Wind, he made his way through the house and out to the backyard where the band was setting up in an astro-turfed corner between the pool and the house. Jesse walked to the back bar, ordered a tequila, and found a white metal chair at the edge of the pool. There were more people than the last time he was here but it wasn't packed. A couple of girls swam around the heated pool in bikinis, while others sat at the tables and lounge chairs. Locals and tourists mingled near the kitchen bar and in the living room. A big moon rose in the east that wasn't quite full, and the sky slowly filled with stars. Jesse took it all in as the band continued tuning up. The Talking Walls were a three-piece consisting of the bartender he met here at the pool bar a few nights ago on bass and the boy-girl couple he'd seen around town a number of times on guitar and drums. They all had longish dark hair and dressed in vintage threads. They kept tuning and tweaking their volume until they fell into a sparse groove, full of reverb and dissonance. It was a sound that called to the emptiness of the desert.

They locked into something reminiscent of Crazy Horse mixed with the ghost of Bobby Fuller. All three of them sang indecipherable vocals in perfect three-part harmony. Jesse got up and walked to the other side of the pool to get closer to the band. He finally recognized the song as a Skip Spence cover, "All Come To Meet Her." More spectators wandered over and got lost in the music. The band ventured into a long spacey interlude. Jesse closed his eyes and let the sounds vibrate through his mind and felt it through his body. The song built to a climax and came to an abrupt stop. The crowd cheered.

"We're The Talking Walls from Delgado . . . for now."

They started up another song and Jesse got lost in it. He hadn't been blown away by a band like this in a while. Probably because the coolest bands were all out here, in the hinterlands of the country, out where actual people could afford to live, out where the creative spirit's not crushed by the ever-rising rents. He closed his eyes and let the sound wash over him for the rest of the band's set, enjoying the haunted melodies and fuzzed-out guitars.

The band played for an hour and took a break. The three of them went back to the pool bar and Jesse followed them to get himself another.

"That was celestial," Jesse told them. "You blew me away."

"Glad you liked it," said the drummer.

"There's been a lot of drama around here the past couple

of days, I don't know if you've heard about any of it," the bass player confided in a serious tone.

"Any of what?" Jesse asked.

"My friend, who I called to get you weed the other night, the cowboy?"

"Yeah."

"He got busted."

"Oh, shit, by who?"

"The Delgado PD. He's out on bail now, but they grilled him about everything. They wanted to know everything he knew, where he got his shit, who he sold to, everything. He said he didn't give them much."

"Is he okay?"

"I think so. He's gonna go hide out in Colorado for a while, I think, but I wanted to tell you the police also asked him about you."

"About me?"

"Yeah, they wanted to know about the guy who drives the white convertible."

"What?"

"Yeah, they mentioned there was some smuggling happening in the Soledad ghost town and they asked what he knew about Cleeve and the guy in the white convertible. He said he didn't tell 'em anything, but I thought you should know just to be careful."

"Man, that is super weird."

The guitarist overheard and said, "Yeah, we may be leaving town because everything's so weird."

"Where would you go?" Jesse asked.

"Not sure yet, just somewhere outta Texas."

"We should go back up there," the drummer told her bandmates.

"Okay, we're gonna play some more. Stick around," the bass player said to Jesse.

"Yeah, I will."

. . .

When the band started playing again, there was a pervading uneasiness to their sound. Jesse slinked along the side of the pool in the direction of the band, and on the way he noticed Frankie and Nina at the inside bar by the kitchen through the sliding glass doors. They were both laughing and splashing around drinks. Jesse's first thought was that he wanted to avoid them and just watch the band, but he soon accepted the inevitability of their meeting. It wasn't long before he felt a pair of cool small hands cover his eyes from behind. Jesse did his best to act surprised, but he didn't believe it and it wasn't a good act. Frankie seemed extra excited as she asked, "Hey! How'd it go today?"

He wasn't sure how to answer, so he just pointed to the band as if he couldn't hear her that well over the music.

"These guys sound great," Nina said.

Jesse nodded and the three of them watched the band for a couple of songs before Frankie pulled Jesse away from the crowd. They stood in the backyard underneath the shadow of a loquat tree.

Frankie seemed a little drunk when she said, "So, sounds like everything went smooth today."

"Yeah?" he asked.

"I mean, you got the contract signed and everything. That's

great! Let's have a toast!" she said, pulling our actor to the inside bar.

They stood in the bright light of the kitchen bar, waiting for the bartender. The sounds of the band outside blared through the speakers in the kitchen. The bartender came around and Frankie ordered something in his ear. Shots were brought and the two of them toasted. Then, Frankie kissed him on the lips. He was confused but went along with it.

"Let's go outside," she said.

They walked back through the house and out to the tree they were just standing under. She kissed him again but his time with tongue. They leaned up against the tree and made out. Jesse slid his hands down her body.

"Should we leave?" he asked.

That snapped Frankie out of it, and she started looking around for Nina. She went back to where the band was playing and Jesse followed. They watched until the band finished their last song and then all walked out to the front of the house.

Frankie pulled Jesse away as Nina went to the big black SUV.

"Hey, I just wanna take things slow, okay?" she said in the street near her truck.

"Yeah, sure," Jesse said, unsure of what this all meant. He felt he should tell her about what happened at the lady in the desert's house earlier, but the timing didn't seem right.

"Let's talk tomorrow," she said and walked to her truck.

Nina stuck her head out of the driver's window and said, "I'll bring the camera on Monday."

Jesse gave her a thumbs-up and watched them drive away.

He walked back to the El Dorado to pour himself a tequila and try to work Frankie out of his head. He opened the door and walked in the darkness to turn the lamp on beside his bed. Before he could turn it on, he felt a presence there—a body in the bed. He turned on the light and saw Dale asleep with his mouth wide open. He walked down to Barbara's room and knocked. She opened the door half-asleep and confused, wrapping a robe around her.

"Your husband's asleep in my bed," Jesse said.

She looked around the room behind her and said, "Goddammit, Dale."

They walked back together and she went in to wake her husband.

"Dale, get up and get out of this boy's room."

Dale woke up startled. "Get up. How'd you even get in here?" she asked.

The old man got up and didn't make a fight to leave with his wife.

"Sorry about that," Barbara said to Jesse as the two of them left.

"You know that's not your room. How'd you get in there?"

Jesse heard Barbara ask again.

"The door was open," said Dale.

Jesse flipped the pillow over, kicked his boots off, and lay down on top of the blanket.

10

I N THE MORNING, HE WALKED OVER to return his Greek tragedy to the library. The Sunday morning church bells rang in the distance. Jesse had been in Delgado one full week and it was the first time the thought of going home crossed his mind. There was something that he was starting to miss about the city; it wasn't the humidity or the traffic, but maybe something to do with the ability to get anything you want at any time. Maybe it was the convenience, maybe the anonymity.

He shuffled around the library and found a room full of local historical texts where the walls were lined with books about Delgado and the surrounding areas. Jesse found a book about the history and people of Delgado. The book was filled with biographies and photos of the families that came to settle in the Delgado basin. He sat at a large wooden table in the middle of the room and flipped through the book. The biographies, dating back to the 1800s, included ranchers, cattle barons, teachers, farmers, miners, railroad men, and a few bandits. Many of the settlers found their way from the East in search of some dream, while others came up from Mexico seeking opportunity in the north. Each biography read like a self-contained Western unto itself.

There was a memoir from a woman named Ellie Ray Stockton, who rode across Texas from Beaumont with her three sisters on the way to their father's ranch near Delgado. She wrote about camping at rivers along the way and how one of their horses was bit by a rattlesnake and her sister sucked the venom out. At one point, they realized they left their deceased mother's wedding veil at their last camp and had to ride back to get it in the heat of the day. They eventually made it to their father's ranch and each married men from the town and all had kids who went on to start businesses in the Delgado Basin.

There was a man named Rafael Menchaca Valdez from Chihuahua, a deserter of the Mexican Revolutionary Army, who came to Delgado, married an Apache woman, and the two of them started a peach orchard that supplied the area with peaches and other produce.

A well-educated man from Connecticut came in on the train headed west. When he got off at the Delgado stop, he favored the climate so much he decided to stay and founded the first town newspaper.

A pair of brothers from Paris, Texas moved here with their wives in 1908 to open the first pharmacy. Their descendants still ran the place as of the time of the book's publishing.

There was story after story of the prominent business people of the area who made their way here and created a community. Jesse was fascinated by all of the stories but started to wonder how his own story would read if he had come here in the early 1900s. What would he have to offer? Would he start the town theater company or just sling cervezas in the local saloon? What story would he leave behind when he was gone? He wondered where the value was in anything he had ever done. Something about this book made an impact and filled him with a sense of purpose. He returned it to its place on the shelf and right there he made a pact with himself: *You finish writing your play and go out there to that ghost town you have at your fingertips and you shoot that thing and send it off to your agents no matter what. It doesn't matter if people like it or they don't, doesn't matter if it gets you a single acting gig, go out there and you give it everything you've got.* He agreed to these words and went back to his room to prepare himself for a dress rehearsal in Soledad.

. . .

He put on his gunslinger getup and rolled a joint. He didn't want to show up to Cleeve's empty-handed. He blazed out of town and out into the wild mountain void. He thought of Frankie as he made his way up into the golden hills that led to Midnight Pass. He thought about their kiss last night and he felt like a fool. He should get another room in another hotel, he decided. It wasn't a good look allowing Frankie to pay for his room. He'd find another place in town, pick up his camera from Nina, and shoot his play tomorrow. That was the most important thing.

His phone went off. He looked down and saw a text from Ben Lipton that said, *Got burned.*

He wondered what to make of the message as he kept driving. He picked up the phone and texted, *Burned?*

Neil took the money and ran.

Jesse found a place to pull off the highway and texted Ben back, *Wtf do you mean?*

He fucking split with the 8k, Ben replied.

Jesse tried calling Ben—he wanted to get the story.

"I can't talk. I'm too busy trying to track his ass down," Ben said as he answered.

"What happened?"

"Gil Phillipe said Neil went to pick up the money and never came back. He took the truck and disappeared. Gil Phillipe's pissed because he had to hitchhike all the way to El Paso and now he's flying back to Paris. Star Colony's off!"

"Are you sure that's what happened?"

"Pretty damn sure. I'll call you later."

"That's strange," Jesse said.

"Be careful who you partner with is all I'll say." Ben hung up.

Jesse sat on the side of the road and thought about it. He thought about the goons he saw at the Star Colony and yesterday at Millie's. How was it all connected, he wondered. For some reason, Millie signed the contract after he left. Maybe her son told her to do it. It felt like there must be more to the story. He pulled back onto the highway and continued to Soledad.

. . .

There was no one around when he arrived at the ghost town, no sign of Cleeve or anyone else. He took the opportunity to stand on his stage in the middle of the street. He planted himself and felt like another mountain in the range. He contemplated the weight of his actions. He heard the voice of Stella Adler say, "*When you stand on a stage, you must have a sense that you are addressing the whole world, and that what you say is so important the whole world must listen.*"

He stared down the main street of Soledad and thought of reflecting his soul out to the cosmos. He noticed a puff of dust around the bend and recognized Cleeve's blue pickup coming up the street in front of him. He stepped back onto the porch of the saloon and waited for his friend.

"Hombre!" Cleeve greeted Jesse as he pulled up to the saloon. He got out of his truck and walked up to the porch.

"Sup, my man," Jesse said, pulling the joint out of his front shirt pocket.

"About time for a drink," Cleeve said as he walked into the saloon.

Jesse followed him inside.

"What are ya having?"

"Same as you."

"Bloody Marias. A friend brought me a new mix. You can try it out and tell me what you think," Cleeve said as he made his way behind the bar and started mixing up a couple of drinks.

Jesse pulled up a barstool.

"They haven't chased you out of town yet?" Cleeve asked.

"Not yet, but it feels like the heat's on."

"Ha, yeah!"

Cleeve continued to mix up the Bloody Marias.

"Speaking of, I ran into a couple of friends last night who told me the guy I bought this weed from got busted."

Cleeve passed Jesse a lighter. Jesse lit the joint.

"How'd they get him?"

Jesse took a drag and passed it Cleeve.

"Not sure exactly, but my friends mentioned that the cops were asking about Soledad. They asked the weed dealer if he knew anything about this place, and apparently, they were asking about me, too."

"What? Why were they asking him about us?" Cleeve asked, passing Jesse a Bloody Maria in a nice glass. "I got some new glasses down in Ojinaga yesterday."

"They're beautiful," Jesse said inspecting the glass. "Not really sure why. You have any ideas?"

Cleeve passed Jesse the joint.

"All I know is the cops have been creeping around here the past couple of weeks and that's a new thing. Seems like they're snooping around for something. You had any more run-ins with 'em?"

"Not really. I saw the deputy that pulled me over a couple of days ago in Vista Acres yesterday, but that's about it."

"Vista Acres? What were you doing over there?"

"I drove out there to take a lady some papers to sign."

"Papers to sign?"

"I picked up a job in Delgado working for a friend of mine. Her dad has a law firm that's helping people fight a pipeline from going in."

"A pipeline in Vista Acres? What the hell pipeline is that?"

"Tex-Mar?"

"Tex-Mar? There ain't no Tex-Mar pipeline going through Vista Acres that I'm aware of."

"Pretty sure that's the name."

"Well, that ain't right. There's only one natural gas pipeline slated to go through here and it's well on the other side of the mountain from Vista Acres. I should know."

"I'm pretty sure that's the name of it and it's going through Vista Acres."

"Let's back up. Why were you taking a lady papers to sign about the pipeline?"

Cleeve showed an acute interest in this story.

"I started working for Frankie, the girl I came out here with the day I met you at the hot springs."

"Right, the Hammer girl."

"The Hammer girl. Her dad has a law firm that's helping property owners from getting their land seized by the pipeline company."

"In Vista Acres?"

"That's where the lady's property was I went to yesterday."

"Well, that don't sound right to me."

"No?"

"No, and here's how I know. I've been working with a group for the past year that's doing everything we can to stop the Tex-Mar pipeline project. It's made up of ranchers and families on both sides of the border that want to keep this thing outta here. We're fighting it because the whole thing's a sham. Tex-Mar says the pipeline'll supply jobs to impoverished communities in Texas and Mexico, but what they're really after is opening up a path for fracked gas from West Texas to get to a port in Mexico, where there's fewer regulations to sell to foreign markets. The pipeline'll do nothing but harm to the ranchlands it's set to go through, not to mention the damage it'll pose to the wildlife. We're doing everything we can to stop the damn thing and there are a lot of powerful people who aren't too happy about that."

"It sounds like Frankie's dad's group is also fighting it."

"That might be the case, but it's not going through Vista Acres, so something sounds off there to me."

Jesse was unsettled and felt like he had no business being wrapped up in any of this.

"The interesting part is that the cops never came around Soledad until we started having the meetings here to figure out what we could do to stop the pipeline, and I have a feeling there's a direct correlation."

"Ya know, the guy who told me the cops were asking about the two of us mentioned the cops specifically brought up something about a smuggling operation coming out of Soledad."

"Smuggling? The only smuggling going on around here is you smuggling me doobies from Delgado. I'll tell you this, we had a meeting here yesterday, there were about fifteen people, and when they left, D.W. Speed himself was parked out on the highway at the turn-in to Soledad watching everyone who rolled outta here. Now, he could've been parked out there looking for clocking cars, but something tells me he was taking notes and letting his presence be known to everyone who attended that meeting."

"Shit, man. You think he's working for the pipeline?"

"Wouldn't be out of character, but if they can imply there's some sort of smuggling going on, they'll have every cop and border patrol from Laredo to El Paso sniffing around. Smuggling people and smuggling weed is their whole trip, that's the thing that gets 'em salivating and justifies their existence. This is all speculation, and I might be paranoid, but things have been feeling just a hair freaky lately."

"I can't believe the cops still make such a big deal about weed around here. It's like the war's over and they didn't get the memo."

Cleeve lit the joint again, took a puff, and passed it to Jesse.

"Well, you gotta think, criminalization began in this state and it'll be the last one to legalize it. This is ground zero for their dumb-ass war and the whole thing is just a racist, convenient excuse to keep black and brown people in check, always has been. The white American male ego is about the most fragile thing on God's green Earth. That's why I know if they're trying to say I'm smuggling weed through here, that means trouble. Hopefully, your friend just has his wires crossed, but I'm thinking it might not be a bad idea to schedule our meetings someplace else." Cleeve thought about it, nodded his head, and said, "Then again . . . fuck 'em."

Jesse passed it back to Cleeve.

"To be honest with you, I made a pact with myself to shoot my play here and I'd like to follow through on that. I'm picking up a camera tomorrow and I'm hoping to get started in the late afternoon. I came out here to do a final rehearsal before the shoot and make sure it was all still cool with you."

"Well, hell, yeah, it is. I need your help getting this place on the up and up and making some productions happen. If I can turn this place into a legitimate money-generating business, it would probably keep the Delgado PD off my ass, and I need a front for my smuggling empire," Cleeve said with a laugh. He walked around from behind the bar and over to the saloon doors. He gazed out onto his ghost town.

Jesse followed him out.

"Hey, what if you're group teamed up with Frankie's dad's group to fight off the pipeline together? Sounds like you have the same goals. I could make the introduction," Jesse suggested to Cleeve as they stood on the porch.

The sound of a truck could be heard roaring up the main street.

Cleeve smiled and nodded. "That's cute, but why don't we just stick to the movie biz?" he said.

The truck came to a stop in front of the saloon doors. Jesse made out Cisco behind the wheel, and Nestor was in the passenger side of the truck.

"We've got some work to take care of up the hill over there," Cleeve said to Jesse, pointing up the hill toward the old silver mine. "Feel free to stick around and do your thing."

"Hollywood!" Cisco yelled at Jesse.

He seemed drunk.

Cleeve walked over and got in the truck.

"Eastwood!" Cisco called out as they drove off in the direction of the road leading up the hill. There was a big blue tarp covering the bed of Cisco's truck. Jesse took notice and wondered what was in there as the truck sped away. The bumper stickers were still there on Cisco's truck: *No Wall, No Pipeline*.

Our actor walked back to his stage on the main street of the ghost street.

After some time going through his actions and scouting his camera placements, he left Soledad.

On his drive out of town, he saw a coyote panting across the road that disappeared into a thick cut of greasewood on the east side of Route 17. Jesse wound around the hairpin curves that led to the top of Midnight Pass. The south side of the pass was shaded from the afternoon sun by the surrounding rocky mountaintops. The view opened up at the top to reveal the golden Delgado Basin spread out before him. The highway went straight down from there, and he trained his eyes on the road's vanishing point, which was washed out by a shimmering mirage.

Mirage, the title of the film that got away. He had his heart set on that role—it could have been the one that changed everything. There was a strong similarity between the Soledad ghost town and the village where a big shoot-out took place on the Texas-Mexican border in *Mirage*. The mental image was almost identical in the mind of Jesse.

The film followed the tale of a young couple, Cy and Ella, trying to make it through Texas to a beachside Mexican resort on the Sea of Cortez as society crumbles around them. A worldwide plague had sent civilization into a downward spiral and all of humanity had been thrown into survival mode. Ella had been working at the resort in Mexico with a group of self-sufficient activists. She went back to Texas to get Cy and drive him to the resort. She knew that if she could get them back there, they would be safe, but they'd have to blast their way through Texas to reach the promised land of coastal Mexico. On the way, the couple tried to help a girl on the run from a gang of lunatics. She has something they were after. All three of them had to fight off these marauding jackals the entire trip. At the climax of the film, they came to a village on the border where a shoot-out took place. There are so many shoot-outs in *Mirage*, it plays like Peckinpah—pure nihilism. It was unclear if the couple survived and made it to the resort or if it was all a death hallucination. At its heart, it was a love story. Ella wasn't sure if she was still in love with Cy, but he proved himself to her throughout the course of the story.

Jesse couldn't help but hang onto a faint hope that if the film ever came back around and it hadn't been cast yet, his Soledad piece could help his chances. He knew it was a long shot; he'd heard rumors of some big names auditioning for the role of Cy, and Zed82 Pictures was the top indie production company out there right now. Zed82 weren't producing blockbusters, but their films always received plenty of press and had solid distribution, both streaming and theatrical. He thought that if nothing else, he could pay homage to that scene, and shoot something similar in Soledad. All of the circumstances felt right to him, and he knew to follow through when things felt right. If nothing else, he'd have the screen test to show the direction he wanted to move in.

He was snapped out of his stoned introspection by the abrupt awareness of a police cruiser blazing past him in the southbound lane of the highway. He looked in his rearview and watched the cop's brake lights flash on before whipping a U-turn in the middle of the highway. The cruiser sped up after Jesse. A wave of panic washed over him as the cop came close enough for Jesse to make out the face of Sheriff D.W. Speed and his deputy. He could see the two officers' cold stares in his rearview, and it disturbed him to his core. He kept his hands steady on the wheel and tried to remember what the speed limit was. His heart began to race; his palms were dripping with sweat. Then D.W. lit up the lights and siren. Jesse pulled over to the shoulder and put his car in park.

He kept his head straight toward the highway in front of him but watched the two of them out of the corner of his eyes in the mirror. The cops kept staring in the same direction. It looked like they were mumbling something, but Jesse couldn't make out the words. They all three just sat there as if they were waiting for something to happen. Jesse realized it was the same damn deputy he saw in Vista Acres yesterday. The cops continued to sit there. "What the fuck are we doing, guys?" he asked in a whisper. The deputy started operating the radio. D.W. Speed kept staring directly into Jesse's rearview mirror. It felt like a psychological game. The deputy hung up the radio and D.W. opened his door. The sheriff put his left cowboy boot on the shoulder of the highway and began to lift the rest of his body out but stopped and sat back down. He sat frozen for a moment before slamming his door. Jesse saw the sheriff pull back on his gear shift and speed off around him, kicking up dust and gravel. The cop car flew away down the highway toward Delgado.

Jesse sat there with both hands still on the steering wheel wondering what to do. Was he free to go, he wondered. Was this a trick? He was still pretty high from the joint back at Cleeve's. He looked all around his surroundings. No other cars were coming from the south or the north. He put the car in drive and crept back onto the highway. The cops were playing mind games with him now, he thought.

Maybe it's time to start thinking about getting back to the city, he told himself.

He made it back to the El Dorado and ducked into his room. The place was dark and cool, he was grateful for that, although a deep sense of paranoia undulated below the surface. He took inventory of his dwindling weed supply and found that there was just enough to roll a sad excuse for a pinner. He'd need to find more but was struck with a fear of going out in search of any in the current police state environment. He relegated himself to what little he possessed and decided to hide away from the outside world for a while as he sparked the pinner.

He walked to the bathroom and gazed into the bloodshot eyes staring back in the mirror. He wondered if there was any future in anything he was doing. He felt he was chasing an illusion. The illusion of success. The illusion of making it as an actor. This illusion of a creative life lived on your own terms. And he felt like a fool for chasing Frankie. She needed an employee, not some dirtbag who could barely feed himself. He had the urge to leave. To get into his car and blaze out of there. Drive north, drive anywhere. Drive to Taos—he'd been there once and visited Dennis Hopper's grave and the old cinema where he cut *The Last Movie*. Dennis Hopper had gone to the brink of madness and made it out the other side. The same couldn't be said for some of his friends back in Austin. Everyone he knew seemed to be on the verge of losing it. It was the times—they weren't easy for many. He remembered the haunting look he saw in Carla's eyes before he left town. That look in her eyes had made him leave without question. He had to get out. He was afraid the same might happen to him. It was happening to everyone. Everyone was teetering. "Tequila!" he shouted to himself.

He poured himself a cup and sat down in his chair. The agave put his mind at ease. He decided he wouldn't go into the office tomorrow morning. He didn't come all the way out here to work in a call center. Even if he *was* helping innocent folk stave off the pipeline, it wasn't a battle he signed up to fight. He hoped he had somehow helped Millie, but he wasn't certain that he did. He could have gotten her in trouble for all he knew. He'd stick around long enough to film his piece at the ghost town and then he'd split. That was that—stick to the plan and get out.

11

His phone went off at 10:25 a.m. with a text from Frankie: *Will we be seeing you at the office today?* He'd been lying awake for a while telling himself he wasn't going in. He contemplated his reply and decided the most honest thing to say was, "No." He sent it and waited as he saw her typing a response. He kept waiting until it looked like she stopped typing. He lay there and relaxed, wondering what to do with himself now. His phone vibrated again. *Can you meet for lunch? I have a check for you.*

At noon he drove over to Saint Annie's, a café bar around the corner from Frankie's warehouse. Inside, the place looked like an upscale home goods showroom. Jesse spotted Frankie and Nina sitting together on a big brown suede couch staring into a laptop. He walked over and sat on an identical couch across from them separated by a raw wood slab coffee table.

"Señor Strange," Nina greeted him.

"Are you taking a sick day or did you decide this wasn't the job for you?" Frankie asked.

"Probably not for me," he said. "No offense, I'm just not looking for . . ."

"No need to explain," Frankie cut him off. "It's not for everyone, but let me give you this before I forget," Frankie said as she handed him a check. "I left the name field blank because

I'm not sure what you use for business."

Jesse looked at the check: It was for two thousand bucks. It seemed like a lot for two days of work. He tried to contain any expression of disbelief. He felt both of their eyes, examining him for a reaction.

"That's your commission."

"Commission?"

He wondered what was sold to earn a commission and what percentage his cut was. He couldn't help but run the numbers. Two thousand was ten percent of twenty thousand, or one percent of two hundred thousand.

"You brought in a new client, and that's your cut. Not bad for a couple days' work."

"I brought in a new client?"

"Yeah, the old lady you went to see in Vista Acres."

"Oh, yeah, Millie."

"I knew you'd be good at this. I was thinking you could take the next couple of days off and focus on your movie or audition tape or whatever. After that, if you feel like coming back to the office, the door'll be open and we'd love to have you. Take a couple of days to think about it."

Frankie's tone was extra accommodating.

"And speaking of, I have the camera for you," Nina said. "It's in the truck if you wanna walk out with me and grab it."

"Sure, should we go now?"

"Let's go," Nina said, standing up.

Jesse stood with her.

Frankie stayed seated on the couch. She looked up at Jesse with her eyes in a flirtatious squint and said, "Gimme a call later, okay?"

Jesse nodded with a half-smile and followed Nina out of the café.

. . .

Nina and Jesse walked around the corner of Saint Annie's and across the parking lot in the direction of Frankie's SUV parked by the warehouse. A light wind whipped around them.

"Are you filming your audition thing today?" Nina asked, looking up at Jesse.

"I'll probably make the day of it tomorrow. It's not really an audition thing though, just something for my reel—a screen test."

"Oh, yeah, Frankie said you don't wanna go to Hollywood or nothing. You just want to be an actor in Austin."

"I don't recall ever saying that."

"Maybe she said you weren't trying to be famous."

"There's more to acting than Hollywood."

He felt silly for saying it as soon as the words left his mouth. Nina seemed to consider his statement.

"I get it. Sometimes people do stuff in the public eye that's not about fame."

"Something like that, yeah."

"Well, it's not bad money working for us, right?"

Jesse still hadn't come to terms with the check. There was a feeling coursing through him that wanted to give it back to Frankie. There was also a feeling of taking the money and leaving Delgado.

Nina unlocked the truck and opened the back driver's side door.

"I think you should really think it over," she said.

"What's that?"

"Coming back to work for us."

"The thing is, I'm not exactly sure what I'm even doing there. I'm still unclear on what the job *is*."

"All you have to do is listen to whatever Frankie tells you and then just let the money roll in. It's really that simple," Nina said as she pulled a Pelican case from the floorboard onto the back seat and opened it. Jesse took a look over her shoulder at the camera inside. Nina took the camera out of the case and passed it to Jesse to inspect.

"I can't tell you much, because I haven't had a chance to use it," she said.

He looked it over, it felt like a foreign object. He wasn't a big camera guy, but he was confident he could figure it out.

"I think everything you need is here," she continued. "There's a charger and extra battery. I brought a tripod, too."

He thanked her and took everything back to his car. He knew he needed to get back to his room and research the camera and make sure he had the proper settings for his shoot tomorrow.

"I'll see ya in a couple days," Nina said as she locked up the truck.

Jesse thanked Nina again on the way to his car and said, "Be seeing ya."

As he began packing the gear into his trunk, he called out to Nina as she was starting her way back across the parking lot to Saint Annie's. "Ahoy!"

She came back to him. She was tiny in a striped dress that the desert breeze blew around. She loosely held her hands to her upper thighs to keep her dress from moving too much.

"You wouldn't happen to know where a guy could get some weed around here, would ya?"

"I think I know someone. I'll put you in touch later," Nina said as she shuffled back to the café in the sandy wind.

Driving back to the El Dorado, Jesse pulled the paycheck out of his pocket, put it on the steering wheel in front of him, and wondered what to do. He was struck with an itch to rip the thing up and toss it into the wind. There was no doubt he could use the money, but something about the payout just didn't feel right. Did Millie pay enough to warrant a commission check of two thousand dollars for legal representation from the Eco group? She didn't seem to know what she was signing and Cleeve seemed confident that the pipeline wasn't set to go through Vista Acres at all. The two goons were also still an unsettling image in Jesse's mind. He kept driving through the town until he was on the other side of it. His foot weighed heavier on the gas pedal in an unconscious gesture of acceleration in the direction of civilization beyond. He zoned out on the two-lane highway and flat desert basin stretching out around him until he looked down into the passenger floorboard and saw the Pelican case containing Nina's camera. He knew the pact he had made with himself was worth honoring, and he slowed the car looking for a place to turn around.

Up the highway on his right, he spotted two palm trees in front of a white one-story building with a rust-colored Spanish tile roof. As he approached, he saw the sign for the Arroyo Inn. He pulled into the paved parking lot to turn around and realized the two palm trees flanked a kidney-shaped pool. There were red and white metal umbrellas shading chaise lounge chairs of the same color spread out around the glimmering azul pool. On the edge of the highway, it was a vision surrounded by the emptiness of the Delgado basin.

He pulled around to a shaded parking spot under a drive-through awning in front of the hotel office. His hair had been blown around from the road; he brushed it back with his hands to look respectable before walking into the office. Inside, he asked the lady at the front desk if she had any rooms for the night. He knew the odds were in his favor considering there wasn't a single car in the parking lot. "Smoking or non?" the front desk clerk asked. He paid for two nights in a non-smoking room, deciding that was all he needed. He'd stay tonight, film his piece tomorrow at the ghost town, and head back to Austin the following day. He walked out of the office with an Arroyo Inn room key, got back in the car, and sped off in the direction of Delgado to pick up his things and check out of his room at the El Dorado.

On his way back, he concluded that he should hang onto Frankie's check instead of cashing it. The check had stirred in him the confidence to pay for his new hotel room, and he thought it might be good to keep it with him for now. He looked forward to spending the rest of the day lounging around the pool at the Arroyo Inn preparing for his shoot. He knew that having a new place to rest his head would help his performance tomorrow.

He parked on the street and walked through the dusty court-yard of the El Dorado. On the way to his room, he saw Barbara walking toward him in her signature white Mexican dress.

"I saw some girl putting something on your door—you just missed her. Is that who you went on your date with the other night?"

"Not sure. What'd she look like?" Jesse asked.

"Oh, she was a hot little thing."

"No clue."

"Well, you'd better go see what she put on your door. I'm going out to find Dale. He worries me, because he's been driving off lately. He used to just sit there on the street, but now he likes to go 'exploring.' I have no idea where he goes, but he somehow always seems to find his way back. We finally got our insurance settlement, so we're trying to figure out our next move. I'd like to stick around here to be near the kids, but Dale is set on going back to Port Olivia. The problem is there ain't no Port Olivia left anymore; the whole place was wiped right off the map. You can't tell him that though."

"Why not?"

"'Cause it won't register—*nothing* registers with that man."

Jesse could see the exhaustion in Barbara's eyes.

"I can stop by later with a little fire water if you're up for it," she offered.

"That's hard to turn down, but I'm checking out of the El Dorado today. I'm just on my way to grab my things."

"Yeah? You going back to Austin?"

"I figure it's time to start heading back that way."

"I can't blame you. I bet you have a lot of fun over there."

"Sometimes."

"Well, I better get out there and wrangle the old man. Maybe we'll still be in Delgado the next time ya visit."

"I'll be sure to look ya up. Thanks for the tequila and the company."

"Anytime, shug."

Jesse continued on to his room to find a white envelope taped to his door. *Have a good shoot tomorrow!* was handwritten on the envelope. When he pulled it off the door and opened it, he found a nice fluffy bud, enough for two small joints. "Saint Nina, coming through with the camera *and* the weed." He promised to do something nice for her before he left town.

Inside room 103, he put his clothes together and collected his things. He surveyed the near-empty tequila bottle: There was only a sip left, and he threw it back, making a note to stop for more on his way to the Arroyo. He took one last look around the room, grabbed the El Dorado Hotel stationery and pen, and walked out.

The front office was empty. Instead of ringing the bell or waiting for the clerk to appear, he pulled a sheet from the stationery pad, wrote *Checking out* in cursive, and placed the key for room 103 on top of the paper on the desk. On his way out of the office, he saw the front desk clerk walking down the shaded corridor toward the office. Jesse nodded and pointed at him as he kept walking out to the street. Jesse hopped in the car and was on his way back to the Arroyo Inn.

He felt liberated. There was something about knowing his room was paid for by Frankie that made him feel he owed her something. The feeling carried a weight that was growing heavier the longer he stayed there. He stopped off at a liquor store and bought a bottle of blanco Siete Leguas and a couple of limes that were losing their color. Back in his car, he cranked up the Stooges and gunned it out of Delgado. No more than a minute later, his joy ride was halted. He took his foot off the gas and turned the music down as he saw a cop car sitting on the other side of the highway, facing the direction of town. Jesse crept past the cop and they both glared at each other. Jesse turned his head forward, and with his left hand out of sight below the window, he flipped D.W. Speed the bird.

The jugular vein pounded in his throat as he sped down the highway. He kept watching the rearview waiting for the sheriff to spin around and come for him. The road out of town ran up a ridge that allowed Jesse to see down the highway at the cop car sitting still on the shoulder. Just as Jesse topped the ridge, he saw D.W. Speed whip around in the middle of the road. In front of him, he saw the two palm trees framing the Arroyo Inn sign about a mile away. He stepped on the gas in hopes he could make it there before the sheriff made it over the ridge. The opening drum roll of *Dirt* rumbled through his speakers, he cranked it up to hear one of his favorite drum beats of all time. "Come on, baby," he said to himself as he kept his eyes peeled on the ridge behind him. His hand flipped on the blinker before he could make the conscious decision to do so as he pulled into the parking lot. He pulled around the side of the white metal fence surrounding the pool and saw the sheriff speeding down the hill. Jesse found the room key in his pocket, which also held the envelope with his weed. He took a look at the room number as he cruised down to room 33 at the back of the building. Turning into his parking space, he saw D.W. Speed and his deputy driving slowly past the Arroyo Inn parking lot, staring straight down at our actor. Jesse saw both of them crane their necks to inspect him as they crept down the highway.

"Well, I guess ya know where to find me," Jesse said aloud. He thought about asking to be moved to another room. He'd prefer to be closer to the pool but reasoned with himself that it wasn't worth the trouble of dealing with the front desk. He also knew it would be easy for the cops to find him if they wanted to, because he seemed to be the only one staying here.

He settled into his new room, poured himself a drink into

another clear plastic hotel cup, and pulled on his swim trunks. He used his room key to saw through a lime and squeezed out every drop of juice. He grabbed his ice bucket and cocktail and headed to the pool.

He spent the rest of the day lounging around the water meditating on tomorrow's shoot. He struggled with what he was trying to express verbally with his piece, so he felt the best thing to do was to keep it physical. He'd go through the motions of the gunslinger from lying on the street to dragging himself to the church steps to die. He would speak with his eyes and his actions, and if the words struck him in the moment, he would recite them. He felt an improvisation would be more powerful than following a script. He would also be the cinematographer on this production and there was a lot to focus on. He wanted to shoot from many different angles to give a voyeuristic view from the buildings of the ghost town of a man dying and that would require a lot of setups and stamina, both mental and physical. He'd need to conserve his strength, get a good night's rest, and not be hungover tomorrow.

He looked down the length of his body lying across a lounge chair. He could see more of his ribs than he preferred and he knew he would go to bed hungry tonight. It was hard to find enough to eat in the desert on an actor's diet. It required a decent amount of effort just to find a place that was open, let alone one that served anything that resembled healthy food.

Back in his room, he sat cross-legged on his bed familiarizing himself with the camera. He scrolled through the camera's menu and found the section for controlling the frames per second. He wanted to shoot in the style that Peckinpah innovated for the final shoot-out scene in *The Wild Bunch*, where normal twenty-four frames-per-second motion would be intercut with varying degrees of slow motion. This editing style was also used in the final shoot-out scene in *Bonnie and Clyde*, although in a much more understated way. He found the settings to shoot in 59.97 frames per second and even slower in two hundred frames per second. He would switch between these three frame rates throughout his shoot tomorrow. Peckinpah had multiple cameras all filming the same shoot-out at different frame rates with different focal length lenses. Jesse would be filming everything himself with one camera doing numerous takes, shot in three different frame rates, with one thirty-five millimeter vintage Zeiss cinema lens.

There would be a lot to focus on tomorrow, so he poured himself one more cup of tequila and tuned in to see what was on TCM. It was a Western from 1950 called *High Lonesome*. The film was a high desert murder mystery involving a drifter played by John Drew Barrymore who may or may not have been set up to take the fall for a series of murders by a couple of outlaws who were presumed to be dead by the townsfolk. It was inferred that maybe the two outlaws were ghosts and the drifter was haunted; he *seemed* haunted by something. Jesse couldn't tell if the movie was good or bad and soon fell asleep with the TV on, missing the ending of *High Lonesome*. A swig of tequila remained in the clear plastic cup on the nightstand beside him.

12

"*T*HE GREAT PARADOX OF ACTING *is that the actor must act real things in an unreal, imaginary setting. You must do everything you can to make the world of the stage real, and you do that by actions.*"

Jesse methodically pulled on his all-black gunslinger outfit and in doing so slipped into character. He didn't *try* to stay in character, he just allowed it to happen. If he drifted off and started getting in his head about camera settings and setups, that was okay, he didn't fight it. He let all of his actions happen as if he were preparing for what lay ahead in Soledad. He laid all of the camera gear out on the bed and packed it up into the Pelican case as if it were his big iron and bullets for the day. Once the gear was packed, he sat down at his table and rolled a joint for Cleeve. Our actor decided he wouldn't imbibe today, but he wanted to show up with his usual offering. He stood up, took a look around the room to make sure he had everything, polished off the remaining tequila in his cup from the night before, and hit the road.

On the stereo, Jesse listened to Stella Adler discuss making an entrance and the need to have a justification for every entrance. "*You must find a purpose for your entrance, meaning you have come from somewhere and you're going some place! A good actor always has a reason to walk on the stage. You don't take the stage because the stage manager tells you to go on, you take the stage for your own justification, something bigger than you."*

He turned it off. He didn't want to think about acting or anything at all. He listened to the road and nothing else and let it clear his head of everything that didn't matter. He'd follow his intuition and rely less on the cerebral today. On the highway up ahead of him, he spotted a caravan consisting of a Delgado PD cruiser, a couple of state trooper and border patrol SUVs, an ambulance, and a fire truck, all coming at him from the opposite direction. As the vehicles made it to the road that led up to Midnight Pass, they all instantly turned on their lights and sirens and blazed away. Jesse approached the turn-off with caution before turning left. By the time he got on Route 17, the caravan was gone. Jesse reasoned there must be something going on at the border.

. . .

On the dirt road leading into Soledad, Jesse spotted a pack of vultures circling above the ghost town. "My welcome committee," he said to himself. He pulled up to the saloon just after eleven a.m. The two front doors were shut and there was no sign of Cleeve's truck. Jesse knocked gently before twisting the knob.

"Jesus, hombre, get in here and shut that thing!"

Cleeve had all the lights off except for a couple of neon beer signs behind the bar. One, a Lone Star beer neon in the shape of a cowboy boot with a small state of Texas for the spur; the other a Budweiser sign with a lizard wearing a sombrero. In front of him on the bar was a bottle of cheap tequila and a shot glass. Jesse's initial read on Cleeve was that he was either still going from the night before or was off to an early start this morning. Jesse kept his distance at the edge of the bar and remained in character.

"Grab a glass from behind the bar and pull up a stool. You look like you need a shot."

Jesse obliged and picked up a tumbler. Cleeve pulled himself up off the bar and stumbled over to the front doors.

"Thought I had these locked," Cleeve said as he slid the bolt latch into place, securing his fortress. He looked out the windows with his right eyebrow raised as he made his way back to his seat. Jesse stayed on the tending side of the bar and blew the dust out of his glass.

"Let me see that thing," Cleeve said, nodding toward Jesse's glass.

Jesse slid it over and Cleeve poured him a couple of fingers' worth.

Jesse told himself this was all he would have today. He didn't come here to drink.

"I think we shut 'em down, hombre," said Cleeve, staring down at his shot glass with distant eyes.

"Shut 'em down, huh? Who's that?" Jesse asked, taking a sip.

"The fuckers, the motherfuckers, we shut 'em down, ha ha!" Cleeve looked over his shoulder out the window again. "They're gonna have a good time trying to run that son of a bitch now."

Cleeve may have been more drunk than Jesse suspected.

"You seen any sleep in a while?" Jesse asked.

Cleeve attempted to pour another shot into his glass, but twice as much spilled on the bar. "The whole thing went —" Cleeve looked up at Jesse, widened his bloodshot eyes, and said, "BOOM!" as he fell out with laughter. "BOOM!" he said again while slapping the bar. "BOOM!"

Jesse nodded and stared down into his tequila wondering what the fuck Cleeve was going on about.

"Damn near blew the face off half of Goat Mountain," Cleeve slurred as he poured another shot.

"Damn near blew the face off, huh?"

"And my woman's a goddamn federale," Cleeve said lifting his glass but not making it to his mouth.

"Your woman's a federale?"

"Why do you keep repeating what I say as if it's a question?" Cleeve asked in an irritated and confused manner. He looked up at Jesse and attempted to focus his eyes on him. "Why don't you just come out ask me something?"

The cowboy was obviously troubled and it seemed like he was trying to confess something to Jesse. Our actor had to think about what his character would ask. What would the gunslinger, who didn't have long to live, ask the owner of the saloon in this moment? Jesse glanced over at the eight-by-ten film still framed on the wall near the door. The late morning light was falling through the window at an angle that allowed him to make out the scene. The gunslinger was frozen in air with his gun to the sky, a split-second after being shot. What would an honorable last question be for a man who was unaware that this might be his last? He tried to see Cleeve in a light that he hadn't seen him in before. He had a flash of him as a little boy walking across the desert to see the healer.

"Why did you walk all that way across the desert to see the curandera when you were a boy?" Jesse asked, referencing the story Cleeve told him the first time they met in the hot springs. "There must have been a good reason to go all that way."

Cleeve began to nod with a smile, pondering the question.

After a moment of silence, he spoke.

"I saw her three times. Once when I was a boy, another time when I was a teenager, and then when I was eighteen. My old man drove me down in his '55 Chevy pickup the first two times. He was a spiritual dude in a very traditional Mexican way and he believed you could get possessed by evil spirits, believed you could get a curse put on you, he even believed something could pass by you in the wind and jump right into your body. I was seven years old the first time he took me to see her. I started having really bad dreams around then; I think it was because I was watching monster movies on the weekends but my father wanted to have me cleansed. He drove me down to her village, a few hours away by car." Cleeve's speech had gained coherence as if the memories had unclouded his drunken haze.

"This little old lady rubbed an egg all over my body and my head. It smelled weird in there, like rotten fruit and Vicks VapoRub—I'll never forget that smell. I didn't like the place, but it was important to my father and afterward, I don't remember having any more nightmares. The second time, I was a teenager and I had a problem with gaining weight. I ate like crazy and I stayed thin as a rail. No matter how much I ate, I kept getting thinner and thinner and it started to scare my family. My dad drove me down again to the little lady. This time she gave me peyote because I was old enough to handle it. She stayed up with me and sang all night and I had a really heavy experience. After that, I was able to keep a healthy weight.

The third time I went to see her I was eighteen or nineteen, coming into my own as a man. This was the time that I walked across the desert. I mentioned that each time she knew I was coming and that was true. My father had also gone to see her as a child growing up, having his spirit cleansed, and he knew that there was no appointment—you just started out on the journey and the little lady would be expecting you. So, I set out on my own journey to see the little lady and have her give me some sort of guidance on the direction I should take as an adult. When I arrived, it was the middle of the night and she was sitting up waiting for me. I remember when you looked into her eyes, it was like looking into space. She gave me peyote again and showed me my whole life's journey."

"Your life's journey?"

"Yeah, she gave me some sort of psychic narration, read my future, told me everywhere my life would go. That was the last time I saw her."

"Was she on the money?"

"To tell ya the truth, she was pretty spot-on. She told me I would inherit a silver mine and I thought that was weird, but here we are. She said my first marriage wouldn't last and it didn't. There were other things that came true and some I just don't like to talk about."

Cleeve paused with a concentrated gaze as if he were attempting to remember what the curandera said. Eyebrows furrowed, he stared down at the bar. He grabbed the tequila bottle and poured both of them another shot.

Cleeve seemed to regain his drunkenness as he held his shot glass up to Jesse.

"To the future, to the past."

Jesse didn't want to drink anymore, but he joined in the toast anyway and threw back the shot.

A silence fell over the two of them, and Jesse found himself staring at the film still on the wall. Cleeve tilted his head up to Jesse and asked, "Did you come out here to make a movie today or what, Sancho?"

"Today's the day," Jesse answered.

"Well, don't let me slow ya down," Cleeve said as he attempted to stand up. "Probably time for me to get bed in there . . ."

He trailed off into some babble that Jesse couldn't decipher. Cleeve planted his butt back on the barstool. Jesse took the joint that he rolled for Cleeve out of his chest pocket, put it on the bar, and walked out the front doors. On his way out, he watched Cleeve pour another shot and say, "If it ain't don't broke fix it," with the weight of his head swiveling on his shoulders, his eyes barely open.

"Oh, yeah, Cleeve?" Jesse called back to mention the caravan of emergency vehicles he saw on the way up but stopped considering the story might take him out of character. Then he saw Cleeve's head gently wobble and come to a rest atop the bar and he knew it wasn't worth bothering him about. The gunslinger continued outside to meet his fate.

. . .

On the front steps of the saloon, Jesse shook off his bizarre interaction with Cleeve and snapped into production mode. He unloaded the gear from his car and began setting up the tripod on the saloon porch. He always preferred to be the one being filmed instead of the one doing the filming, but today he'd have to do both.

For the first shot, the camera would be on the ground filming the fallen gunslinger lying on the dusty street. He double-checked all of the camera settings and adjusted for the high noon light. He placed the camera on the ground, framed up the shot, and pressed record. He lay down in front of the camera with the bottom of his boots closest to the lens. He stayed there with his face on the ground and remained lifeless for a good ten seconds. He got up and played back the shot; it wasn't bad, but he felt it would be a better frame if he moved his body further from the camera and stretched his legs out a bit more. He hit record and went to his new mark. He repeated the action and held it for another ten seconds before going back and having a look. This take was better, but he felt that if he crossed his ankles, stretched his legs even more, and laid himself across the frame, it would be a better shot. He rolled the camera and tried it again. This time he was happy with the playback and proceeded to set up the next shot.

The next shot would be from above, looking down on the fallen gunslinger. Jesse set up the tripod and used a rock to find the center of the frame. He rolled the camera and positioned the area just below his belly button on top of the rock and lay still on the street. After a few seconds, he opened his eyes and slowly clutched his abdomen. He got back up, checked the playback, and decided it was a keeper. He set up the next shot.

This would be a wide master shot from a low angle. He moved the camera and tripod to the middle of the street and let the ghost town buildings fill the edges of the frame. He started recording and walked back to his spot on the street and lay down. He took a moment to align with his character and began to lift his body off the ground. He lifted himself to his knees, then used his left leg to stand up and swing around to face the camera. He was still hunched over and holding the bullet wound on the right side of his stomach. He kept his hand there to keep his guts from spilling out of his body and onto the street. He scanned the town with one eye to see where the bullet came from. He stared straight down the main street beyond the camera and began walking slowly.

The next setup would be from the second story of the building next to the saloon. Jesse leaned the tripod and camera on his shoulder and took them inside the Soledad Inn. He went up the stairs and to the window looking out on the town. He set up the camera and centered the frame on the spot where his body had just lay. He hit record and ran back down the stairs to his mark on the street. He repeated the previous action of standing up and scanning the town as he held the bullet wound on the side of his abdomen. He made sure to look directly at the camera and give it a "go-to-hell" look before he started walking. Then he ran back up the stairs to retrieve the camera and set it up across the street.

This time he placed the camera in the window of the general store with half a lace curtain in the shot. He walked back out to the street and drug himself through the frame; again he made sure to stare at the camera. He wanted to create a voyeuristic effect that felt like the town was watching the wounded gunslinger make his way down Main Street.

He took the camera, carried it in his hands, and focused on the church at the end of the street. He walked with the camera to show the point of view of the gunslinger attempting to make it to the church. He stumbled a number of times with the camera in his hands.

He continued in this way as he dragged his dying carcass down the main street of the ghost town. He'd set up a wide master shot and walk toward the camera, then he'd run and put the camera in the window of a building and walk through the frame. He was driven and methodical and worked with a feverish focus. He began to experiment more with the perspectives and framing. He put the camera at his eye level and walked into the camera, turned it around, and filmed his back stumbling away for a walkthrough shot. He set up a couple of Dutch angles on the wooden sidewalk platform. He put the camera on the ground and just filmed his boots. In his mind, he was waiting for another bullet to hit him from one of the second-story windows.

He went back to the second story of the Inn and filmed himself stumbling down the street with the church in the distance. He ran back and retrieved his camera. All of the running back and forth was making him sweatier, dirtier, and more worn-out, and it all worked for the look and energy of the dying gunslinger. He kept going, setting up more shots on his way to the church. He put the camera on the ground and fell to his knees less than a foot from the lens with an equal look of fear and determination in his eyes. He needed redemption and salvation from a lifetime of killing. He pulled himself back up and continued walking past the camera, all while holding the bullet wound on his right side.

He ran and set up a wide shot beyond the church. He filled the left side of the frame with the white adobe church and steeple and the right side with the ghost town buildings across the street. He started recording, then ran back to his last mark and continued to stumble toward the church. He used his natural exhaustion as the gunslinger took his final few steps.

He retrieved the camera and brought it into the church. He set up the tripod at a low angle just in front of the pulpit with a view of the pews and the open wooden doors; in the background, you could see the crooked white crosses of the cemetery across the street. He was proud of this shot. *Classic John Ford doorway framing*, he thought as he hit record. He ran out of the church. The gunslinger took his last steps as he came into the shot and collapsed on the floor of the church, his head and torso in the house of God, his legs still in the sun outside, the graveyard in the background behind him.

He got up and took a look at the playback. The shot was better than he ever imagined it would be and it filled him with excitement for the entire project. He couldn't wait to edit the footage. Now he needed to go back and film his body lying halfway in the church and halfway on the church steps from all of the buildings of the ghost town, showing the voyeuristic perspective. This shot had given him the strength to continue with the last few setups.

He slung the camera and tripod over his shoulder and set up a shot in the cemetery with the white crosses in the foreground and the church in the background. He rolled the camera and fell into the church again.

From here on, it would just be a shot of his body lying halfway in the church. He set the camera in the middle of the street and filmed himself dead in the chapel. He ran to the town post office and set up a shot inside, looking out the window, of the gunslinger lying on the church steps. He filmed another angle from the Soledad Inn. With each shot, he had to run further with the camera and further back to the church. He went back and forth with a number of these shots until he felt he needed only one more.

He sat in the entryway of the church and looked back at the second-floor window of the general store across from the saloon. This would be his final and longest shot, both in depth and the amount of time it would take to go to and from. He'd need to go back to the Inn and take the camera across the street to the general store, record, and then run all the way back to the church. He decided that once he set up the camera in the window of the general store, he would go through the entire motion of stumbling through the town and collapsing into the church.

Upstairs in the general store, he framed the shot, it was wider than he saw it in his mind. He wondered if it was worth it but reasoned with himself that this shot was important and would offer a good amount of coverage. Suddenly, he was hit with the realization that he didn't have a gun. In the film still in the saloon, the gunslinger has a revolver in his hand. He worried that this whole piece wouldn't make any sense without a gun. He sat down and leaned against the wall contemplating the situation and was struck by an image that hadn't fully registered with him when he saw it.

When he was talking to Cleeve about visiting the curandera, he noticed a pistol on the bar about an arm's length from the cowboy. He didn't think much of it because it wasn't an out-of-place object—he'd seen the same gun behind the bar by the cash register on a previous visit. He was sure Cleeve would let him use it, but he wondered if he really had it in him to reshoot the entire thing with a pistol in his hand. Maybe if he reshot the first couple of scenes with the gun in his hand he could drop it in the street, because the gunslinger realized that he didn't need it anymore and that would make a powerful statement. That would allow our actor to salvage the rest of the shots and it would all make sense. He sat there leaning against the wall and decided to go ahead and shoot the final long shot of the gunslinger lying on the church steps. Afterward, he'd check in on Cleeve and see about borrowing the pistol.

Outside, he heard a car rumbling up the gravel road into Soledad. He peered out the window and saw the police cruiser driven by D.W. Speed and his deputy creeping into the ghost town. Jesse ducked behind the window frame and watched the cops come to a stop in front of the saloon. He pulled the camera toward him into the lower corner of the window and tilted the viewfinder down so that he could surveil the scene. The officers got out of the car and started looking around the ghost town. Jesse framed them in the shot and hit record. D.W. leaned into his cruiser and gave two quick honks on his horn.

"Anybody around?" he called out. "We're looking for Cisco Maines."

The deputy went to a window at the saloon and took a look inside and quickly walked back to D.W.'s side. The doors to the saloon flung open and Cleeve stepped out wearing nothing but a pair of white underwear and tube socks. In his right hand, he held a pistol. Both cops froze and put their hands on their holsters.

"What in the hell's going on out here?" Cleeve asked drunk and stumbly.

"We'd like to have a word with Cisco Maines. Heard he might be here. You seen him around?" asked the deputy.

"I'd say you need to get the hell off my property."

"Why don't you put the pistol away and go inside, put some clothes on, and come back out and talk to us?" Sheriff Speed reasoned with Cleeve in a cool tone.

"I'm not putting anything away or on. This is my goddam

private property and you don't have the fucking jurisdiction to be here, so see ya later."

"There's a good indication there might be a little smuggling going on around here," Jesse heard D.W. say, although it wasn't easy to hear from his camera perch in the general store window. "Word has it there's been quite a bit of weed flowing through Soledad, maybe a few illegals, too."

"*Illegals*? What the hell are you talking about illegals?"

Jesse had a hard time making out what the officers were saying because they spoke in a calm tone.

Cleeve raised his voice. "You know goddam well there ain't no weed being smuggled through here."

"It'd make us feel a whole lot more comfortable if you went ahead and put the gun down, Cleeve," Jesse heard the sheriff say.

"I don't have to put anything down. I know what this is really all about. I know who you work for."

"Put the gun down, Cleeve!" the deputy yelled. D.W. put his hand out to the deputy in a gesture for him to stand down.

"And who do we work for?" asked the sheriff.

"You know I know who you work for," said Cleeve.

"Our duty is to the citizens of Delgado."

"More like Bob Hammer and Tex-Mar."

"Why don't you regain a little dignity and let's talk about it?"

"Right now, you're on my private property and I'm telling you to get the fuck off it."

"Right now, we're investigating a federal crime, Cleeve, and we'd appreciate your cooperation," the sheriff said calmly.

"I don't give a flying fuck what you're investigating, I want you off my property!" Cleeve yelled and motioned the cops out of there with his gun. As he turned to walk back inside, the deputy drew and shot him. Cleeve dropped. Jesse gasped, not believing his eyes.

"Jesus Christ, Grady," D.W. said.

"He pointed that thing right at us, D-Dub."

"Call the goddam EMS."

Jesse looked for Cleeve in the viewfinder, but he was blocked by the cruiser.

The deputy got into the car and called for help on his radio. D.W. walked around and took a look at Cleeve on the ground. The two officers discussed the situation, but Jesse couldn't hear what they were saying. D.W. went over to Cleeve's truck as Jesse realized his car was parked next to the pickup. The sheriff waved the deputy over and they looked through both vehicles. D.W. started scanning around the town and the mountains.

They're fucking looking for me, Jesse thought to himself.

The two cops walked back to the saloon and went inside. When they came back out, they walked to the middle of the street, and gazed around the buildings. Jesse knew they were looking for him, and he gently pulled the tripod and camera away from the window. He could hear sirens approaching and soon the ambulance was pulling up to the scene of the shooting. Jesse glanced out the window and saw the paramedics loading Cleeve's body onto a stretcher and into the ambulance. The cops got back into the cruiser and both vehicles drove off with their lights and sirens blazing. The battery light on the viewfinder began flashing red and the camera shut off. Jesse tried to turn it back on, but it was dead. He listened to the emergency vehicles go up and over the pass, and when the sirens faded, he grabbed the camera and ran out to his car.

He sat there and considered his next move. He knew the

cops would be interested in finding out why his car was parked at the saloon, where he was at the time of the shooting, and what he saw. He thought they may even be waiting for him out on the highway back into Delgado. He remembered the rocky mountain road Frankie took to the hot springs on his first day out here and he felt confident he could find that route and navigate it back to town. He grabbed the camera and tripod and walked downstairs to the doorway of the general store and took a look around the silent ghost town bathed in magic light before running to his car.

He knew he needed to go south toward the border and find the highway that ran along the Rio Grande. The sun was setting, but there was still about an hour of light left before night would fall. His mind raced as he flew down the south side of Midnight Pass toward Mexico. A green and white border patrol truck blew past in the opposite direction. His eyes darted between the descending road in front of him and the rearview mirror. He decided he needed to leave town tonight. He'd go back to the Arroyo Inn, gather his things, and hit the road back to the city. His hands shook on the steering wheel. His entire body vibrated with nervous energy. He couldn't believe what he had just witnessed. He tried to clear it all from his mind and focus on getting out of there.

He came to the T at the border road. All that lay before him was Mexico; in the other three directions was Texas. He turned right toward the west. He remembered there was an old adobe convenience store on the corner of the road he'd need to turn on to get back to Delgado. They called it the Back Door Road because it turned into a residential street in Delgado, a less conspicuous approach in and out of town. It was almost certain the cops would be looking for him soon, and Jesse remembered that they saw him pull into the Arroyo Inn. He wondered if they would be there waiting for him. He assured himself they didn't have anything on him, he hadn't committed a crime, and they didn't know he was filming. Still, he was paranoid that they somehow knew he saw the shooting go down and it was obvious what they were capable of. He saw the adobe store coming up on his right. He pulled around to the back of the store to keep his car out of sight from the border road, got out, and packed the camera back into its case in the trunk. He didn't want to have a camera in the back seat if the cops caught up to him.

The Back Door Road was paved at the bottom portion near the border, but he remembered the road became rocky and uneven for miles around the top of the pass. He hoped his car had a high enough clearance and knew he'd have to take it slow. He raced up the paved section trying to gain distance and beat the night back to town.

He wondered why the cops had shown up at Cleeve's in the first place. They said they were looking for Cisco and mentioned something about smuggling weed, then they shot a good man. From Jesse's perch in the window of the general store, it looked like the deputy shot Cleeve in the back as he turned around to walk back inside. He hoped he had it all on film. He remembered the battery dying in the middle of the last take and wondered if the footage of the shooting was actually on the card or if he lost the shot because of the battery. He wanted to stop right there and take a look, but he knew that would be foolish. The road turned to gravel and Jesse had to slow the car to keep it from shaking apart. The terrain changed the higher he went up the mountain, and the giant boulders he passed looked like they could come dislodged and roll right over him. He wasn't confident his car would make it to the top and knew there would still be miles of worse conditions on the other side. This started to seem like a bad idea. It became harder to see the massive holes that felt like canyons in the road and he had to drive even slower to navigate all of the obstacles. He pushed it as he climbed higher. He felt that if he let off the gas he would slide backward down the mountain. As the thought of being stranded on this road overnight crossed his mind, he reached the top of the pass and a long flat straightaway along the ridge of the mountain. His car still shook out of control, but at least he wasn't climbing.

The last hues of dusk were leaving the sky. He felt a sense of relief. He stopped the car on the side of the road, got out, and took a deep breath. He shook all of the tension out of his arms and legs and let the howling mountain wind blow over him. It would be night when he reached Delgado. He hoped the cover of darkness would work in his favor. He put the top up on his car thinking it would help him stand out less in town, and noticed a pair of headlights coming toward him from the direction of Delgado. He got back in his car and tried to stay calm as he pulled onto the road. He knew the approaching vehicle was probably the border patrol and decided he'd tell them he was just coming from the hot springs, even though it looked like he had just come from a gunfight at the Soledad ghost town. As the truck came closer, it stopped in the road. Jesse tried to keep his eyes straight ahead like nothing was out of the ordinary, but then he recognized the truck and its driver. It was Dale from the El Dorado Hotel, Barbara's husband. They stared at each other, and Jesse stopped the car beside him.

"This the road that spits ya out in the Gulf of Mexico?" Dale asked.

"What are you doing out here, Dale?"

"I'm trying to get to Port Olivia. A fella back in town told me this road takes you all the way to the Gulf."

He looked lost and a little worried about the darkness he was driving into.

"This isn't the right road, Dale. Why don't you follow me and I'll show you the road to take?"

"You know how to get there?"

"Yeah, you'll just have to turn around and follow me."

"Well, that's the way I just came. Port Olivia's that way," said Dale, pointing in front of him.

"I just came from that way, and this road won't take you to Port Olivia. If you wanna get there, you'll have to go back the way I'm headed."

Dale weighed his options. Jesse planned to have Dale follow him back to the El Dorado Hotel and find Barbara. If anything went down with his car or with the cops, having Dale with him would be good cover. Dale turned his pickup around and Jesse kept driving toward Delgado. After a few miles of more gravel, the road turned to paved asphalt. Jesse felt comforted with Dale behind him and smooth blacktop under his wheels. When they arrived in Delgado, Jesse drove straight to the El Dorado. He wondered if Dale would recognize where they were going and turn around, but he kept following. Barbara was pacing the sidewalk in front of the hotel smoking a cigarette. She threw her arms up in exasperation when she saw Jesse and Dale. Dale pulled into his normal parking spot and Barbara went to his truck. She looked at Jesse idling in his car and shook her head.

Jesse shrugged his shoulders and waved before driving off.

He drove slow through the middle of town and stopped at every street corner looking around for any sign of the cops. The place was still and Jesse wondered if any news about Cleeve had made its way to town yet.

On the highway leading east out of Delgado, the Arroyo Inn sign stood as the last light of town on the edge of the pitch-black desert. Jese turned into the parking lot and drove slowly down the opposite side of the hotel from his room. He kept his eyes peeled for the law. There were a few cars in the parking lot now, which made him feel more at ease. The cars looked like they belonged to tourists, clean and new, with Texas plates. He pulled around the back of the hotel. He parked in front of a room a couple of doors down from the one he was staying in. He thought maybe if the cops came, they'd knock on the door in front of his car and he'd hear it, that would at least give him a heads-up. He got out, popped the trunk, grabbed the camera case, and took it into his room.

Inside, he looked through the camera case and found the card reader. He took the card out of the camera and offloaded it onto his laptop while he gathered his belongings and rolled a quick joint for the road with the rest of his weed. He planned to drive through the night back to Austin, but he wasn't sure what to do with the camera. Nina was kind enough to let him borrow it, and he wanted to get it back to her. He decided he'd leave it at the front desk for her to pick up later. He packed everything into his bag and placed it by the door.

After the card had finished offloading, Jesse double-checked that everything was there. He'd need to erase the card and format it before leaving it with the camera. He watched some of the clips as he checked the footage. He looked at a few of the early takes that he shot of himself. They weren't bad—the light could have been better—but he knew going in that he wasn't shooting in the best light. He went to the last clip and it was all there. He watched the beginning of the clip and saw D.W. and the deputy calling for Cisco, then Cleeve coming out in his underwear holding his pistol. He turned up the volume all the way on his laptop, but it was still hard to make out everything that was said. He knew he could get help boosting the audio when he got back to Austin. Everything was filmed up until the battery died around the time that D.W. and the deputy began driving out of town behind the ambulance. It was hard to watch, but it also showed that Cleeve was turning around to go inside when the deputy shot him. The magnitude of what he had just filmed washed over him and he felt lightheaded. Then there was a knock at the door.

It was a gentle knock, not a cop knock. Jesse froze and took a look around the room. He put the camera and laptop into the case and tucked it under the bed. He went to the window and saw an attractive lady dressed in black standing at his door. With little thought, he opened it

"Hi, sorry to bother you," she said with a nervous smile. She had a black bob haircut and full red lips, she kept her hands in the pockets of her black trench coat. "But I was wondering, well, there's not an ice bucket in my room and I can't find anyone at the front desk, and I saw you when you pulled in, and so I was wondering if I could borrow your ice bucket, just to fill up some ice in my bathroom sink, then I'd bring it right back."

He looked around the parking lot behind her.

"Do you have one?" she asked.

"An ice bucket?"

"Yeah," she said.

He thought about it and said, "Nah, I don't have an ice bucket."

"Oh." She looked a little letdown and confused. She stood there, then looked up and scanned the room over Jesse's shoulder. "I can see one right there on the table."

Jesse looked back at the ice bucket on his table. He walked over and grabbed it.

"It's all yours."

"I'll bring it right back."

She flashed him another nervous smile. Jesse wondered what she was doing out here alone knocking on strangers' doors.

"Don't bother, keep it. Ice machine's down there by the office," he said, pointing toward the front of the hotel.

"Yep, I'll be right back."

She walked off down the sidewalk toward the office in a pair of stiletto heels. Jesse closed the door. He looked back at his table: All that was left was an empty plastic cup and his bottle of tequila. He went over to the bottle and turned it back. He filled his mouth with the fiery agave and was grateful that he'd have the tequila to keep him company on his drive back through the night. He walked around to the other side of the bed to finish packing his suitcase.

There was another knock.

She stood there holding the bucket full of ice in her hands. Jesse opened the door.

"I'm sorry, but I saw you getting out of your car and I felt like I knew you from somewhere, and then on my way to the ice machine, it hit me. You were in *Dust Devil Heat*, weren't you?"

"Yeah, yeah, I was. You saw that?"

"I thought you were really good in it. You were in *Welcome Home, Gilley*, too, right?"

"That's right."

Jesse found her even more appealing now, but he had to get out of there.

"I actually had a little, well, when I saw you get out of your car . . . This is just so random that you're here, just a couple doors down, out here in the middle of nowhere."

He glanced around the parking lot from the doorway. He didn't see anything that looked suspicious.

"I'm sorry to bother you," she said. "You probably have better things to do."

"No bother at all but you caught me just as I was walking out the door."

She stood there batting her eyes at him with an inviting smile.

"I guess I've got time for a quick drink if you wanna bring that bucket of ice inside. I've been working all day and could use . . ."

She stepped inside and shut the door behind her. Jesse went to the bathroom to get another clear plastic cup from the sink.

"Are you working on a film out here?"

He came back with the plastic cup and filled both with ice and tequila.

"Something like that. It was more of a screen test for something I'm trying to make happen. Care to sit down?" he asked as he handed her a cup of tequila and motioned to the only chair at the table. She sat down, and he sat on the edge of the bed. "So, where did you see *Dust Devil Heat*? I didn't know there was any more than a cast and crew screening for that."

"I saw it in an acting class. There was something about your performance in that film that really stuck with me."

"An acting class, really? So you're an actor?" Jesse asked.

"Yeah, well, I'd like to be one."

"Are you out here working on something?"

She took a swig of the tequila.

"Actually, I'm here for a wedding and was waiting on my girlfriend that I'm sharing a room with to come back, and I heard a car that I thought was hers, but when I looked out the window, I saw you getting out of your car and it didn't make sense to me why you would be here, this actor whose films I just watched in my acting class. I was a little tipsy from the wedding, so I made up an excuse to come and see if you were really who I thought you were."

She rose from the table and stood in front of Jesse.

"I hope that's not weird."

"Not at all, but you watched my films in your acting class?" Jesse asked.

"We did, and I can't believe it's actually you. What are the odds?"

"Don't know what the odds are."

They finished their drinks, and she took his cup and poured them both another.

"I have to come clean though," she said.

"Okay."

"I didn't need an ice bucket."

She slowly unbuttoned her coat to reveal a black lace negligee. She approached him on the edge of the bed. He grew nervous. She brushed his hair back, and ran her hands through his hair. He leaned into it. She pushed him back on the bed and fell down beside him with a seductive laugh. They stared into each other's eyes as she inched closer. Her lips met his and he wrapped his arms around her. She slung her long brown legs around his waist and straddled him. She grabbed his hands and ran them over her breasts. He inched himself to the center of the bed and kicked off his boots. She stayed on top of him, unbuckling his belt and unzipping his pants. He slid the trench coat off her shoulders and kissed her neck as she flipped the light switch on the wall behind the bed, turning off all the lights in the room. They made love for half an hour before collapsing into each other's sweaty arms.

In the dark, Jesse held onto the stranger in his bed.

"I have to admit, I've thought about you a lot," she said in a quiet voice.

"What's your name?"

"I don't want to say."

"Why?"

"It's Marisella," she whispered as she started crying.

He wasn't sure what her tears meant. "It's okay, Marisella," he said as he held her in his arms.

"I shouldn't have done that," she said.

They continued to lay there as she sniffled.

Jesse didn't want to upset Marisella anymore, but he knew he needed to get out of there. He was sure the sheriff and his deputy would come looking for him soon. He thought about how to tell her he needed to leave, but nothing felt right. He was exhausted and decided to just lay there with her.

"Jesse?" she asked.

"Yeah?"

"I have to tell you something."

"Okay."

"Everything I told you was a lie. I'm not here for a wedding. I'm here because someone put me up to it."

"What do you mean, put you up to it? Who?"

"Frankie," she said, still sobbing.

"Frankie?"

"Frankie Hammer. She told me to come and see you and do whatever it took to make you feel better."

"Why would Frankie do that?"

"I don't know. I assume it was a test. I came here to Delgado to work for her, and I just did what she told me to do and now I feel terrible about it. I don't want to work for her anymore. I fucking hate her."

Jesse's wheels began to turn.

"Did Frankie tell you why she wanted you to make me feel better?"

"No. She told me to go to this hotel and wait for you to show up."

"What the fuck? So, you didn't actually see any of my movies?" he asked, certain of the answer.

"No."

It stung, but he turned his anger to Frankie.

"Why did you want to work for her anyway?"

"I had a friend who worked for her and made a lot of money, like *a lot* of money."

"Doing what?"

"It had something to do with high-end real estate acquisitions, but really whatever Frankie asked her to do. She put in a good word for me and Frankie had an opening. There aren't many good jobs back in McAllen."

"That's where you came from?"

"Yes."

They lay in each other's arms, her head resting on his shoulder.

"I think I need to leave," he said.

"Can we stay like this just a little longer? I need you to comfort me now."

Jesse stayed in this position with Marisella until they were both asleep.

13

JESSE STARED AT THE CEILING replaying the events that led him here. He knew he had to leave, but he couldn't bring himself to disturb Marisella sleeping beside him. He kept still until she began to stir. He closed his eyes and turned on his side away from her when she pulled her legs out of bed and hurried around the room to collect her things. On her way out the door, she paused and stared at him before leaving. He wondered what was going through her mind. He heard her car door slam and looked out the window to see her peeling out of the parking lot in a candy-apple red Mustang. He almost fell back to sleep until the fear of D.W. and the deputy stopping by for a visit got him up.

He pulled his laptop and camera from under the bed and double-checked that he had all of the footage. When it was clear he had everything, he erased the card in the camera and decided to keep it with him to be safe. As he ran around the room throwing everything into his suitcase, he thought about Frankie and wondered why she'd put Marisella up to such an act of seduction. On his way out the door, he texted Frankie: *Why would you do that?*

Her response was immediate: *I need to see you. Can you come to my place today?*

I'm leaving, had enough fun, he replied and put his phone down on the table.

He opened the door and took a look around. Nothing seemed out of place. He stepped outside to his car and scanned the highway beyond the parking lot. All was clear. He heard a train horn in the distance pulling through Delgado. He darted back inside to grab his suitcase and the camera. He saw another text from Frankie on his phone that said, *I have your money.*

This irritated him. It was obvious she thought she could buy and sell people. He contemplated what to say as he put the camera and suitcase in the trunk. *Just ignore her*, he thought—it was probably the thing that would say the most. He pulled around to the front office to drop off Nina's camera with the hotel clerk. He'd tell Frankie he left it there when he was far enough away.

His phone lit up with another text from her: *The cash in the blue bank bag you left at the theater. We have it.*

He paused to consider what this meant. How did she get the money after Neil skipped town with it? Did Neil pay her dad's law firm for protection from the pipeline after all? Why would Neil leave town if he paid the retainer?

It's like 10k, you should probably take it with you.

He was conflicted but decided it would be worth it to get some answers and bring the money back to Ben Lipton.

I can swing by on my way out. Where should we meet?

My place. 4 Wild Horse Way.

He looked up the address on his phone and pulled out of the Arroyo Inn in the opposite direction of Delgado.

Every car he saw appear on the highway looked like the cops, but it never was. After a few miles on the highway, he veered right onto a road that ran south up into the mountains. The road became sharp and winding with steep cliffs dropping off inches from the blacktop. He ascended a rocky plateau and turned left onto Wild Horse Way. It was a smooth white dirt road that cut through a flat golden grassland. He began to see massive wooden stables with well-kept quarter horses milling around the field—nothing wild about them. Just beyond the stables, he saw the hacienda spread out on the plateau. There was no sign, just a giant iron entry gate with a single horseshoe affixed to the top. He pulled through and continued toward the main house.

The road ended at a circular driveway in front of a white stucco archway that led into a courtyard. He parked and pulled the camera case from the trunk and made his way through the courtyard along a stone pathway that ran through a desert garden containing large saguaros, blooming palo verdes, desert willows, a couple of date palms, and an assortment of well-placed Spanish dagger yucca and prickly pear.

Before he reached the glass front door, he saw Frankie running barefoot down a Mexican-tiled hallway coming to greet him. She swung open the big glass door.

"Come in, come in," she welcomed.

She was wearing a white rope cover-up over a bikini, the same thing she wore when she took him to the hot springs.

"I just made breakfast. Are you hungry?"

"No."

He had to remind himself that he was here for business, though he couldn't help but delight in the sight of her.

"Then I'll make you a Bloody Maria, I know you want one of those. Come on," she said as she led him back down the hallway. Along the walls were huge framed ancient maps of the desert regions of Texas, photos of racing horses, and a stuffed Buffalo head. At the end of the hallway was a great room with a wall of glass offering an endless view of the Chihuahuan Desert stretching into northern Mexico. To the left of the great room was a kitchen and bar.

"Are you sure you don't want food?" Frankie asked as she started mixing up a cocktail.

Jesse stopped at the bar and got lost in the infinite vista.

She poured his drink over ice in a glass and brought it to him. He took a sip but tried not to let his guard down. She brought a plate of over-easy eggs to the bar and nibbled at it.

"So, before my family bought this place, it was a cattle ranch. It's still a cattle ranch, but that's all it was back in the day, and in 1965 there was a movie filmed here called *Sunset on the High Plains*—there's a poster for it on the wall over there."

Frankie pointed to the poster across the room. Jesse was intrigued and wanted to take a look but instead pulled out his wallet and retrieved the two-thousand-dollar commission check. He tossed it on the bar and said, "I don't want your money, but I'll take what belongs to my friend."

"Jeez, okay. But I don't want that back, you earned it," Frankie said.

"I don't believe I did, and I don't want it."

"Is this about Marisella?"

"That's part of it."

"Yeah, she called to scream at me on her back to McAllen."

"I'm sure we all understand why."

"I just told her to go check in on a friend who was probably having a hard time. I didn't tell her to go and fuck your brains out."

"I'm not sure why you felt I needed comforting so bad."

"I heard about the shoot-out in Soledad."

"That news traveled fast."

"As it does around here."

Frankie started mixing another cocktail.

"So, what'd you hear?"

She grabbed another glass, filled it with ice, and poured herself a Bloody Maria from the shaker. She brought it over to Jesse and said, "Let me see your glass."

Jesse slid it to her and she emptied the shaker into his glass.

"I heard Cleeve and that guy Cisco blew up some bridge and the cops went to Soledad to question them. Then Cleeve pulled out a gun and they shot him."

"Blew up a bridge?"

"Yeah, they dynamited a bridge that was built to carry the pipeline across a canyon and some bridge worker was hospitalized because a boulder fell on him. It was pretty stupid and dangerous and now the cops are trying to find Cisco."

"And so, you heard about all of this and decided to send Marisella on an assignment to comfort me? How did you know the cops didn't have me in jail or full of bullets? You knew I was filming out there."

"I told Marisella to keep an eye out and let me know if you didn't show back up at the Arroyo. She saw you pull up and texted me you were there and I told her to go check on you and apparently, she just couldn't contain herself."

"If you were so concerned, why didn't you check on me yourself?"

Frankie stood there pushing the fork around her eggs.

"I'd like to get that cash and leave now," Jesse said.

"You'd really just drive away and leave all of this behind?"

"Yes, and I plan to do it as fast as possible."

"Why? You didn't do anything wrong."

"I was there at the ghost town when the shooting went down."

"What were doing there?"

"I was making a movie."

"Well, is there anything illegal about that?"

"No, but the cops know I was there."

"If you haven't done anything wrong, you should have nothing to worry about, right?"

He thought it sounded like something a cop would say.

"It's time for me to get back to my life."

"Back to your burgeoning acting career in Austin?"

"It beats telemarketing in the middle of nowhere."

Frankie laughed and took Jesse's glass with her to the cocktail station on the other side of the bar and began mixing another. He picked up the camera case at his feet and placed it on a barstool. "I want to make sure Nina gets her camera back."

Frankie brought him a fresh drink and said, "Perfect, you can give it back to her in person. She's on her way out here right now bringing your cash from the theater. Let's take these out to the pool and wait for her."

Jesse started to feel like he was getting the runaround.

"I have something you might be interested in," Frankie said as she disappeared through a door behind the kitchen. Jesse took another sip of his Bloody Maria.

Frankie came back through the kitchen door with a blue and white Mexican platter and set it in front of him. It was full of weed with a grinder, a lighter, and a pack of rolling papers.

"Let's go out to the pool and you can roll one up while we wait for Nina."

"I don't think I'm in a sitting around a pool kinda mood."

"Oh, come on, it's a gorgeous day out there," Frankie said on her way through the sliding glass doors that opened to the patio.

He looked out on the glimmering pool down the hillside surrounded by oleanders and potted olive trees and wondered if he really had anything to worry about. Maybe Frankie was right, he didn't do anything wrong, and if he had to wait for Nina, why not do it out there by the pool?

He took the weed and his drink and followed Frankie outside and down a flight of tiled stairs to the pool. When they got to the bottom, Frankie turned back to Jesse and said, "Oh, wait, you don't have a swimsuit, do you?"

"I don't need a swimsuit," he replied.

"See, that's why I like you, you're always up for a good time."

Frankie took off her cover-up and dove into the deep end of the pool. Jesse sat down on a lounge chair and took off his shirt and boots. He sat cross-legged in the chair with nothing but his jeans on and rolled a doobie. He lit it and took a couple of puffs. Frankie swam over and motioned for him to bring it to her. He brought her the joint and she took a long drag. She saw her maid on the patio as she blew out the smoke and called out for her to bring them another round of Bloody Marias. Then she yelled, "Wait, la botella!"

Jesse wondered if this was a normal Wednesday morning for Frankie.

"Taking a break from the office today?" he asked.

"I'm *so* over that place," she said, holding herself up on the lip of the pool. "I need to travel. God, I miss traveling just for fun. Just going somewhere far away. Do you wanna go away somewhere with me?" she asked in a seductive voice. "Just me and you. Somewhere far away from all of this?"

Jesse stayed silent as he stood up on the side of the pool.

"Why don't you jump in?" she asked.

He dove headfirst in the direction of the deep end and swam underwater to the edge.

"I think I got too high," she said with a laugh when he reemerged. "That's why I don't smoke."

The maid came back with a tray consisting of a clear bottle of tequila, lime wedges, blood orange slices, a small pile of salt, and two shot glasses. The maid set the tray down on the side of the pool in front of Frankie. Frankie poured each of them a shot and she told Jesse to come over and have one. Jesse pulled himself up on the edge of the pool and sat there in his jeans. Frankie stayed in the water and they both took a shot.

Frankie rested her elbow on Jesse's knee. She looked up at him and smiled.

There was a voice in the back of Jesse's head telling him that he needed to get out of there and back on the road, but the more he drank and smoked, the less he could hear it.

"You know what I'd like to know?" she asked.

"What's that?"

"Why'd you drop off all that cash at the theater?"

"How do you know it was me?"

"We didn't at first. Nina found the money and it was a mystery to us for days. We thought it might be ticket money from years ago, but that didn't make sense the more we thought about it. Then, yesterday, we had the bright idea to check the surveillance camera and there you were sliding that bank bag through the ticket slot like you were in a starring role. But the mystery remains. Why? Who was all that cash for?"

"A friend of a friend."

"A friend told you to drop off all that cash at the Delgado Theater for another friend?" Frankie asked as she stared off into the desert.

"Yeah, but for some reason they didn't pick it up."

"Hmmm."

They lingered there on the side of the pool.

"I'll stop asking questions. I'm just glad the money's going back to its rightful owner," said Frankie.

"I'll make sure it gets back to its rightful owner."

"Speaking of your money, where the fuck is Nina?"

Frankie pulled herself out of the water and walked to retrieve her phone on a lounge chair.

"She still hasn't responded to me," she said, staring at her phone. "We need to go find her."

Jesse lay back in the sun on the cement surrounding the pool. Frankie threw a towel on his stomach and said, "Come on, let's go find her."

Jesse picked himself up.

"Grab that," she said, pointing to the plate of weed, "and I'll grab this." She picked up the tequila tray and made her way up the stairs.

In the kitchen, Jesse sat at the bar while Frankie got ready. He looked through a massive book of oil field photography that he found on a table between a pair of leather chairs. The book contained photos of oil wells and pump jacks spread through-out a bleak black-and-white landscape of flatland Texas. He wondered why her dad ran an eco law firm fighting a pipeline if her family money came from oil. Was he some sort of reformed oil man or did he just follow the money? He put the book back down on the table and noticed a printed land survey for the Soledad ghost town. He was a little high, so it took him a second to realize what it was, and he only caught a glance before Frankie came out and asked, "You ready?"

Jesse put the book down. Frankie grabbed the tequila tray and the keys to Jesse's car and told him to bring the weed plate and Nina's camera case.

"Señor, su billetera," the maid called out as she came in through the patio doors holding out Jesse's wallet.

"You might need that," Frankie chuckled as he took the wallet and slid it into his back pocket.

They walked back down the long hallway and out into the blazing courtyard.

"I'm driving," Frankie said.

"No, I don't like other people driving my car."

"You've drunk way too much already."

"And you haven't?"

"Not as much as you, and besides, I drive this road every day. I know every twist and turn all the way to Delgado. You take a curve too sharp and we'll wind up in the bottom of a canyon, so that means I'm driving."

Jesse was uneasy but got in the passenger seat. Frankie put her tray of tequila in the back and Jesse put the weed plate on the floorboard between his boots.

She pulled out of the circular drive and sped off down the driveway and out onto Wild Horse Way. She swerved on the gravel road attempting to reach something behind her seat.

"Whaddaya need?" he asked.

"The bottle, man."

Jesse reached back and grabbed it. She took it from him and put it between her legs. She pulled the cork out of the bottle and it made a thump. She took a big swig and passed it to Jesse with a wild look in her eye. Jesse took a drink and held onto the bottle. She pointed down to the floorboard and brought her thumb and forefinger to her lips in a joint smoking gesture. Jesse leaned down into the floorboard and lit the joint.

"So, what are you going back to in Austin, anything?"

"My life."

"Your life? Back to the way things were before? Back to everything you left behind?"

"Yeah, all of that."

Jesse passed Frankie the joint and she took another hit.

"What did you come out here for?"

"To get away from everything."

"No, what did you come here *looking* for?"

Jesse considered her question over the roar of the road and said, "I think I came out here looking for something real."

"And did you find it?"

She made a sharp turn onto the highway without slowing down or looking for other cars coming around the blind curve. Jesse held onto the side of the car.

"I love your car," she said, laughing. "Even though it's a piece of shit, it's cute."

She passed the joint back to Jesse as she whipped around the twists of the road.

"So, did you find it?" she yelled in the wind.

"What?" he yelled.

"What you came here looking for, something real?"

"I don't think so."

She took another curve too fast and lost control of the car a bit.

"You mind slowing down?" he called out to her.

"This is the best part of the drive!"

There was a straightaway and she floored it. Jesse couldn't bring himself to look at the speedometer.

"Play some music, please!"

He plugged his phone in and tried to find something that he thought would calm her down, but he couldn't decide on anything.

"So, you really don't remember the night we met at the hotel in Austin?"

"I don't have a clue as to what you're talking about," she said.

Jesse looked straight at her. She looked back at him and laughed. He knew she was full of shit.

She glanced up at the rearview, adjusted it, and said, "Uh oh, we're in trouble now!"

Jesse looked at his side mirror and saw the cop car in the distance behind them.

"We'll just fuckin' outrun 'em!" she said as she drove even faster. She looked over at Jesse and said, "Don't worry, I'll lose 'em."

The straightaway ended as the highway curved back around the mountain. Frankie zipped around the twisting road.

"Take it easy," Jesse pleaded.

"I wanted you to be my actor," Frankie said, pressing the gas with an abandoned gaze.

The car fishtailed on the shoulder.

"It's not too late," she said as she sped around a corner too fast. The car slid on a patch of loose gravel, spun around, and slammed into a boulder.

They sat there in a state of shock. They took a look at each and both seemed okay. The front passenger side of the car was banged up where it hit the boulder, but things could have been much worse.

The cop car took the turn around the mountain, came to an abrupt stop behind them, and threw on the overhead lights. Jesse surveyed the weed scattered around the floorboard and the bottle of tequila at his feet. He looked back and saw the doors of the police cruiser opening. Jesse used his boots to sweep the weed and plate under his seat but before he could make much progress. D.W. Speed and his deputy were standing over the back of the car looking down on them. The sheriff seemed to be holding back a smile when Frankie and Jesse faced him. D.W. and the deputy looked happy.

The deputy walked around to the passenger side of Jesse's car and noticed everything on the floorboard.

"I think I spy more than reckless driving and speeding over here, D-Dub."

"Yep, we're gonna need to check the BAC. You two in decent enough shape to step out of the vehicle or do I need to call an ambulance?"

"I think we're okay," said Frankie in a shaky voice as she opened her door.

Jesse couldn't fully open his, so he climbed out.

"You two stand still at the back of the car. I don't wanna hear any talking or shuffling around, just stand there and be quiet. I'm gonna have a look around and the deputy's gonna give you a breathalyzer test."

"I can already see they've got an open container right here, D-Dub."

"I can see that, just go and get the test ready," D.W. said to the deputy. "Y'all been doing a little day drinking?""I'm not saying another word or taking your test until my lawyer arrives."

"That's okay, all the evidence I need is right here on the floorboard," said D.W. "Anybody wanna take responsibility for this marijuana? Looks like y'all still got a joint smoldering on your console there."

"It's mine, officer," Jesse said.

"No, it's mine," said Frankie.

"Well, in that case, I'll just assume it belongs to the both of ya."

The deputy came back and said to Frankie, "Ma'am, I'm gonna need you to submit to a breathalyzer."

"No, thanks."

"Well, ma'am, we already have probable cause to make an arrest, so it doesn't really matter if you blow or not."

"Okay, then, why waste any more of our time?"

"All right, then, I'll have to place both of you under arrest," the deputy said as he began reading them their rights. "You have the right to be silent. Anything you say can and will be used . . ."

"Looks like my attorney's here," said Frankie.

A black Mercedes sedan pulled up behind the cruiser and a slick middle-aged blond man who looked like Robert Redford stepped out.

The deputy continued, ". . . against you in a court of law. You have the right to an attorney . . ."

"Okay, okay, what's going on here?" asked the blond lawyer.

"Sir, your client is being arrested for speeding and reckless driving."

"Well, those are only ticketable infractions, officer."

"We also have 'em on possession of a large quantity of marijuana, open container, and DUI," the sheriff chimed in.

"They're lucky to be alive," the deputy added.

The attorney looked at both Frankie and Jesse and said, "I'll meet you at the station. When we get there, you do exactly as I say, got it?"

"Yeah," said Frankie. She looked at Jesse and said, "Do exactly what he says and he'll get us out of this, all right?"

Jesse nodded.

The deputy placed them both in handcuffs. Another cop car arrived and the deputy led Frankie to the back seat of the new cruiser. Then he put Jesse in the back of the car he and D.W. were in.

The deputy got behind the wheel and drove slowly through the desert—he was in no hurry to get back to Delgado.

"I knew it was only a matter of time before I'd find you sitting right there in that back seat, my friend," the sheriff said to Jesse, looking at him in the mirror of the flip-down passenger side visor.

Jesse stayed silent.

"We're not quite sure what you're doing out here, but something just don't seem right about ya. Now, seeing as you weren't driving your car . . ."

"And that is a pussy ass car," the deputy chimed in.

"Shut up, Grady. Seeing as you weren't driving," D.W. continued, "all we have you on is a possession of Mary Jane charge and an open container—neither one of those add up to too much, but they will go on your record and we could place a couple of hefty fines on ya. Or we could make all this go away. Take a look out your window and you'll notice an infinite expanse of desert stretching out in every direction. There's a lot of space for a person to disappear out there. And over the years we've found some pretty good hiding spots, haven't we, Grady?"

"That's right, there's some places out there that there ain't a soul laid eyes on."

Jesse looked out onto the desert rolling by his window and felt the magnitude of what these cops were laying down.

"I consider myself a measured man, but my brother-in-law here, I can't say he doesn't have a few screws loose and restraint is not a capability that he possesses. We've done a little research on ya and we know where you live there in Austin," said the sheriff. "We're not quite sure what you're up to out here, but something just don't add up with ya in our minds. So, the way we see it is, you're gonna get booked at the station, spend a night, and when you're let out, you're gonna get back to your funky little life in Austin just as fast as you can and keep your mouth shut or we'll make sure that you're never seen or heard from again. And if you choose not to comply, you will know hell on this earth. That's more of a promise than a threat, just so we're clear." D.W. Speed tilted his wire-rimmed Ray-Bans up to the mirror, looking directly at our Jesse.

Jesse locked eyes with the dark lenses in the mirror and nodded as he realized that the camera and his laptop containing all of the footage from Soledad were sitting in the trunk of his car on the side of the highway.

"To tell ya the truth, sheriff, I was planning to leave Delgado today for good and I'd be happy to continue on my way. If you wanna take me back to my car, I'd drive out of here without looking back." Jesse delivered in a tone that made it clear he fully understood the situation.

"Like I said, son, it's not gonna be that easy. You'll be arraigned, you'll spend the night in jail, you'll see a judge, and when you're out, you can pick up your car and go back to where you came and that's just the way it's gonna be. We have to follow a certain protocol."

"Do you know where I'll be able to track down my car when I get out?"

"Don't worry, we're not gonna leave it out there on the side of the highway. It'll be towed to the pound and you can pick it up when you're out."

"When you grow up around this much bullshit, you know it when it stings your nostrils."

"What the hell's that supposed to mean?" the sheriff asked the deputy.

"Means I don't believe he's gonna leave. I'm gonna turn left on this old dirt road up here and see where it goes, because I'm not sure what this punk thinks he saw yesterday in Soledad."

"No, no, he didn't see anything that wasn't a by-the-book procedure and I trust that when he gets out of the Delgado jail he'll get back in his car and drive right on outta here and if his car won't drive because his girlfriend crashed it, well, he'll just get on the first Greyhound or train that comes along. That sound like a plan, bud?"

"Yes, sir. I'm fully on board for that plan."

"Fuck all that, we're about to get down to the truth of the matter," the deputy said as he whipped a left onto the dirt road.

"Grady, what the hell are you doin'?" asked the sheriff.

"I know exactly what I'm doin', D-Dub."

The deputy sped down the dirt road until he came to a quick

stop far from the highway. He got out and walked around to the passenger side and pulled Jesse out of the cruiser. The sheriff got out and all three of them stood there in the midday blazing sun.

"I'm sorry, son, I was hoping to keep a level of decorum, but my deputy has a mind of his own," said the sheriff.

The deputy looked at Jesse and pointed out into the desert and said, "Walk."

"What?"

The deputy shoved Jesse in the back and demanded he start walking.

Our actor did as he commanded and started off into the flaky white shale and creosote. The officers followed him out. All three of them kept their eyes on the ground, looking out for snakes. After about fifty feet, the deputy told Jesse to stop.

"Get down on your knees and you keep looking straight ahead."

Jesse followed the deputy's orders and planted his knees into the desert rock, his hands still handcuffed behind his back. He felt the touch of the cold hard steel at the back of his head.

"Now, why don't you tell us what the hell you were doing in Soledad yesterday," commanded the deputy.

Jesse's thoughts raced, searching for the best response, but before he could answer, the deputy fired a round into the dirt to the right a few yards from where he stood.

"Goddammit, Grady," said the sheriff.

"Thought I saw something slithering over there. I was just scaring it off," said the deputy as he placed his pistol back behind Jesse's dome. "So, what were you doing in Soledad?"

"I was location scouting for a movie, I swear to God," said Jesse, staring out into the endless desert.

"You believe that shit, D-Dub?" asked the deputy.

"Nope.

"Where were you when we were paying Cleeve a visit? We know your car was there, so you must've been lurking around."

"I was up hiking around near the mine, like I said, looking for filming locations for a movie. I heard a gunshot and saw an ambulance show up, but by the time I got down the hill into the town to see what was going on, everyone had cleared out, so I wasn't sure what happened."

"Did you see Cleeve pull his pistol on us?" asked the deputy.

"I didn't see anything."

"You sure about that?"

"One hundred percent."

"What I wanna know is who you're working for," said the sheriff.

"I'm working for myself."

"Why are you out here in the first place?"

"I came out here to work on a screen test and ran into Cleeve and he said I could use his ghost town, and that's what I was doing. Just looking for a good location for a possible production down the line."

"How do you know Cleeve?" asked the sheriff.

"I met him at the hot springs, randomly. He got into a tub I was soaking in and he told me he owned a ghost town and I should check it out."

"He did like to hang out at the hot springs," the sheriff said to the deputy.

"I don't buy it," said the deputy, still holding the pistol to the back of Jesse's head. "What I think happened is you came out here as part of some hippy Austin environmental outfit to work in cahoots with Cleeve and his pipeline group."

"I have no idea what you're talking about."

"You're telling us you don't work for the people fighting the pipeline?"

"I'm an actor. I came out here to work on a piece and I didn't want to get involved in anything other than that."

"It still don't add up to me. I'm pretty sure you must've been working for somebody," said the deputy.

"You can look me up. I'm an actor, I swear. You'll see my face and everything I've been in."

"You looked him up, right?" the sheriff asked the deputy.

"I looked him up in *our* database, I didn't Google him or nothing."

"Well, let's look him up."

The deputy took the pistol off the back of Jesse's head and pulled out his phone. Jesse continued staring out into the desert. The two officers stood together looking at the deputy's phone.

"That's him right there, ain't it?" asked the sheriff.

"Looks like him, all right. Okay, get up, Pretty Boy Floyd," said the deputy as he pulled Jesse off the ground by his right arm.

The officers walked Jesse back to the cruiser and put him in the back seat. They drove to Delgado in silence. Jesse assumed they were all considering the various angles of the story they found themselves in. They must have been following him since he left the Arroyo Inn this morning, he reasoned. They tailed him to Frankie's and waited for him to leave. He imagined they weren't too happy about seeing Frankie behind the wheel of his car, but when they saw her driving like a maniac, they had probable cause. He hoped Frankie's attorney would be there waiting for him when he got to the Delgado jail.

. . .

As they came into Delgado, they got held up at a four-way crosswalk.

"Jesus, would you get a load of these two?" D.W. Speed said, referring to a couple of tourists crossing the road. "Looks like they're high out of their minds."

The girl was wearing iridescent bellbottoms and a big puffy sweater with smiley faces printed all over it. The guy had spiked Rod Stewart hair and looked like a relic from the Sixties' swinging London.

"What I wanna know is where do they all come from and what the hell are they coming here for?" Deputy King asked the sheriff.

"Beats the shit out of me," the sheriff said under his breath. "That's the sixty-four-thousand dollar question isn't it?" D.W.'s window was down, and when the couple crossed in front of the police car, he asked in a polite manner, "How y'all doing today?"

The couple both flashed big goofy grins.

. . .

At the police station, there was no sign of Frankie's attorney. Jesse was booked into a small jail cell with a solid door, a metal cot with a paper-thin mattress, and a steel toilet. He had the place to himself and was relieved to be in there all alone after waiting in the station holding room for hours while they processed him. He stretched out on the cot and considered his predicament.

He thought about Frankie and the time he spent with her earlier. Something about her story and Marisella didn't add up to him. Why would she go to such elaborate lengths to "comfort" him? Why would she tell Marisella to pretend she knew about his acting and the films he'd been in? And why didn't she come to the Arroyo Inn herself if she was so concerned about him?

He worried about the condition of his car. He worried about all of his possessions sitting in the trunk: Nina's camera, his laptop with the footage of the shooting in Soledad, and most of all, the hard work he had put into his ghost town screen test. He thought about all of these things being towed through the desert and sitting in an impound lot.

He rose from the cot and started pacing the cell like a caged animal. What were the thoughts of an animal taken from the wild and locked in captivity? Fear, hunger, confusion, anger. He walked the tiny room back and forth in a trance. He'd use this experience to inform his acting, he told himself. If he were cast in the role of the prisoner, how would he move? What vision of freedom would he dream of? He tried to keep his mind occupied on his craft, but soon a tsunami of worry, fear, and anxiety washed over him and he found himself exhausted and sad, curled up on the cot. He wanted more for his life than this jail cell in a hell-hole Texas desert town. He had come out here to find some form of clarity and sanity, and this is where it got him. He called out to any higher power that might be listening, "God, Universe, Ganesha, whatever, put me to work. Use me as an instrument to convey something of substance, something important that could touch just one person. Allow me to do the thing I was put here to do. Get me out of this cell and onto great things, big things, meaningful things. Please. Please. Please." He squeezed his knees closer to his chest.

14

"**S**TRANGE. GET YOUR ASS UP, Strange, your attorney's here."

An overweight officer was standing at his open jail cell door. He had a thick mustache and wheezed from the short walk.

"Vamanos," the officer commanded.

Jesse pulled himself off the cot and followed the officer down the corridor to the same waiting room he had been processed in.

"Take a seat," the officer instructed.

One other person was sitting in the waiting room, and they locked eyes. It was a familiar face.

"Jesse?"

"Maggie?"

"Oh, my God, what the fuck?"

Maggie was a producer he'd worked with on several projects in Austin. She was dialed into the big tech firm marketing departments and she'd landed him a few well-paying commercials over the years. He felt ashamed to see her here but realized she was being booked in the Delgado jail just the same as he was.

"What are you doing time for?" she asked.

He thought about it and decided the easiest explanation was, "I got pulled over and they found a little weed on me."

"Dude, same. I didn't realize it was even a thing anymore."

"What happened to you?" he asked.

"You remember my girlfriend Camille?"

"Of course."

"She's been stressed out with a ton of work and family shit lately and I took her out here to get away from it all. We stayed at these amazing hot springs last night and it was just beautiful. I was trying to do something nice for her, and this morning we were driving around sightseeing and we got pulled over by these small-town dickweeds as we were smoking a joint."

Jesse nodded and said, "I know the feeling."

"Same thing happened to you?"

"Yep."

"Damn. I'm just glad they didn't find the mushrooms or the molly," Maggie said as she broke out in laughter. "They let Camille go, and she's out there now trying to get my bail sorted. I just feel bad for her because this was supposed to be her getaway and here we are dealing with this shit. Jesus, man, how long have you been in here?"

"Since last night. What time is it now?"

"Probably close to noon. We were out trying to get breakfast. Oh, my God, wait, congratulations on *Mirage*."

"*Mirage?*"

"I heard its back on."

"What?"

"You haven't heard anything?"

"No."

"Oh, shit, well, I'm not sure if I'm supposed to say anything, but I heard you had it."

"I had it?"

"Yeah, have you talked to your agent, what's his face?"

"Rich?"

"Yeah, Rich."

"I haven't heard anything."

"Well, this is all just happening, but you should call him as soon as you can. I've been able to get a few of my clients on, but I heard you were attached as the lead. It's not filming in Austin anymore, but they're using some of the cast and crew that they had on initially."

"What?" Jesse said as his head began to swirl.

"Yeah, I think it's gonna be big. I just heard about it on my way out here, so I'm trying to get back to Austin as soon as possible. You need to call your agent, dude."

A door opened and in walked the Robert Redford-looking attorney from the crash site.

"All right, Mr. Strange, I've come to get you out of here," said the attorney.

Jesse rose and looked back at Maggie. He was still processing what she told him.

"Wait, can you help her, too?" he asked the lawyer.

The attorney looked at Maggie and asked, "She a friend of yours?"

"Yeah, she's a good person to have on your side. She makes a lot of people money."

"I'll see what I can do. Let's get you out of here first."

"Thanks, Jesse," Maggie said. "I'll be okay. Call me and let me know about *Mirage* when you hear something."

"I will."

Jesse followed the attorney out of the holding room, down a hall, and into an office. On one side of the office was a counter in front of a reception window. He noticed someone pacing back and forth behind the window performing some administrative task.

"Have a seat, let's talk," the attorney said as he sat down in one of the older plastic chairs. Jesse followed his lead.

The attorney placed the briefcase he'd been carrying in his lap and pulled out a stack of paperwork and a gold pen. "Have you been arrested before?" he asked with a slight Southern lilt and sympathetic eyes.

"A couple of times when I was younger for stupid shit, nothing serious."

"Well, then, you've probably been through this process. As of now, you have two options," the attorney said. "You can wait to see the judge, he'll hear your case, and set your bail. Then you'll need to find a bondsman to post bail for you. The problem with that option is that the county judge operates on Delgado time and I've seen people sit in here for a week waiting on him to show up. Now, he could show up and see you in the next hour, or you might not see him for days."

"I'd be interested to hear my other option."

"I don't blame you. The other option you have is to sign this contract granting me the power to legally represent you and I'll go over and see the lady behind that window and all of this will go away and you'll be on your way."

Jesse knew his phone was probably on the other side of that window with a possible missed call, voicemail, text, or all three from his agent.

"If I chose the second option, what would I owe you?"

"Nada, it's a pro bono favor for Francine that I gave her my word I'd follow through on. There is a catch though."

"Okay."

"The catch is, I have to walk out of this police station in exactly"—the attorney shook out his arm and took a look at the gold Rolex on his wrist—"six minutes and fort-eight seconds to drive to the Degaldo Airstrip and catch a flight to attend a conference in Santa Fe. So, you're gonna have to make your decision in the next three minutes, because I will not miss my conference for screwing around getting someone off a pot charge."

The attorney clicked the ink pen and slid it over to Jesse with the contract on top of the briefcase.

"Feel free to scan through, but if it's not signed in the next two and half minutes, I'm walking out that door."

Jesse attempted to play out both options.

"I sign this, I'm free to go?"

"Yep, and the whole thing'll be expunged from your record. I'd suggest getting out of town as soon as possible though."

"What about my car?"

"The lady behind the window will let you know. I'm sure it's across the street at the impound lot. One minute."

Jesse flipped through the pages without reading anything.

"Just need your signature on that last page underneath your name there and we're set."

Jesse signed his name with a nervous hand.

The attorney took the pen, signed contract, and his briefcase without haste, and walked to the reception window. Less than a minute later, he turned around, walked across the room and out the door without even glancing at Jesse. The lady at the reception window waved Jesse over. She unlocked and slid open the window and handed Jesse a clear Ziploc bag containing his phone, wallet, the erased media card, and his sunglasses.

Jesse looked the bag over and asked, "What about my car keys?"

"I don't know, they're probably still in your car."

"You know where I can find it?"

"Across the street at the impound lot. You're gonna have to sign this," the lady said, passing him a sheet of paper.

"What's this?"

"It's to say you've been released. You don't sign it, you stay here."

Jesse signed it.

"Walk out this door and then out the front doors and the lot's across the street. That piece of paper in your bag has the ID number written on it. Show 'em that and they'll show you to your car."

Jesse left the room and made his way to the front doors of the police station. He pulled his phone out of the plastic bag and saw a missed call, voicemail, and text from his agent Rich that said, *Huge stroke of luck! Call me.*

Jesse called Rich as he walked out the front doors and made his way down a set of stairs that led to the sidewalk. There was no answer. Jesse listened to the voicemail.

"Strange! Where the fuck are you, man? *Mirage* is back and they want you. Call me!"

The missed call and voicemail were from 3:54 p.m. the previous day. Jesse looked across the street at the impound lot surrounded by chain-link and razor wire and walked over.

On the other side of a rusty metal door was another reception window. Jesse went to the window and rang the bell on the counter. An old man appeared after a couple of minutes covered in oil and dirt.

"You picking up?"

"Yeah."

"Got your ID number?"

Jesse slid the man the small piece of paper with the number written in marker.

"Okey doke," said the man as he disappeared around the corner.

Jesse called Rich again, but it just rang and went to voicemail.

The man behind the counter came back and said, "Here's your keys, but the car's totaled."

"Totaled?"

"Yep, you ain't driving that outta here. The front end's all busted and it's pretty much just scrap parts at this point. You'll have to tow it somewhere or you can donate it, but it has to be out of here in the next forty-eight hours."

"Well, shit, can I take a look?"

"Yeah, it's your car."

The old man buzzed the door to the side of the window and opened it. Jesse walked through and followed the man out to the lot. He led Jesse down an aisle of cars and at the end was his. The front passenger side bumper was crumpled and pushed into the tire. He got down on his hands and knees and peered underneath. It was banged up, but he wanted a second opinion.

"Do you have a mechanic you trust?" asked Jesse.

"Well, yeah, but no one that'd wanna jack with that."

"You said I have to tow it out of here, right?"

"Yeah, you can't leave it here."

"Okay, then, I'd like to tow it to a mechanic here in Delgado that'll give me their opinion. At this point, I'm not going to donate it, so I don't see another option. Do you?"

"Nope."

"Can you suggest a mechanic?"

"Nope, but there's the yellow pages in the office. I'm sure you can find something in there."

"I'll just look on my phone, thanks."

"Do your thing, just come back inside when you're ready to settle up," the old man said as he walked off.

Jesse went to the trunk and opened it. The camera was gone. He looked all over, but there was no sign of it. His suitcase was still there in the trunk. He found his laptop in the bottom underneath his clothes. He still had the footage, but someone obviously wanted to know what was on that camera.

He searched for a mechanic on his phone and didn't find many options. He clicked on one of the few and recognized the photo of someone he remembered talking to at the Bodhi Wind hanging around the Talking Walls. His name was Antares. Jesse called him.

Thirty minutes later, Antares himself showed up in his tow truck. He took a look at the car and said he could probably fix it but wanted to get it back to his shop to get underneath it. Jesse rode along with Antares back to his shop.

After a thorough inspection, Antares said, "I'll have to rebuild parts of the front end and suspension system, and you'll need a new tire, but I think I can get it into good enough shape to drive it back to Austin. It'll take a day or two and cost fifteen hundred."

Jesse took out his wallet, though he knew he didn't have enough cash. He took a look at a couple of credit cards but didn't think he had fifteen hundred dollars on either of them. Then something caught his eye. The commission check from Frankie was still in the cash pocket of his wallet. He didn't put it back in there. He tossed on Frankie's bar before they went to the pool. He thought back to sitting at the bar looking through the oil field book while Frankie was getting ready to leave and he didn't remember seeing it. Then he flashed to the maid bringing his wallet in from the pool. Frankie put her up to it, he thought, but why?

Jesse asked Antares if he could sign the check over to him since the name field was still blank. Antares took a look at the check, shrugged his shoulders, and said sure, although he gave Jesse a suspicious look.

"But you don't have to pay until it's ready," said Antares.

"I'd feel better if you just took it now," Jesse said, handing over the check.

Luckily, Antares didn't seem to be too busy with anything else at the moment, and Jesse left him to it. He reached under the passenger seat and found his copy of *The Art of Acting* and put it in his suitcase. He stood there in the parking lot and wondered what to do.

Across the street from Antares's shop, there was a shaded little park with a cienega and picnic tables. Children splashed around in the water. Jesse walked over and sat on a bench in the shade. As he was sitting there contemplating his next move, he noticed a clean-cut guy in a starched white dress shirt standing at the right side of the bench.

"Mind if I have a seat?"

Jesse looked around at a number of empty benches but gave the man a nod.

"Mr. Strange, my name's Detective Vernon Hayes and I'd like to have a word with you today about your connection to the Hammer Family. Let me start by saying you are not a suspect in our current criminal investigation, but your cooperation would be greatly appreciated."

"Okay."

"Mind if I ask you a few questions?"

Jesse was intrigued enough to say, "I can't see why not."

"I take it you know Miss Francine Hammer."

"Yes."

"How would you describe the nature of your relationship with Miss Hammer?"

"The nature of our relationship?"

"Romantic, platonic, professional?"

"I guess borderline all three."

"How long have you two known each other?"

"A little over a week but maybe longer? You mind telling me what this is all about?"

"I'm investigating a series of land scams perpetrated by the Hammer Family and their associates and I've been hired by a collective of parties who have fallen victim to these scams. I believe you may have been set up to take a fall for a number of these crimes."

Jesse didn't detect a Southern drawl or any hint of cowboy in this guy.

"Whaddaya mean set up?"

"You were just released from the Delgado Police Station, correct?"

"That's right."

"And you worked with an attorney to arrange your release. Do you know who that attorney was?"

"Frankie's guy."

"That was Robert Hammer."

"Frankie's dad?"

"That's correct. And he had you sign some sort of contract?"

"Yeah, just something that gave him the power to represent me."

"We believe that may have been something that would prevent you from legally testifying against the Hammers."

"Testify for what?"

"Did you read the contract you signed?"

Jesse sighed. "I didn't get the chance to fully read through it. The attorney was in a hurry."

"He was in a hurry all right. Mr. Strange, this is a far-reaching investigation that implicates a number of prominent, well-respected members of this community including local law enforcement. That's really all I can tell you at this time. We've built a strong case but could use any information you'd provide us. Would you be willing to come in for a formal on-the-record interview?"

"Interview?"

"You'd meet with my partner and me and we'd ask you a series of questions. You're under no obligation at this point, but it could be a huge help to our investigation as well as the victims."

"I don't know. To tell ya the truth, I'm just waiting on my car to be repaired, then I need to get back to Austin as soon as possible for work."

"If you're still here tomorrow morning and you have the time, please give me a call. It would be great to discuss what you know more in-depth."

The detective gave Jesse his card and left the park.

Jesse sat there and watched the kids jump into the cienega. He wasn't sure what to do with himself, and after some time spent processing recent events, he stood up with his suitcase and started walking into town. He was uneasy. He felt like a fly trapped in the web of the scam that was unfolding in his mind and he didn't know who to trust. The only thing that made him feel better was the idea of getting in his car and leaving, but he knew that wouldn't be happening for a while.

He felt he was being watched. He felt like with every move he made someone was keeping tabs on him. The detective knew where to find him and knew Frankie's dad sprung him from jail. He wondered who else was watching him. He wanted to find a place to hide until his car was ready. He felt eyes everywhere, though there was hardly a soul around.

When he made it to the town square, he headed in the direction of the blank marquee of the Delgado Theater. He knew that it would most likely be vacant and had the thought of finding a way in, maybe through a door or window in the alley. He walked to the ticket window and noticed the poster for *The Border* no longer hung there. In its place was a white letter board that said *Don't know where, Don't know when* in black letters. He stared through the window into the dark empty lobby and was struck by another pair of eyes looking back at him in the back of the foyer. Nina stepped into the lobby and looked at him like she was staring at a ghost; he stared back at her in the same way. She came and opened the front door as she glanced nervously around the town.

"You look like a man who could use a place to hide. Come in," she instructed.

He stepped inside and scanned the room.

"It's just me," she said.

She wore a red jumpsuit and gazed at Jesse as if trying to get a feel on his mood.

"What's playing tonight?"

"I have a print of *Rio Conchos*. Ever seen it?"

"Can't say that I have."

"I haven't either, but it seems like a good one to show for this summer's series. Not sure that anyone will see it now."

"Why's that?"

"Frankie left this morning and I'm not sure she's ever coming back. That means the future of this place is up in the air."

"Frankie left? For where?"

"Not sure exactly. Somewhere out of the US. She knew it wouldn't be safe to tell me."

Jesse's phone went off in his pocket. He pulled it out and found a text from his agent Rich that said, *Sorry, stuck in meeting. Call you in an hour.*

"Have you heard anything about your camera?" he asked Nina.

"Heard anything? Whaddaya mean?"

"Well, I think the cops stole it."

"What?"

"It was there when the cops arrested Frankie and me, but when I got out and picked up my car from the impound lot, it wasn't in the trunk. You heard about me and Frankie getting arrested, right?"

"Yeah, I know about that."

"This town doesn't do secrets too well."

"Nope. But who the hell has my camera?"

"My guess is the cops."

"Why would the cops take it? Was anything else missing?"

"Everything else was there, they just took the camera."

"Why would they do that?"

"No clue."

Jesse kept his suspicions to himself as to why the Delgado PD would steal the camera.

Nina looked around with paranoid eyes and said, "Let me show you the theater."

He picked up his suitcase and followed her into the grand theater with red-draped walls and ancient wood-framed folding seats. Nina turned on the house lights. Jesse reveled in the beauty of something so untouched by time. It felt like a holy space to him, like the church in Soledad. It was a space where transformation was possible. A place where people came to find something bigger than themselves and hear stories that gave life meaning. A place where generations had come to dream of a life outside of this town in an area where many movies were set but few were filmed.

"It'll probably be a boutique hotel if the developers have their way."

"So, Frankie's dad owns this?"

"Yeah. We've fought to preserve the theater and keep it for the community, but her dad's developer buddies have been trying to convert it into something else for years. Now that she's gone, it's probably over with."

"I'm gonna guess that Frankie didn't leave the country because of the trouble that she and I got into."

"I'd say that's a good guess."

"What else can you tell me?"

"I can tell you that Frankie doesn't care about anyone but herself and she'd been waiting for someone like you to come along."

"Someone like me?"

"Some charming stranger from the city, an actor, who had

never heard of her family, someone she could put the blame on if things got heavy and you fell right into her lap."

"And what kept you playing along?"

"Growing up poor and being blinded by not wanting to be poor anymore. Frankie's good at spotting desperate people. She offered me a way out and I took it. I can see that now. I was naive. The difference between me and Frankie is I'm willing to pay for my sins and not run away from them. If I were you though, I'd probably run away back to my life as soon as I could. I'd say you're pretty sin-free in this situation."

"Thanks to Frankie, it looks like I'll have to wait around awhile. You know we were coming to find you when we got arrested."

"Oh, yeah, the cash. Let me get it," Nina said as she turned to walk up a staircase at the back of the theater.

Jesse's phone rang.

"My man."

"Strange, are you sitting down?"

"Should I be?"

"Why don't you go ahead and grab a seat?"

Jesse walked over, plopped into a theater seat, and kicked his legs up on the back of another.

"*Mirage* is back and they want to keep you as the lead."

"Holy shit," Jesse said. He stood up. "No fucking way. It's back on?"

"Yep, it's back on, and this is huge because they're only sticking with a couple of people from the original cast. They said they can't imagine anyone else in the role."

"What?"

"Yeah!"

"What's the deal?"

"The thing is, in order to secure funding, they have to shoot outside of Texas for the tax breaks. The majority of the production is happening in northern Mexico, with a bit in New Mexico, and some around LA. Where the hell are you?"

"Uh, I'm in a movie theater in Delgado, Texas."

"Oh, what are you seeing? Should I call you back?"

"No, no, now's perfect."

"Delgado? What's the deal with that place? Everyone keeps talking about it. Supposed to be magical or something?"

"That's what they say."

"Okay, we need to get you to LA like tomorrow to start read-throughs. The production schedule's tight as fuck on this one. How soon can you get back to Austin?"

"I should be back tomorrow."

"Get here as soon as you can and I'll get you on a flight day after tomorrow. I'll go out with you and make all the introductions, get you set up. You may be there for a while, so we'll need to get you a place, but we'll figure all of that out. Just get back and pack your bags. Are you ready for this?"

"Yeah, of course, I'm ready."

"This is big, man. Zed82 has everything behind them and there's already a ton of buzz. This means the festival circuit, Cannes, Sundance; this means press, interviews, a full theatrical release."

Jesse paced the aisles full of excitement.

"First things first," Rich continued, "let's get you out there and get you set up to knock this thing outta the park."

"You got it. I'll get back to Austin tomorrow."

"I'm pumped for you, man. I have a good feeling about this."

"Same here, Rich. Thank you."

"Okay, enjoy your movie, then get the fuck back here."

Jesse's hair was tingling and his mind was racing as he continued to pace the theater. Nina came back down the flight of stairs holding the blue bank bag.

"I couldn't help but overhear," she said, "sounds like you landed a role?"

"I didn't think it was coming back, but now it's happening."

"What's the film?"

"It's called *Mirage*. It's like a road thriller, dystopian *Bonnie and Clyde* style story set in modern-day Texas and Mexico."

"That sounds cool."

"I love the script."

Nina handed Jesse the bank bag.

"Neil filled me in," she said.

"What do you mean Neil filled you in?"

"He called me a couple of days ago and told me to look for the money, but I'd already found it. Frankie and I were trying to figure out where it came from for days until we checked the surveillance video and saw you dropping it off, which made us even more confused. Oddly enough, a few hours after we saw you on the surveillance video, I got a call from Neil."

"So, what happened to him?" Jesse asked.

"He's not really sure. Sounds like he had some sort of breakdown and wound up in a tiny village on the other side of the border. He said he thought people were following him, so he hid out down there for a few days. I think he has a history of mental health issues. He used to work here in the summers when we needed extra help, so I got to know him. He's better now, back with his family in California, but he wanted to make sure the money got back to the person it belonged to."

"Did he tell you what the money was for?"

"He said it was seed capital for the Star Colony from some investor in Austin. He said a guy came out here to deliver it and I realized he was talking about you. He asked me about a week ago if he could have something dropped off here. I guess that's what he meant."

"I wonder why he didn't get in touch with me—he had my number."

"I think he's having a hard time facing his friends after dropping the ball on the resort. And by the way, I never told Frankie about my call with Neil."

"Why not?"

"I felt like I should keep it to myself and reach out to you directly about it. Then I heard about the shoot-out in Soledad and everything went to shit. You were there, right?"

"Yeah." Jesse paused to consider how much he wanted Nina to know. He still wasn't sure if he could trust her.

"What happened?"

"I was there filming my piece and just as I was about to wrap, the cops showed up and for some fucked-up reason, they shot Cleeve."

"Did you see anything?"

"I'd just ducked into one of the buildings in the ghost town to film a scene and I saw the cops pull into town, I heard some yelling, and then a gunshot. I hid out in the general store until the ambulance came and everyone left, then I got outta there."

"Jesus, man. I heard Cleeve pulled a gun and shot at them."

"Uh, no. I was there and there was only one gunshot and it came from the cops."

"Wait, if the cops stole my camera, does that mean they have your footage?"

"Nope," Jesse said as he pulled the erased media card out of his pocket and showed it to Nina. He wanted to keep his smoke screen intact, just in case. "I was hoping I could hang onto this card and send you a new one."

Nina nodded.

"So, the cops stole the camera out of the trunk at the impound lot?" she asked.

"That's my theory. The only other explanation is that someone came along and took it while the car was on the side of the road."

"Did the cops see you in Soledad?"

"I don't think they saw me, but my car was parked next to Cleeve's truck and I know they saw that."

"Hmm, interesting. So, the cops saw your car parked in the ghost town. Then you got arrested and they found a camera in your trunk and took it. Sounds like they wanted to know what was on the camera."

"That's what it sounds like."

"But there was nothing on the camera because you had the card the whole time?"

"Yep."

"Interesting."

"Yes, and what's more interesting is that after I had my car towed to a mechanic, I was approached by someone who claimed to be a detective."

"A detective? What did he want?"

"He wanted me to come in for an interview to tell him what I know about the Hammer family."

"Did you do it?"

"No, don't think I feel like sticking around or getting involved."

They stood there in the theater. Nina in her red jumpsuit, leaning back against the crush red velvet wall, and Jesse, leaning on the back row of seats. She seemed to be considering all of this new information.

"What if you could help someone?" she asked.

"How would I do that?"

"By talking to the detective and telling them what you saw."

"I don't think they're interested in what happened in Soledad. They want dirt on the Hammers and I don't wanna get wrapped up in any of that."

"I see your point, but sometimes you have to stand up for a thing you believe in."

"I believe I'd like to just blaze out of here as fast as I can."

"I understand, but you still have to wait for your car, right?"

"Yeah."

"And what'll you do until then?"

"Not sure. Hide somewhere?"

"Well, why don't you just stay here? It's safe. There's a couch up in the projectionist's booth."

Jesse nodded his head in contemplation without committing.

"You can trust me," she said.

"Not so sure about that."

"You can. Let's go up and take a look. I think you're gonna want to see it. I think you're gonna flip."

Nina led Jesse up the stairs at the back of the theater that led to the projection booth.

Upstairs, the walls were lined with shelves that held the cans of films on thirty-five millimeter. Jesse browsed the titles on handwritten pieces of tape stuck to the cans. There were Westerns: *Today We Kill Tomorrow We Die*, *Destry Rides Again*, *Beyond The Law*; biker movies: *Werewolves on Wheels*, *The Wild One*, *Run Angel Run*; Giallo flicks: *Cat O' Nine Tails*, *The Bird with the Crystal Plumage*, *Deep Red*; teen rebellion films: *The Legend of Billie Jean* and *Badlands*, and of course, *The Last Picture Show*.

"What a collection," Jesse said.

"Someday you might be in one of these films sitting on a shelf in the projection booth of a small-town movie theater."

"Wouldn't that be something?" Jesse said with a grin.

"What should we watch?" she asked as they perused the shelves of the projection booth. "Could be the last one ever played here."

"How about this one?" asked Jesse as he pulled out a can.

"Good choice," said Nina.

"I've never seen it on the big screen before."

"Well, then, it's time."

Jesse watched Nina thread the film through the projector and onto the take-up reel. She seemed like a sweet girl who got in over her head and was now left behind to face the consequences. There was a part of him that wished Nina was the girl he met that night at the hotel in downtown Austin instead of Frankie. She flipped on the projector and arc lamp and the two of them went back downstairs and grabbed a couple of seats in the middle of the theater. Just before the movie started, Nina pointed to the emergency exit to the left side of the screen.

"In the morning, you can leave through that exit, but just be aware that if it closes you won't be able to get back in. If you need to go out and get back in, if you go out to get coffee or whatever, just use a rock to keep the door propped open. There's one painted red back there in the alley that works perfect."

"Got it," Jesse whispered as the opening credits came up.

15

J ESSE STRANGE ROLLED OVER ON THE COUCH in the projectionist's booth. The smell of dusty celluloid and ancient carpet filled his nose with a lingering hint of the projector motor and popcorn. He thought of the road leading out into the wide open desert and there was a feeling of hope that today would be the day he left Delgado. He pulled on his boots, grabbed his suitcase containing the eight thousand dollars cash and his laptop, and proceeded down the stairs to the back exit.

The door opened into the rocky alley and he found the red-painted rock right away. He moved it with his foot in between the door and the jamb. He wasn't planning to come back, but it was good to know he could if he had to. He hadn't called Antares to find out if his car was ready. His thought was that even if it wasn't ready, he'd hang around and do whatever he could to help. And if for some reason he wouldn't be able to drive out of here in his car today, he'd find the next bus, train, or hitchhike if it came to it. He had to get back to Austin today no matter what.

On the street leading down to Antares's shop, he stuck to the shady side. The high desert morning air was biting in the shade, but he felt it best to stay inconspicuous from the eyes of town. Delgado was silent except for the rusty sounds of iron squeaking in the wind and a few pickup trucks he could hear rumbling around the surrounding streets. He saw no other signs of life the entire way to Antares's.

After about eight blocks, he made it to the mechanic's shop on the edge of town. There was no one in the office, but he saw the back of his car through a window that looked into the garage. Antares stood up from the front of the car as if he knew there was someone there. He waved to Jesse in the window and came around to the office to greet him.

"How's it looking?" Jesse asked.

"It's not looking too pretty, but I think it'll drive. I need to take it out and make sure everything's holding up. You have a few minutes?"

"Not really, but I can sit tight while you take it for a spin."

"Okay, hang out here and I'll be quick. I need to get out on the highway and see how it handles."

Antares went back into the garage and Jesse watched him as he pulled his car out. The front bumper was missing entirely and the license plate was on the dash. Two neon green ratchet straps ran along the length of the hood holding it to the frame. Like Antares said, it wasn't pretty, but hopefully, it would make it the seven hours through the desert back to Austin. He watched his car speed off onto the open highway headed west and listened to the engine until it faded away in the distance.

He paced around the office with nervous energy and noticed a pot of burnt coffee sitting on a small folding table next to the front desk. The pot was still warm, and he poured himself a Styrofoam cup full. He took the cup and walked outside to sit in one of the chairs lining the front of the building. On his way out of the office, he saw a copy of the Delgado Dispatch and brought the local newspaper out with him for a distraction. As he sat down, he registered the headline on the front cover: "Shoot-out in Soledad." He turned his focus to the article that followed.

"Local rancher and land owner Cleeve Barón Menard shot down by deputy Grady R. King after Menard pulled his pistol and fired on Delgado Sheriff D.W. Speed and King. King said the two officers were following up on a lead about a possible marijuana trafficking operation in Soledad and found evidence pertaining to the Palo Blanco Bridge explosion. Menard was pronounced dead on the scene in the Soledad ghost town. Neither officer was harmed. The investigations into the PB bridge explosion and trafficking operation are still ongoing and the police are unable to make further comment at this time but do encourage anyone with leads to come forward and contact local law enforcement."

Jesse reread the article a few times and grew more pissed off with each reading. The idea that these cops were being made out as heroes for shooting Cleeve in the back didn't sit well with him. The thing that stood out was the fact that the cops never asked him anything about weed or a smuggling operation when they had him on his knees in the desert. They seemed more concerned with him working for an anti-pipeline environmental group. It was just like Cleeve said: They were looking for an excuse to come in there and bust up his group. They didn't care about weed. All they cared about was Cleeve and his group standing in the way of the pipeline. Jesse fumed sitting in the chair in front of Antares's shop and he was reminded of Nina encouraging him to stand up for a thing he believed in.

He was rattled by the sad sight of his car pulling back into the parking lot. The mechanic got out and said, "I think you'll be all right to make it back to Austin. I can't say you'll make it much further than that, but I think you'll be okay if you drive slow and don't take it on any bumpy roads."

The two of them went inside to settle up. Antares pulled a wad out of his cash register and handed it to Jesse.

"I haven't tried to cash the check you gave me yet, but here's the change."

"Man, you're too kind, but you should keep it," Jesse said.

"You're gonna need it," said Antares.

"I want you to have it. You're saving my ass here."

"Okay," Antares said as he put the cash back in the register. "Oh, by the way, the cops came by last night asking about your car."

"What?"

"Yeah, they asked me what was wrong with it and if I'd be able to fix it. They wanted to know where you went from here and what we talked about. They kinda spooked me out. Did you run over somebody or something?"

"I didn't run over anybody. I let someone else drive it and they ran it into a boulder, but thanks for the heads-up."

"You got it, man. You should come see my band the next time we play in Austin."

"I will. What's it called?"

"Quiet Earth."

"I'll keep an eye out."

Jesse threw his suitcase into the back and sat down in the driver's seat of his car. He slipped his hand into the right front pocket of his jeans and pulled out the card the detective gave him the day before. Nina's voice echoed in his head, something she said to him yesterday in the theater.

Sometimes you have to stand up for a thing you believe in. He wondered if he'd ever stood up for anything in his entire life. Nothing hit him. *Why not?* he thought and dialed the number on the detective's card.

Detective Hayes was anxious to speak to him and gave an address for their field office on the south side of town. Jesse drove out on the highway for twelve tortuous miles in the direction of the border before turning into an RV park and making his way to a Holiday Rambler motorhome parked in site #16.

Detective Hayes greeted him at the door of the RV and welcomed him inside. He was introduced to another detective inside by the name of Gibson. Hayes sat with Jesse at the foldout table and Gibson sat on a small couch across from them. On the table between Jesse and Detective Hayes was a digital audio recorder. Hayes wasted no time getting into it.

"Okay, I'd like to thank you for coming in and speaking with us today. I believe the information you're willing to provide us will go a long way in helping a lot of people."

Gibson nodded in agreement as he leaned in on the couch.

"Can you start by stating and spelling your full name?"

Jesse complied.

"What's today's date?" Hayes asked.

Jesse told him.

"You stated previously that the nature of your relationship with Francine Hammer was part romantic and part professional. Can you elaborate on that a bit and tell us how the two of you became involved with each other?"

"Well . . . I met her playing pool at some bar out on the highway the night I came to Delgado. I don't remember the name of the place."

"So, you two met in a bar? Did you have any previous knowledge of who Francine or her father were before you met her?"

"No, and honestly, I'm not that interested. I do have some information about the shooting that occurred a couple of days ago in the Soledad ghost town, as I was an eyewitness and have evidence that refutes what the police say happened."

This grabbed both detectives' attention, and they looked at each other wondering how to proceed.

"Well, that's very interesting to hear and I look forward to exploring your evidence and full account, but I think we should follow the chain of events that led us to the point we are today. Now, I'd like to know more about the professional side of you and Francine's relationship. Can you tell us how that come about?"

"We hung out a couple of times and she asked me if I'd be interested in coming to work for her."

"And what was the nature of the work she wanted you to do for her?"

"She said it was sales and she was persistent about me working. I imagined because it was hard to find people around here who could deliver lines or follow a script, although I hated that she put it that way. I'll say I was apprehensive to take on the work, but I thought there was a chance I'd be good at it and I figured I could use the money."

"What did she have you selling?"

"Like I said, she made it *seem* like a sales job, but it was more like telemarketing."

"How so?"

"I just called people from a list and asked them if they'd received some information about the pipeline coming through and then asked if they wanted legal help from Frankie's dad's law firm. Supposedly, the pipeline company had some sort of federal right to claim people's property for the pipeline construction and the eco group was there to help."

"Do you remember the name of Frankie's eco group?"

"Not off the top, no."

"Friends of the Basin Ecological Survey Group sound right?"

"That sounds right, something like that."

"What else did you do on the job?"

"I called a list of names and read the script. Most people said they weren't interested or hung up and that was that. Then, the next day, she had me deliver some paperwork to a lady out in the desert."

"And what can you tell us about that?"

"Frankie gave me a contract and asked me to drive it down to a subdivision of ranches called Vista Acres and told me a lady would be expecting me and I'd have her sign the papers."

"Did she sign them?"

"I told her not to."

"You told her not to?"

"She seemed confused and didn't know what she was signing. I looked over the contract and told her she should have an attorney take a look before she signed it."

"Do you have any idea what the contract was about?"

"It was supposed to be a contract between her and the eco group for legal help to fight the seizure of her land from the pipeline company, but when I skimmed through it, there seemed like there was more to it than that."

"Like what?"

"I don't know, I'm not an attorney, but it just seemed off and I made up my mind not to work for Frankie anymore. I had better things to do with my time and I really didn't care if the lady signed it or not, and honestly, I just didn't want to be involved."

"So, then what? You left the contract with the lady?"

"Yeah, I left the contract with her and drove away. That was it."

"That was it, huh?"

"Then I noticed a couple of guys in a big SUV that looked like hitmen pull into the driveway after I left and drive up to the lady's house."

"Hitmen? What do hitmen look like?"

"They didn't look like cowboys or ranchers. They looked like they were in the Mob or something. I saw a cop car sitting on the side of the road and told the cop about the two guys and asked him to go check it out. Then I drove back to town."

"Did the officer check it out?"

"I assume he did, but I didn't stick around."

The two detectives looked at each other and nodded for a moment.

"I'm gonna stop this," Hayes said as he paused the recorder. "We'll speak off the record for a bit because I'm sure you have plenty of your own questions."

"We believe those two men you encountered," Gibson spoke, "the men you called hitmen?"

"Yeah."

"We believe they worked for Robert Hammer and their purpose was to intimidate the potential scam victims."

"Create paranoia for landowners who believe their property may be taken away by the government," said Hayes.

"We believe you were set up to finesse the lady into signing the contract and when they found out you didn't get it signed, they went and intimidated the lady. That was their job."

"So, your instincts were accurate," Hayes said. "That contract signed over the mineral rights of this lady's estate and countless landowners have fallen victim to this exact scam perpetrated by Bob Hammer and his associates."

"The Friends of the Basin Eco Group had two goals. One, to spread misinformation in the community about where the Tex-Mar pipeline would go."

"Two, to find unwitting land owners to sign over the mineral rights to their land in a false exchange of legal representation"

Gibson continued, "Then, Hammer & Associates could sell the mineral rights to Tex-Mar or any other mining, fracking, or drilling endeavor for additional profits. This is all part of a long history of land scamming by the Hammers."

"Jeez, seems pretty out in the open. How did they think they'd get away with it?" Jesse asked.

"That's the deal, Jesse, it is out in the open and it involves people in the highest echelons of power at the local and state level. Bob Hammer's been at this for a long time and he's always gotten away with it."

"People like Bob Hammer, with the connections he has, tend to keep cases in perpetual litigation. That's why your first-hand information is so valuable. Thank you for talking to us. It requires a lot of courage."

"And just so you know, Bob Hammer was apprehended last night at an executive airport in San Antonio attempting to flee the country. He's being brought back here to Delgado as we speak on a separate federal fraud charge."

"What about Frankie? Was she with him?" Jesse asked.

"Not that we're aware of."

The weight of the situation began to dawn on Jesse. He realized that if this was as big as the detectives made it out to be and he got caught up in a high-profile legal case, it could affect his future film role in a negative way. It could shut his whole career down. He felt sick.

Panic flooded him. He felt trapped and wanted out. His legs were shaky as he tried to stand up.

"Okay, guys, I have a long drive ahead of me and I'd like to get on the road. I'm starting a new job tomorrow back in Austin, so thanks for talking to me today."

"Hold on just a sec there," Hayes said, "we still haven't heard what you know about the shoot-out in Soledad and that's another important piece to this puzzle."

"It may be one of the most important pieces to this puzzle and we'd be very interested in what you know," Gibson added.

"To tell ya the truth guys, I think maybe I should have a lawyer if I'm gonna say anymore."

"Okay, okay, just wait. How about we tell you what we know about Cleeve and you tell us what you know? You see, Cleeve Menard does play a big role in all of this and you can't tell us you were a witness to the Soledad shooting and then leave us hanging. We'll start with what we know."

Jesse sat back down at the table. "Okay, guys, but I really do need to get going soon."

"We'll all make it quick," Hayes assured as he started the recorder again. "Now, there were a couple of people that were part of an organization that Cleeve Menard was also a member of who initially reached out to us about this entire case. A group of local ranchers, property owners, and environmentalists got together to try and figure out what they could do to stop the pipeline. A lot of the meetings for the organization took place at the Soledad Saloon owned by Mr. Menard. He opened up his place to them and was a vocal opponent of the pipeline. As the organization was researching the pipeline, they started uncovering more and more of Bob Hammer and his associate's involvement with Tex-Mar."

"Not only that," Gibson chimed in, "but a few of the folks who were involved in the organization had also been victims of these mineral rights scams, so there were a lot of discussions happening about the correlation between the pipeline and the mineral rights scams. And as slick as Bob Hammer and his associates have always been about covering their tracks, things started to become apparent to some of the members of the organization fighting the pipeline."

"Our theory is that Bob Hammer started to feel the heat and he saw Cleeve Menard as a ringleader of this organization that was digging a little too deep into his affairs," said Hayes.

"On top of that, it's been rumored that Bob Hammer has always wanted Soledad for his own development project."

"So, we think the Delgado police were trying to bait Cleeve Menard into committing a crime or setting him up on a bogus charge to get him out of the way, possibly by planting a provocateur in the organization to carry out the Palo Blanco Bridge explosion."

"A provocateur?"

"We have reason to believe there was someone on the inside encouraging the organization to carry out a felony. Unfortunately, when the Delgado PD showed up to question Cleeve about the crime, it sounds like he fired on them."

"That's what we know and why we're more than interested in anything you can tell us about what you saw go down in Soledad the day the shoot-out happened."

"So what were you doing out there in Soledad?" asked Hayes.

"I was working on a screen test for my acting reel. The first time I laid eyes on the ghost town, I knew I wanted to film something there. Cleeve and I got along pretty well, and he allowed me to come out and work on my movie. So, the day the shooting happened, I was busy filming."

Jesse stood up, and both detectives kept their eyes on him.

"I just need to go out to my car and grab my laptop so I can show you what I have."

The two detectives rose from their seats and remained focused on Jesse as he walked to the front door of the RV. Hayes followed him, opened the door, and watched Jeese pop his trunk and pull the laptop from his suitcase. Jesse came back in and placed the computer on the table. Before opening it, he said, "In exchange for what I'm about to show you, I have a request."

"What's that?"

"I need to know that by showing you this I'll remain as anonymous as possible. Treat this like a crime stopper tip or something, because I can't have my career affected in any way. My agent would kill me. Can you promise me that?"

"Well, we're not sure what you're about to show us, so it would be hard for us to make any promises," Gibson explained.

"I can't get wrapped up in some sensationalized news story, and this seems like it could be a big one. So, is there a way to keep my identity anonymous?"

"Like Detective Gibson said, we don't know what exactly it is we're about to see, so it's not easy for us to commit to keeping you an anonymous source, but we can give you our word that we'll do everything we can to shield your identity from the spotlight of a public trial if it comes to that."

"You said the contract I signed for Frankie's dad would keep me from testifying against him, right?"

"Well, we're not sure what you signed, and even if it was something that kept you testifying, it would be hard to hold up in court. These things tend to fizzle out in a federal case."

The detectives were being coy, but Jesse went ahead and opened the laptop. He found the folder of footage from the Arri and clicked on the last clip.

He expanded the file to fill the screen and the three of them stood around the table watching the scene unfold. It began with a wide shot of the main street shooting in the direction of the church. Jesse paused the footage to provide context. "I was filming the last scene of the day. I went up to the second floor of the general store and set up my camera to film one last shot down the main street of Soledad in the direction of the church. My intention was to get the camera rolling and then run down the street all the way to that church in the background and lie down on the steps halfway in the door of the church, but just as I got the camera set up and rolling, this happened."

Jesse continued the clip.

The detectives watched as the Delgado police car, D.W.'s Mustang, came into the frame and drove down the main street of the ghost town. The camera panned with the cruiser until it came to a stop in front of the saloon. The sheriff and deputy got out of the car and called out for Cisco. Jesse turned up the volume on his laptop. The detectives watched as Cleeve appeared from out of the saloon doors in his skivvies, holding the pistol at his side. Cleeve drunkenly swayed as if the breeze was blowing his thin frame around. The deputy kept his right hand on the holstered handgun on his hip. The discussion between the three men continued until Cleeve waved his pistol in the direction he wanted the cops to leave and turned around to go back into his saloon. A second later, the deputy drew his gun and shot Cleeve in the back. Cleeve's body fell on the steps in front of the cop car, out of the camera's view. The detectives watched with their jaws on the floor as the two police officers looked around the ghost town.

"Wow," said Gibson. "We're dealing with a clear homicide captured on video."

"I have to say, this footage looks incredible. It's like watching a movie," said Hayes.

They watched the video until the ambulance arrived and everyone left the ghost town. Jesse kept his eye on the sheriff. There was a moment as the cops were leaving Soledad behind the ambulance that he thought he saw D.W. Speed gaze up at the second-story window of the general store and look directly at the camera.

The two detectives seemed stunned.

"All I can say is, holy shit, I've never seen anything like this. This clearly shows Deputy King shot Cleeve in cold blood," Gibson said.

"Would it be possible for us to obtain a copy of this?" asked Hayes.

Our actor was apprehensive about sharing the clip with them but decided to do it for Cleeve and all the other scam victims.

"Where would you like me to copy it?"

Jesse copied the clip to a thumb drive that Gibson provided.

Both agents bubbled with excitement, which they did their best to contain. When the file transfer finished, both detectives shook Jesse's hand.

"You've done a great service by cooperating and sharing what you have with us," said Hayes.

"Well, I just hope this helps to clear my friend's name."

"It most certainly will."

"And I'd appreciate it if I could remain anonymous on all of this."

"We'll do everything we can."

"I think the best thing you can do now is go back home to Austin. Probably wouldn't be a good idea for you to linger around here much longer. You'll hear from us if we need you," Hayes said.

. . .

On the highway heading north back toward town, Jesse couldn't help but think of Frankie. He wondered what was going through her head when she drove his car into the side of a mountain.

He was certain the whole thing was orchestrated to get him arrested and put in a position to sign the contract for her dad, but damn, she was reckless about it. *Hell of a performance*, he thought. He wondered where in the world she was and what would become of her, now that he'd given his confession to the detectives. He remembered a passage in *The Art of Acting* about the concept of confession and how it carried with it a sense of purification, how a confession was often a cleansing experience for the soul. He couldn't say he felt cleansed, but he was hopeful that he'd done something to help clear Cleeve's image in the public eye.

Just as he reached the southern edge of Delgado, he glanced in his rearview and saw the black-and-white speeding up behind him. D.W. Speed and Deputy King were tailing him once again. In front of him was the turn-off to the highway that led back east in the direction of home. He put his blinker on, came to a stop, and turned onto the highway. Maybe the sheriff and his deputy were giving our actor a friendly escort out of town. Or maybe they were following him out to the middle of the desert.

Jesse's eyes darted and he couldn't catch his breath. What if the detectives had been working with the cops all along to find out what our actor saw in Soledad? He knew it wasn't beneath them to wedge him out on some back road and leave him rotting in the desert. If they took the camera from his trunk and didn't find any footage on it, they probably wanted to know if Jesse had anything and where it was. He thought of the footage on his laptop sitting in the suitcase on his back seat and felt dizzy. He made a split-second decision to turn left onto the last possible road back in the direction of the Delgado town square. He decided that if they were going to try something, they'd have to do it in public for the eyes of town to see.

He sped up through the empty unpaved streets. The cops continued to trail him but kept their distance. He turned right onto Main Street and drove in the direction of the square. He pulled into a parking spot and came to an abrupt stop in front of the storefronts facing east, grabbed his suitcase from the back seat, and ran into an alley. He turned a corner and widened his pace down the hardscrabble pathway that led to the back door of the theater. It was still propped open by the rock, and as he ducked inside, he took a look in both directions and saw no sign of the cops chasing him. He closed the door.

The only light in the theater came from the doorway that opened into the lobby on the opposite side of the room. Jesse walked through the theater and sat down in a seat in the last row. He kept his eyes on the back door for any sign or sound of police activity. He found himself in a void of silence and took a moment to calm his heart and breath. He reckoned the theater would make a good lookout spot to keep watch of what was going on out on the street. He could keep tabs on the cops from the windows and wait for the right moment to attempt another escape from town. As he sat there in the darkness, he was struck by a vision of himself. He saw himself on the big screen in his leading role in *Mirage*, first in the movie itself, then sitting on set with the lights and the crew. He was smiling and felt very at ease. He was proud of himself and more ready than ever to get out of this theater and this town and onto his future.

He decided to go out to the lobby to have a look outside, but when he stepped into the light, he saw the sheriff and deputy both gazing through the glass doors. He ducked back into the theater and heard the sound of breaking glass and the lock of the front door being unlatched. He ran along the back wall and climbed the stairs into the projectionist's booth. Looking around in a panic, he noticed a ladder that led up to a roof hatch. He climbed the ladder, pushed open the hatch, and crawled out onto the roof with his suitcase. He could hear the footsteps of the cops pounding up the stairs to the projection booth as he closed the lid.

He made his way across the rooftops that ran along the main street in the direction of the courthouse spire. He came to an extension ladder laid across a missing rooftop on one of the buildings. He tested the sturdiness of it and crawled across on his hands and knees, pushing the suitcase in front of him. The ladder bowed with the weight and Jesse could feel the sweat on the palms of his hands sliding against the cold metal. Below him was the rubble of an old storeroom full of busted-up cement and ancient lumber. He looked back to see Deputy King crawling onto the roof of the theater. He figured the only reason they'd be chasing him like this was that they knew he had the footage of the shooting. He stood up when he made it across the ladder and ran to another roof door on the next building. He tried it, but it didn't budge. Scrambling over a brick barrier to the next rooftop, he turned back to see Speed and King inspecting the ladder laid across the roofless building for another way around it.

"You need to stop right there!" Deputy King called out as he saw Jesse look back at him.

Jesse caught a glimpse of King pulling the gun from his holster. He kept on to the next roof hatch, pulled on it, and it opened. He climbed down a ladder, shut the hatch above him, and locked the bolt latch on the bottom.

He ended up in a drafty attic full of boxes of a similar shape and size and found the staircase leading down to the ground floor. He descended the staircase into the town hat shop. The shop girl behind the counter noticed Jesse coming down the stairs and greeted him with a smile.

"Oh, hello," she said.

"You might wanna keep your roof locked," Jesse said as he dashed through the shop room, "You never know who could come down it."

He walked out of the front door onto the sidewalk and took a look down both sides of the street. To his right, he saw his car parked a block away in the direction of the theater. To his left was the courthouse, where a big crowd had gathered and spilled out onto the sidewalk and lawn. He wondered if he could make it to his car and blow out of there while the cops were still fiddling with the hat shop roof hatch. He took one quick step toward his car and saw King and Speed coming out of the empty building a couple of doors down the street, patting the dust off themselves. They were all three startled by the sight of each other. Jesse turned around and sprinted to the crowd at the courthouse.

"Stop!" Speed called out.

He noticed news trucks and state trooper SUVs among the malaise of people gathered in front of the courthouse. He ran across the street into the chaotic scene on the courthouse lawn hoping the crowd would serve as a smoke screen or at least provide witness to whatever the cops were planning to do. Everyone was gathered around a black Dodge Ram parked in a handicap space. News anchors talked into their microphones, facing away from the crowd, the photographers held their cameras high trying to get a shot. A Texas Ranger attempted to push the crowd back as he opened the back door of the truck. Jesse did his best to stay in the mix of people. He looked back and saw no sign of Speed or King. The back door opened and the Texas Ranger pulled Bob Hammer out of the back seat and onto the pavement. A politician's plastic smile stretched across Hammer's face, and his hands swung free at his sides. Cameras clicked in rapid fire. Reporters yelled questions. Locals gawked. Two Texas Rangers guided Bob Hammer, who seemed flattered by the media circus, onto the sidewalk. The crowd engulfed the rangers and Hammer and moved with them across the courthouse lawn. Jesse stayed swept up with the people looking for his escape from the sheriff and deputy—there was still no sign of them. Out of nowhere, he saw a familiar face appear in the crowd. The face carried no expression, only a stone gaze as it cut through the throng. Jesse heard Cisco say, "Hey, Bob! This is for Cleeve, you son of a bitch," as he fired three rounds from a pistol into Bob Hammer's stomach.

The crowd erupted in hysteria. Bob Hammer fell to his knees while the Texas Rangers shielded him and called for backup on their walkies. Jesse saw Cisco sprint across the lawn and jump into an old blue pickup truck waiting on the street. As the truck peeled away, Jesse spotted the Sheriff and Deputy blazing around the corner of Main Street in their cruiser in pursuit of Cisco and his getaway driver.

Jesse backed away from the crowd, straightened his posture, and tried to look nonchalant as he stepped across the street and down the sidewalk in a beeline to his car. He heard the shriek of sirens echoing around the town in all directions. He felt the chaos stirring behind him but didn't turn back to look. When he reached his car, he threw the suitcase into the back seat and hopped in. As he adjusted the rearview mirror, he became distracted by the sight of a starry-eyed couple gazing around in wonder with goofy smiles on their faces. The tourists ambled down the sidewalk in front of him, fresh from the faceless city, in awe of this place full of possibility and hallucination. He realized it was Friday and the weekenders were arriving. He took a deep breath and brought his eyes back into his own in the cracked rearview, brushed his hair back, put the car in reverse, and gunned it out of Delgado.

16

OUT UPON THE GOLDEN PLAINS, the highway stretched through a patch of massive black boulders shooting up from the earth. To his right lay the mountains of Mexico spread out in the late afternoon light when the shadows begin to bend eastward. *Hang onto this thought to write down later*, he told himself. *Keep Mexico on your right side. You'll be working there soon and it's a place of great mystery and wonder.* The road weaved between the molten boulders scattered along the plateau. It was about an hour before the magic hour.

Jesse glanced back at the suitcase on the floor behind the passenger seat and smiled. Inside was the eight thousand cash and a new piece of work he was proud to be going home with. He felt he was far enough away from the jurisdiction of Delgado to reach his hand down below his stereo and open the hiding spot in the console. He kept his eyes on the road as he felt around until the thing he was feeling for fell into his hand. It was there, his last joint, the one he rolled for the road back at the Arroyo Inn. He sparked it and gazed out upon the surreal landscape.

The shadow of a circling vulture glided across the hood of his car and he caught a glimpse of its ragged owner before it disappeared behind him in the endless sky. He looked back to

Mexico and something distant caught his eye. The silhouette of a cowboy on horseback rode along the horizon among the boulders. The horse's gait was swift. It seemed to be keeping pace with the car. Jesse looked down at the speedometer to confirm his speed of just above seventy miles per hour. *Must be something to do with the perspective*, he told himself.

The horse and rider seemed to be heading in a diagonal direction toward the highway. They kept their speed, and Jesse shifted his view back and forth between the highway stretched out in front of him and the approaching cowboy and steed. As they drew closer, Jesse wondered how it was possible this horse was running so fast. He lost sight of the cowboy as a boulder came between the two of them, but soon the horse and rider reemerged about twenty-five yards to the right of the car, running at the exact same speed with effortless grace. Something about the cowboy seemed familiar. Jesse strained his eyes but couldn't make out the details of the rider's face, though he felt a big smile emanating from the cowboy.

The cowboy lifted his hat and waved it at Jesse. He wondered if it was someone he knew. Jesse lifted his left hand and returned a wave with his peace-sign fingers back at the faceless cowboy. The man gave a cool nod as he maintained his speed and distance. Jesse glanced back at the road and saw for the first time an approaching bridge that stretched across a canyon. He began to worry that the cowboy wouldn't see the cliff in front of them and fly right off it into the rocky abyss. Just as they reached the cliff, the cowboy waved his hat again and he and the horse turned to run along the cliffside before heading back west and riding off into the golden plains toward the sunset. Jesse kept glancing back as he drove onto the bridge that ran across a massive river gorge. A giddiness washed over him. The air hung electric as he made his way beyond the chasm.

. . .

With the sunset behind him, he began to think of the future that lay ahead and all that he was driving toward. He thought of the film he'd soon begin working on. He'd always felt the role was made for him. He played the story through his mind from beginning to end as he drove into the night. He knew it by heart because the story spoke to him on a deep level and he knew his connection to and awareness of the work were the things that would bring truth to the fiction.

Mirage was ultimately a love story with a nihilistic twist and an open ending. After an abrupt collapse of society, two ex-lovers set out on a drive for The Mirage, a Mexican seaside resort where the girl has worked since their breakup, a place where their safety will be guaranteed and the possibility of a new beginning exists. Along the way, all hell breaks loose and the couple is forced to blast their way through Texas while working to reconcile their relationship and figure out if they still love each other. It's never revealed if they make it to The Mirage or if they perish on the border in a shoot-out with a roving pack of bandits hell-bent on the apocalypse. Our actor liked to think they make it to The Mirage and a new dawn, that love overcame the nihilistic state of our world *and* the story. He hoped the audience might feel the same.

He looked forward to working on the picture outside of Texas. He thought it would probably do him good to get out of there for a while. *You stick around one place too long, and people start to look at you like a local,* he thought. He wasn't tied to Austin or any other place—he'd go anywhere for the right part. There was a whole wide-open world, and he figured he wasn't doing himself any favors by hiding away from it. The more he thought about it, the more excited he was to leave, but *tonight*—tonight would be spent on the town, back in the city on a Friday night.

He had a feeling it would be one of those nights. The kind where the temperature was perfect with low to no humidity, just a cool dry breeze blowing in from the west. The stars were out, everyone you know was there, they were all smiling and high, the drinks flowing, the women beautiful, everything sparkled, and there was a band blowing the crowd away like a sonic boom.

If his calculations were correct, he'd be driving into downtown around ten p.m. He was about an hour away when he remembered his favorite radio show, *Slip Inside This House*, was on Friday nights from eight to ten on KVRX, a show that played psychedelic music from all over the world. He switched his radio to the frequency, hoping to catch a little bit of it as he came into town, but he was still too far away. Static howled in between a cacophony of multiple frequencies from across the area battling for the airwaves. He heard the crackling voice of a pastor giving a sermon about the carnage of a beast and the wrath of God. There was talk of a tornado touching down in Acuña. A crazed conspiracy nut screamed about indoctrination. Tejano music emanated between the dissonance. Random news filtered in and as he turned down the noise, then something faint caught his ear.

"High-powered Texas attorney Robert Hammer was shot down at the Delgado county courthouse this afternoon . . ."

He tried to fine-tune the frequency but it kept going out.

"The local lawyer turned land developer was said to have amassed

a fortune of more than fifty million dollars from a series of land scams perpetuated on unwitting victims across West Texas. He was pronounced dead on the scene. The suspected gunman is still at large."

The station faded out before more news was beamed in.

"Today, the United States government historically voted to repeal the federal prohibition of cannabis. The sweeping legislation will make the plant federally decriminalized and legal for recreational use in all fifty states."

The static roared back.

He picked up what remained of the joint resting on the console and lit it again. He wondered what it all meant. The semblance of a thick bassline and a slinky guitar drenched in reverb could be heard. He turned up the radio as the static faded and the transmission came in strong. A swirling psychedelic funk song with a Middle Eastern groove rumbled in through the speakers. It was the sound of the city, the sound of promise. The highway turned to a wide open lane freeway, nice cars zipped around at top speed. Jesse loosened his grip on the wheel. Excitement bubbled up and something wild stirred within. Jesse topped a hill and saw the glimmering skyline spread out before him. The night was just beginning.